"Falling for You"

An MM Gay Romance

The Colors of the Heart
Volume 3

Jerry Cole

This book is intended for Adults (ages 18+) only. The contents may be offensive to some readers. It may contain graphic language, explicit sexual content, and adult situations. May contain scenes of unprotected sex. Please do not read this book if you are offended by content as mentioned above or if you are under the age of 18.

Please educate yourself on safe sex practices before making potentially life-changing decisions about sex in real life. If you're not sure where to start, see here: http://www.jerrycoleauthor.com/safe-sex-resources/.

This story is a work of fiction. Names, characters, businesses, places, events and incidents are the products of the author's imagination or used in a fictitious manner and are not to be construed as real. Any resemblance to actual persons, living or dead, or actual events is purely coincidental. Products or brand names mentioned are trademarks of their respective holders or companies. The cover uses licensed images and are shown for illustrative purposes only. Any person(s) that may be depicted on the cover are simply models.

Edition v1.00 (2021.05.10)
http://www.jerrycoleauthor.com

Special thanks to the following volunteer readers who helped with proofreading: Jim Adcock, Bob, Julian White, Earleen Gregg, RB, Big Kidd and those who assisted but wished to be anonymous. Thank you so much for your support.

Prologue

The Kincaid home was beautifully appointed, and Isaac Hamilton smiled as he checked out his handiwork on his way out. The two tablescapes had been a delight to design, and along with bouquets in strategic posts in the living and dining rooms and on the back patio, he was sure the happy couple would be pleased with his work. Mrs. Kincaid's color choices were on point, as always. As the priest's wife, she had shown herself to be a woman of great taste for all the years that she and her husband had served in their parish.

He smiled as he watched her coming in from the front of the house carrying her granddaughter, followed closely by a man Isaac had never seen before but whom he recognized as one of her sons. The family resemblance was obvious. He was carrying the little girl's overnight bag.

"You're early," Bennett, one half of the happy couple and the one hosting the party said, walking over to hug his brother.

"I finished my reports sooner than I thought I would."

The man returned his brother's hug and then stepped back. His eyes caught on Isaac, who found himself unable to stop gazing like a starstruck idiot at the stranger. He wasn't too out of it to notice that the object of his attention was returning it in equal measure. It was as though there was some invisible tension wire stretching between them, trying to make a connection. After a long moment, Isaac came back to his senses and looked away. Whatever it was about the younger man that had caught his attention, he wasn't there to socialize or encourage it.

Thankfully, Bennett broke the charged silence, snapping the chord trying to pull them together.

"Adam, this is the genius who did the floral arrangements for me today. Isaac Hamilton, this is my brother, Adam Kincaid. Adam, Isaac and his son, David."

Adam's cheeks, ruddy from the cold, creased in a friendly smile. Was that a dimple in his left cheek? Damn, that was cute!

"Nice to meet you. The flowers are gorgeous."

Isaac blinked. "Thank you." Time to get out of there.

They shook hands and then Isaac moved purposefully toward the front door, barely managing not to close his fist around the feeling that still tingled on his palm from where Adam had touched him. His whole body was buzzing from that simple touch and he had to slow his breathing while Bennett went to get his coat for him. He shrugged into it and fixed the collar on his son's before reaching for the door.

"Goodnight," he said, before passing through the door Bennett held open for him.

David followed him into the cold evening, walking silently beside him, his hands in the pockets of his jacket.

"Thanks for coming to help me, son," he said, passing a hand over his teenage son's back.

David was fifteen now, and they'd been together, father and son, since David was four years old. Eleven years alone, raising the boy who was the best thing to come of his too-brief marriage to Rowena, the love of his life. It was a bittersweet coincidence that this day, when Bennett would ask

David's math tutor, Jordan O'Leary, to be his husband, marked the anniversary of his marriage to Rowena. The pain was merely an echo of itself these days…more of a sad memory than the deep and unrelentingly awful wound it had remained for years after her passing.

"Mr. O'Leary's cool," David said, strapping himself in once they got into the truck. "I'll bet none of the kids at school even know he's gay. He doesn't look like it."

Isaac chuckled. "Are you saying gay men look a certain way?"

David shook his head impatiently. "You know what I mean, Dad," he protested. "Most people think gay men are girlie wusses. Mr. O'Leary is a big, tough guy."

There was a little bit of hero worship in David's tone, but Isaac could understand that. Jordan O'Leary was a big guy, and Isaac could appreciate his masculine beauty, with those wide shoulders, chiseled jawlines, and that salt-and-pepper look.

"As long as we're clear that stereotyping is wrong, even the one about girls being wusses, everything will be fine," he replied, pleased with his son's response.

He would never fail to caution his son about making judgments about people based on their race, social status, gender, sexual orientation, or religion. He'd lived too long with the social stigma of his race to allow his son to participate in that kind of bigotry.

"I know, Dad," David said, the eye-rolling sigh unvoiced but clear in his response. "I don't care that he's gay. It's kind of cool."

Isaac rolled his own eyes, though David didn't see it. He remembered having crushes on the teachers he'd thought were the hottest back when he was a teenager. He hadn't had a father to talk to about them, though. He'd had a drill sergeant and a commanding officer instead. Even now, as weakened by age and illness as he was, his father was still Major Hamilton to everyone, even his own grandson, who had shortened it to Maje back when he was a baby and couldn't say the whole word.

That had been one of the strongest reasons for Isaac refusing point blank to enlist. He never wanted to be the man his father was, because he hadn't been emotionally available to his son, even after he was honorably discharged for injuries received in the line of duty. He remained as unbending and aloof as ever, until he was forced by his illness to go into an assisted living facility.

These days, the Major was subdued and regretful, though not enough to allow anyone other than his grandson close enough to see the scars he carried on his body and in his soul. Isaac was thankful for that, at least. He would never be close to his father, but he was happy that David had found another, softer side to him.

"Dad?"

"Hmm?" He had completely zoned out, and apparently his son had still been talking to him. "Sorry, son. What was that?"

"I just asked if we were gonna eat out since we're already out."

Isaac grinned at the hopeful note in David's voice. They didn't spend too much money on eating out, because he could cook and he preferred to eat his own cooking. It was healthier, unless they went to a fancy restaurant, and cheaper as well.

"Is that your way of asking to have an unofficial junker night, son?"

Friday nights were their usual junk-eating nights, whether they ordered in or ate out. But today had been pretty hectic, between getting the flowers ready for church and then doing the Kincaid house for the party. He didn't mind another junk-food night, but he had one stipulation.

"If we go fast food tonight, Friday night we stay in and cook. And since you're the one making the request, you get to make the meal."

"Sure, Dad. I'll make something really healthy, I promise." David's expression said he was crossing his fingers at that statement, which made Isaac grin, though he didn't respond. "So, can we go to Elbows? A friend at school says his big brother works there and that the mac and cheese dishes are killer."

The one thing David could not resist — and for all his size he was a very picky eater — was macaroni and cheese. It was his go-to dish when he was cooking, and when they went out to a place that had it on the menu as an option. Isaac had heard of Elbows. It was an English-style pub in the trendier part of town, with reasonable prices and exceptional food, as well as a full bar. He could take his son there because they served food and he wouldn't drink while he was out with him, so he was happy to agree.

"Put the address in the GPS," he told David, and soon they were parking in the crowded lot.

Isaac wondered for a moment if they'd even have room for him with a minor anywhere in the establishment. He needn't have worried though, since once they got inside the warm space, the server led them to the far side where a couple of empty tables waited.

"Would you like a coffee or tea while you wait for your order, sir?" she asked, glancing at David.

Isaac chuckled, causing David to look at him curiously as they took their seats. He wasn't about to explain to his teenage son that his height had made him the focus of the older server's attention. She didn't look much past eighteen or nineteen herself, so in another decade or so their age difference wouldn't matter. But it never failed to amuse him that his son's six-foot height brought him all kinds of inappropriate attention, of which he was still, thank goodness, blissfully unaware.

"Coffee, please," he said. "Cream, no sugar. David, do you want a hot drink?"

David shook his head with a mumbled "No" without looking up and the young woman said, "I'll be back to take your orders in a moment, sir." Her words were addressed to Isaac, but her eyes were now on his son.

He'd start to worry when David finally figured out that he was a…what did the young people call it these days? A chick magnet with his height and broad shoulders. He had an innocent beauty to his face, just as his mother once had, and Isaac could understand anyone being captivated by it. But his son was jailbait and he would always protect him from predators. Their server didn't give off a predatory vibe, so he'd just watch her and hope she didn't forget her purpose, which was not to hit on his underage son. Still, he'd point it out if he had to.

When she returned, she carried a coffee pot, a pitcher of water, two glasses and a cup and saucer on a tray. "Are you ready to order, sir?" she asked cheerfully as she placed the items on the table and took out her pad and pen. She was clearly trying hard not to ogle David.

Isaac fought the laughter that threatened to spill from his chest. "David, what would you like, son?"

David turned to look at his dad instead of at the pretty girl watching him. "Can I have a double chocolate fudge milkshake, please, Dad? And can I have ham mac and cheese?"

"Sure thing," the server answered for Isaac, and when David finally looked at her, she smiled widely at him.

"And I'll have the Cajun mac and cheese, please." Isaac was pleased to see his son return her smile politely before returning to his game. "What beer would you suggest I have with my order?"

Isaac wanted to see if the girl was worth her salt. Her immediate response pleased him.

"You would need a light, citrusy beer to complement the spicy flavors, sir. We have Pilsner on tap or Blue Moon. Have you tried either of those?"

Isaac had had both. "I'll have the Blue Moon this time, thanks."

The girl smiled at him, then said, "I'll be back with your order presently, sir."

Flashing another quick look at David, who was too busy on his phone to notice her, she walked away, and Isaac couldn't keep the laugh in this time. He kept it low and short, glad that David was too engrossed in his game to care why his dad was laughing randomly.

Maybe if his son were older, he'd sit back and see whether or not he'd get a clue, but he was relieved that, at least for now, David retained the innocence of his childhood.   He sipped the water at his fingertips and thought about why it was that his only child was so unaware of his appeal to the opposite sex. Maybe it had something to do with the fact that his dad had not been in a relationship of any kind since his mother's untimely death. Isaac just hadn't been interested in trying to find anyone else. Rowena Bray had fit him so perfectly that he doubted any other woman ever would.

His thoughts went for a moment to his priest's son, Adam. He was such a beautiful man, all tall lean muscle and quiet strength. Something about the young man had sparked an awareness in him that he didn't know what to do with. His magnetism was almost palpable, almost as though Isaac could hold it in the palms of his hands. That had been what had sparked the shock between them when they shook hands. Isaac couldn't remember ever having been so acutely aware of another person as he had been of Adam.

What it meant, he couldn't say. If anyone had ever asked him, he'd have said he was a straight man. He couldn't recall ever having been attracted to anyone other than a woman before. But he knew himself well enough to know that he loved people in general, and he had never been one to qualify or quantify his feelings in terms of what gender someone was. He found, as he considered his reaction to the younger man, that the idea of being attracted to a man didn't freak him out quite like he thought it might have. He certainly didn't think there was anything more to it than the impact of a powerful personality. He wasn't lusting after the man, nor did he feel any overwhelming urge to be or do anything sexual because of the pull he felt toward him.

Even the infrequent physical attraction he'd felt to one or two women in the last eleven years had not been enough to make him do anything more about it than jack off in the privacy of his shower. His left hand was good enough to meet his lackluster sexual needs. His libido seemed to have gone into hiding when Rowena died, and that was fine by him. With a now teenaged son, the last thing he needed was the inconvenience of a sexual attraction to anyone. He couldn't imagine managing his own lust at the same time as he was trying to steer his son in his own sexual discovery…assuming it would happen any day now.

What would he do when David decided he was more interested in girls than in games? He knew his son had reached puberty a couple of years earlier, so it wouldn't be long now before he'd need to have the next conversation, the one about birth control. He'd prefer for his son to wait to have sex, but he knew that was likely not to happen. He supposed there were still virgins in the world — Rowena had been one when he married her — but he would guess that they were far fewer than they used to be.

The server returned with their food and drink orders, placing each before them and then stepping back to say cheerily,

"Enjoy your meals, gentlemen."

Isaac ate quietly, enjoying the silence and the flavors that burst across his tongue with every mouthful. Once he was done, he leaned back to sip his beer and watched his son slurp more of his milkshake.

"Hey, Dad," David called to him, his eyes bright. "We had a visit from a few college reps at school on Friday. They brought some packages with them and stayed half the day."

He paused, as though gathering his thoughts, sipped some more of his liquid dessert, and then plunged on with his questions.

"Did you always know you wanted to start your own business? I mean, why didn't you join the Army like Maje? And what did you need to study to become a businessman?"

Isaac had never really talked to David about his choice of a vocation, though he had told him he'd started this shop and bought the farm with his mother. He certainly hadn't expected those to be the questions he got asked at this point.

"Where's this coming from?" he wondered aloud.

"Well, I'm gonna have to keep my grades up if the colleges I apply to are going to take me seriously," David explained, sucking in more of his shake. "And I don't even know what I want to be."

Ah! Now things made sense, though Isaac wasn't sure what had sparked the thought at this moment.

"I didn't want to join the military," he told David, though he didn't explain why not.

That was a conversation for another day, especially as he would need to tread carefully in discussing his relationship with his father, because he didn't want to spoil what David had going with him.

"I just knew that I didn't want to work for anyone but myself, which meant I had to start a business. That's what helped me decide what to study in college."

"Did you go beyond a bachelor's degree?" he wanted to know next.

"I did. But I did it all online so I could run the business and not have to take time off to go to school."

That had been a challenging time for him, coming so soon after Rowena's death. He had done it as much for the added security of the qualifications he would earn as for the distraction it provided from the pain in his broken heart.

"Is there something you're thinking about studying in college, son?"

David shook his head just as the server reappeared at their table.

"Did you enjoy your meal?" she asked with a smile for each of them.

"It was delicious, thank you," Isaac said.

David just smiled and nodded. She returned his smile quickly as though she thought she would lose his attention if she didn't get right on it.

"Would you like dessert, or more coffee, perhaps?" she asked next.

"No, thank you, we're good. You can just go ahead and let me have the check now, please." Isaac accompanied his request with a smile of his own.

"Right away, sir," she said, hurrying off to do his bidding.

The conversation she had interrupted continued once they were strapped into their seatbelts and waiting for the truck to warm up.

"What if you didn't like owning a flower shop, Dad?"

Isaac looked over at his son for a moment, wondering what thoughts he was wrestling with but knowing he would tell him when he had figured out what he wanted to say.

"If you're asking me what I would have done if I found I didn't enjoy the work I was doing, I don't know, son. The thought never occurred to me. I had chosen a path, and I was determined to follow through. There wasn't any time for liking or disliking in those early days. There was only time for hard work."

Then after Rowena had died, the business had still been new enough that he couldn't afford to think about enjoyment because he had bills to pay and a son to raise. Only in the last few years had he been able to relax enough to realize that he liked what he did. So, he had never stopped to think about what he would do if he hated the work.

David remained quiet the rest of the way home. Once they were inside, their coats draped over the coat rack by the kitchen door, David turned to him and said,

"I guess I'm not sure if there's anything I like to do. Maje asked me the other day what I wanted to be when I grew up and I didn't know what to say."

Isaac wondered what his father's response had been to David's silence but didn't ask. It was clear his son wasn't happy with not knowing and he didn't want to cause any more discomfort.

"Don't worry about it too much, son. Some folks don't know what they want to be even when they're grown up and they still manage to do okay. It'll come to you when it's time."

Yes...nothing happened before its time. He knew that. He hoped that learning that wouldn't be too hard on his son.

Chapter One

Fridays were typically pretty busy days at Wine and Roses Flower and Gift Shop. and today was no exception. Isaac had just finished sending out the last bouquet for the bachelorette party, for the Mayor's daughter, that was being held later that evening. He was exhausted, and his back hurt from all the work he'd put into the two wreaths for the doors, the centerpieces for the two tables as well as the tablescape pieces, and the corsages for the ladies…all ten of them, not counting the bride, who had her own specially-arranged one.

Reaching for the Hydro flask that he'd filled with water and ice earlier, he took a long swig just as the swinging door to the workroom opened. He had had the saloon doors placed instead of regular ones so he could use his hips or other body parts to open them instead of having to put his creations down to open the door the usual way.

"Have you had lunch as yet, Boss?"

His store manager, a feisty fifty-something, poked her head in. Isaac loved her like the big sister she pretended she was, even if she never called him anything other than Boss.

"Not yet. Why?"

He knew better than to waffle about when she asked him about his meals.

"Because I've brought you a wrap sandwich and a bottle of water."

He accepted the food she came through the doors to hand to him, and then reached out to give her a one-armed hug.

"Thanks, Peaches."

He ate quickly, then went to relieve her so she could take a break off her feet. She would never complain, but he knew she sometimes hurt from the long hours standing and tending to the customers' needs. She smiled at him as she passed him to go into the staff break room and he stepped behind the counter just as the bell over the front door opened. He looked up, a practiced smile ready on his lips.

Adam Kincaid walked in, looking around him as he entered, not yet noticing Isaac standing at the counter. He seemed to be looking for something specific. Isaac ignored the warm feeling invading his chest and spoke.

"Good afternoon. Welcome to Wine and Roses. How may I help you?"

"Oh, hi, Mr. Hamilton," Adam replied, looking up with surprise and something else in his eyes. "Yes, I'd like to get some flowers for a new mother. What's good?"

"Please, call me Isaac," he told Adam, before turning to his left to the already-made bouquets and pulling a fresh one that he'd just made that morning. The tulips were yellow and white, and the lilies were a pale pink.

"I just made this one earlier. Is she already at home, or is she still in the hospital?"

"She'll be at home by the time I get to her," Adam said.

"Would you like it in a vase, or as is?"

"In a vase, please." He paused, as though he was thinking, then added, "Do you have any gifts for music lovers? I'm looking for something unique."

Isaac smiled and led the way over to a section of the gift shop that held trinkets, figurines, and music boxes. He turned when he noticed that Adam had stopped before the display of delicate music boxes. He watched as Adam picked up a black lacquered music box with a pink ceramic rose atop its domed cover. He lifted the lid and a tiny crystal ballerina slid up. He looked at Isaac, who nodded, pleased that Adam didn't handle the delicate toy without permission.

Adam closed the lid and turned the box upside down so he could wind it up. Righting it, he reopened the lid and the little ballerina rose, twirling in place on her pedestal. The music was soothing and Isaac watched as Adam's shoulders visibly relaxed as he listened.

"Do you like music boxes?" he asked, going to stand next to Adam.

The younger man looked up at him. "Yes. I started to collect them when…" he paused. "Four years ago, before my daughter was born."

Something shifted in his expression, but he didn't add any more. Isaac wondered what had happened when his daughter was born.

"I'm sure your wife and daughter must love them," he said, wanting to fill the silence and saying the first thing he could think of that he didn't think would sound inquisitive.

Adam's reaction was entirely unexpected. His face closed and he put the music box back on the shelf in the exact spot it had been before and turned away.

"I'm not married," he said quietly. "Thanks for letting me look. I'll just pay for the flowers now."

He walked away before Isaac could reply, leaving him to wonder what he'd said to upset the man and how he could fix it. He hadn't meant to be offensive. He stepped behind the counter, making quick work of tying a white bow around the neck of the vase, and then rang up the sale, taking Adam's card and sliding it into the card reader. Then he pushed the receipt across for him to sign. He spoke as Adam leaned in to leave his signature.

"I'm sorry if I offended you back there," he said.

Adam didn't look up until he had signed the receipt and pushed it back across the counter. Then he stared quietly at Isaac for a long moment before replying.

"It's fine. I'm not offended." He took the gift-wrapped vase and turned away, then turned back to say, "Thank you. It was nice to see you again."

Then he walked out, leaving Isaac feeling curiously empty. He watched until he could no longer see Adam, who had stepped off the sidewalk and crossed the street before hurrying down to the public car park and disappearing. Not understanding why he felt so unsettled, he shook his head, put the receipt in with the other sales for the day and set about emptying the box of knickknacks that had been delivered the day before. He had identified a place to put them in the gift shop, but they'd need to be inventoried first.

By the end of the day, all the newly acquired pieces had been inventoried and set out on the shelves, he'd sold a number of figurines, a lot of flowers, and one music box. He was tired. He had sent Peaches home, promising not to work late, but he knew he couldn't leave until he had finished the last of the bouquets he needed to have ready for an order that had been called in late that afternoon. The client wanted delivery by ten the next morning.

As he was cleaning up and resetting the shop, the back door opened and David walked in.

"Hi, Dad," his son said. "Ready to go home? I have a new recipe I wanna try."

"A new recipe for…?"

"Mac and cheese, of course," the teenager said with a grin. "And you can make the salad, if you like."

Isaac grinned at his son's attempt to be slick and pass off part of the dinner prep onto his shoulders.

"Sorry, buddy, it's all yours tonight. I'll set the table and choose the game we'll play after we watch Jeopardy!"

David sighed. "Okay, fine!" He sounded defeated for a moment, then asked, perking up, "Can I get something extra if I win more points than you tonight?"

Isaac paused for a moment before answering. "Let me think on that. I'll let you know after dinner."

Isaac let David drive the last five minutes home, which he knew always thrilled his son. He had been giving the boy lessons since he turned thirteen, and though most of his driving had been done on their farm, once in a blue moon he let David drive part of the way to or from the store. He knew his son could hardly wait to take the driving test so he could have an official learner's permit, and he fully intended to sign him up for a state-sanctioned learner driving class, but he liked to see his boy smile.

The cats all greeted them when they walked in the door half an hour later. The old farmhouse had seen a lot of changes since Isaac and Rowena had bought it all those years ago. They had wanted to preserve its original bones as far as possible, while updating it with the most modern amenities that would fit their lifestyle. Rowena had done a lot of the work before her untimely death, and for a while after it, Isaac had done nothing.

Back then, the very thought of finishing the changes she'd begun had filled him with dread and a pain so acute that he had completely shied away from it. But as he had learned, time does heal all wounds, and he had finally been able to complete the changes they'd agreed to right when they had first bought the place. Now it was a warm, rambling, family space, and he loved that he could remember her without pain in every room of it.

David went up to change while Isaac fed the animals and then when the boy came downstairs, he went up to shower and get comfortable. He set the table, as he'd promised, and decided they'd play Checkers after Jeopardy! Then he sat in the armchair by the fireplace in the living room, watching his son and petting their oldest cat, Sadie, whose place in his lap was uncontested by the two female kittens and the old tom who also lived with them. He must have dozed off, because his son's voice startled him.

"Dinner's ready, Dad."

He pushed up out of the chair, went to wash his hands in the powder room that used to be part of the parlor and then went to sit at the big farm table. David had already put the bowl with the salad and dish with the steaming mac and cheese in the center, along with bottled balsamic vinaigrette dressing.

"What do you want to drink, Dad?" he asked.

"I'll have water for now, son, thanks."

They settled in to eat, and Isaac noticed that the mac and cheese was baked. He raised his eyebrows.

"Where'd you get the recipe for this?" he asked. "It looks great, David."

David preened. "My friend said her brother showed her how to make this at home, and she added the bacon strips for some extra protein." He warmed to his subject, going on without being asked. "I used a packet of the French onion soup you had as well as the Cheddar cheese you had left over."

Isaac smiled and helped himself to a heaping bowl of salad, dressing it and settling in to enjoy his food. They didn't talk much, mostly because they preferred to concentrate on the food. But Isaac couldn't help exclaiming when he had his first taste of David's mac and cheese.

"Mmm! This is delicious, son!" He raised his glass and tipped it to David. "Well done!"

After dinner he helped David clean up, then cut two pieces of apple pie and added a scoop of vanilla ice cream for each of them and took their dessert out to the family room where David had the television on, waiting for the gameshow to begin.

"Dessert," he said, handing David his bowl.

The boy's eyes lit up. He was a growing boy, so the extra food wasn't unwelcome plus, his favorite dessert was apple pie with ice cream.

"Thanks, Dad." He settled back into his seat and polished off the treat by the time the announcer was declaring "This is Jeopardy!"

The rest of the evening went as usual. David won the game show this time, and Isaac handed over the sixteen dollars he'd earned, one for each question he'd gotten correct. That was the standard. Isaac had decided that the extra would be letting him have an extra hour with his friends on whichever Saturday he chose. He could either have them come over, or he could spend that time with them doing whatever they got up to at his friend's home.

They played Checkers for another couple of hours, before Isaac said he was tired. It had been a long day. He left David watching some sport or other on the television and went up to bed. Lying in bed in his boxers, his mind went back over his day, and lingered on Adam Kincaid's part in it. That man was fine by any stretch of the imagination. That long blond hair, those gray eyes, that sweet dimple in his left cheek, were all so attractive on the guy. Even his height, which was still shorter than Isaac's own six and a half feet, was a treat. He wasn't a short man and Isaac had liked that Adam hadn't had to crane his neck for their eyes to meet.

And why was he liking that their eyes had met more than once this afternoon? That was new. As new as him appreciating how beautiful the man was. As new as him noticing how when Adam had told him he wasn't married, they had grown dark, as though all the light had been extinguished from them. As new as him wishing he could fix whatever had made the light go out.

He turned onto his side, trying to get the pretty man out of his mind. But nothing seemed to be working, so he relaxed and let his thoughts center on him some more. He didn't know much about the younger man, aside from who his dad was and that he was one of three sons and older than Bennett, the one who was engaged to David's teacher. What did he do for a living? What had happened to his daughter's mother? Was he a widower, like Isaac was? That might explain the darkness in his eyes.

Isaac would never wish the kind of pain he'd felt when Rowena had died on anyone. At thirty-six, a part of his soul had died with her, a slow, horribly painful death. He could never have imagined such pain, nor had he ever thought he would lose his heart. She had been his heart and soul, and recovering from the loss had taken a long, long time. No one should have to suffer that agony.

He wondered how old Adam was. He had a youthful face, and his daughter didn't look to be more than two or three years old. She was a pretty little thing, just like her dad, with the same blond tresses but with blue-gray eyes. He knew how difficult it was to work a full-time job and still be a good parent for a toddler. He admired the man for that just on principle. And a little girl had to be harder than a little boy.

At least with a boy, he knew how everything worked, how they'd feel about things, how to help them. He would have no idea how to raise a little girl. Yet Adam Kincaid was doing it, even if he had his parents to help him. And why was a handsome dude like him not already married again or at all? Adam didn't seem to be shy or socially awkward, but then, he had only interacted with him twice, and not for long enough to know if that assessment was accurate.

Turning again, he plumped his pillows and chastised himself for wasting good sleeping time thinking about a man. A man he would not normally even have noticed. So, what was up with this strange preoccupation? He didn't understand it.

"Go to sleep, Zac!" he told himself sternly. "You've got another busy day tomorrow."

He slowly relaxed his body, starting with his neck and moving downward. He didn't know when he fell asleep, but the old rooster crowing woke him up. He rubbed his eyes and sat up, checking the time on his clock. Dawn was just about to break, so the sky was still gray but lightening. He got out of bed and pulled on a robe before heading down to the kitchen. The television was still on, and he found his son wrapped in a blanket, sound asleep on the big old leather sofa.

Isaac smiled and shut the TV off, then padded into the kitchen to make his coffee. By the time he was pouring himself his first cup, David was up and wandering into the kitchen, yawning hugely.

"Hey Dad. Morning. Sorry I fell asleep in the couch again." He looked sheepish.

Isaac smiled indulgently. "Morning, son. What have you got going on today after work?"

David spent four hours every Saturday working in the shop, and Isaac paid him to do it, because it was important that he learned the value of a dollar, as well as the pleasure of working with his hands. Then he spent his Saturday afternoons and evenings with his friends. He had to be home by ten, though, and if he weren't going to go home with his dad, he'd have to let him know how he planned to get home.

"I told the guys I had an extra hour so we're going to go bowling and then go play video games at Alex's house. He says his dad will bring me home."

Alexander Mansfield was David's best friend, and only one of three guys he hung out with on Saturdays. Isaac had met Alex's dad a few times. The man was a cop, so he felt safe having his son spend time with Alex. They'd even had a few sleepovers, though mostly it was because it had been too late to ask either parent to take them home.

"Okay. Well, we have a little time before we need to head out. Do you want me to make you breakfast before we leave?"

"No thanks, Dad. I'll have the leftover mac and cheese."

Isaac grinned. Why was he not surprised? He didn't mind what David ate, as long as he ate something before he started his day. Maybe that was bad of him, maybe he was being a neglectful parent, but so far in fifteen years, he hadn't seen his son choose to eat anything that was inherently bad for him at breakfast time. Mac and cheese was fine.

Isaac went up to shower and change, then returned to the kitchen to make himself an omelet and toast, which he slathered with butter and marmalade. Then he took his breakfast out to the covered back porch and sat at the table, letting the peace of the morning wash over him. The sun was up now, and Old Yeller, his loud rooster, was silent again, having done his civic duty and all. The sky was a glorious mix of blue, pink, peach and gold. He savored the food and sat long after it was done sipping his coffee and planning his day.

Aside from the usual tasks — making the flower arrangements for the sanctuary and sending the weekly bouquet of daisies to old Mrs. Thornton from her son — he had two new events to plan for, as well as the weekly visit to the hospital to give away any unsold flowers over a few days old. When he got back inside, David was waiting to go outside to back the car out of the garage as was his custom.

Once at the shop, Isaac left David to park the car in the back while he went in to open up and get started. There was a lot to do. David came in and immediately began to sweep. Isaac left him tidying the front of the shop while he went ahead and began the tasks for the day. First, emails. People often left him messages regarding changes they wanted made to their orders, or left fresh orders for immediate or long-term delivery. Next, he checked his answering machine, happy that the only message was from the nursing home to say the Major had a physical coming up on Monday and they'd like him to be there to discuss his progress.

He'd call at lunch time. Right now, he needed to start gathering together the flowers for the two new projects. He heard the bell over the front door jingle and listened as his son greeted the customer. David knew to come and get him if there was anything he couldn't handle, so Isaac concentrated on the flowers the first client wanted included in her arrangements. They had come in the day before and he got them now and set about making the five garlands and the large bouquet she wanted. They'd be coming to get them at noon, and he wanted to be ready to handle the sale, especially since that was when David was scheduled to leave.

By late afternoon, Isaac was tired again. David had left promptly at noon, asking if Isaac wanted him to get him lunch.

"No, thanks, son. I'll duck out in a bit. Have fun."

"Later, Dad!"

He'd order something from the diner and have them deliver it so he wouldn't have to leave the shop unattended. His other teenaged helper wasn't due until one, and then he could get back to work in the workroom. By the time his fried chicken and waffles order was delivered, along with a bottle of beer, Isaac was more than ready to chow down. He sat in the little alcove behind the counter, next to the cash register but out of sight of the front of the shop and ate his lunch while he watched the world go by through the side window. When Shannon, his other Saturday helper arrived, he gladly relinquished the shop to her and went back to work.

The last thing he did before closing up at five was to prepare the flowers for the sanctuary. Mrs. Kincaid liked bright colors, and since he always made four arrangements for the spaces both at the altar and in the back, he chose to frame the flowers he used with dark green foliage. He included peach and yellow carnations, pink gerberas, white roses, and baby's breath. He knew someone from the church would be along to pick them up before he closed, though he had delivered them once or twice when there had been the need.

He had just put the finishing touches on the bouquets when the door to the shop opened. He heard Shannon greet the customer and stretched his back before heading to the front to see who was coming in so late. Adam Kincaid looked over at him as he pushed the doors open. The younger man smiled and Isaac's belly tightened. Ignoring the inexplicable reaction, he returned the smile.

"Adam! Happy Saturday!"

"Afternoon, Isaac. Thank you. I just came to get Mom's arrangements for the church. She can't come herself and Mrs. Thompson, who runs the Flower Guild, is sick this week."

"Not a problem, Adam," Isaac said, turning to head back into the work room.

"How's your mom, Shannon?" Isaac heard Adam ask as he picked up the first arrangement.

"She's much better, thanks, Dr. Kincaid. She has another appointment at the hospital next Tuesday."

Dr. Kincaid? Adam was a doctor? How had he not known that? He walked out with an arrangement in his hands.

"Show me to your car. There are three others," he said.

What he wanted to do was ask a bunch of questions. What sort of doctor are you? How long have you been a doctor? Are you off this weekend? Instead, he followed Adam out the door and waited while he opened the back of his SUV and placed the flowers gently inside.

"I'll come help you," Adam offered.

Leaving the trunk open, he walked back inside after Isaac, who asked him to wait. He didn't need Adam's crisp-looking white shirt and dark trousers to get messed up in his workroom.

"I'll bring it here," he said and turned away, returning a few seconds later with a second arrangement.

He followed with the third one, and before long they were all settled in the back of the vehicle. Adam closed the hatch and stepped back.

"How much?" he asked, reaching for his wallet.

Isaac smiled. "The Flower Guild has an account with us," he said, "and arrangements for the sanctuary are paid for from their budget. It's covered."

Adam's cheeks turned a light shade of pink, as if he were embarrassed not to know how the flowers for the church were paid for. Adorable as ever! The thought crossed his mind without any conscious effort on his part, astonishing him immensely. Since when did he find anything about a man adorable? Lord help him!

"It was good to see you again, Isaac," Adam was saying, extending a hand.

"Yes."

Isaac felt silly standing there unable to say more because he was so caught off guard by his reaction to the younger man. Gathering himself, he shook Adam's hand and added after a moment, "Please say hello to your parents for me."

Which wasn't much better, since he was likely to see them tomorrow morning in service. Shaking his head at himself, he registered the tingle he felt at the touch of Adam's hand, and the warmth that flowed up his arm at the firm clasp of that hand on his.

"I will."

Adam raised a hand in farewell before getting into his vehicle and driving away, leaving Isaac standing there on the sidewalk staring after him like a befuddled idiot.

Get a damned grip, Zac! Yep...that's precisely what he needed to do. Turning sharply on his heels, he made his way back inside in time to give Shannon her weekly pay and smile at her as she wished him a good afternoon and went home to her mother.

Chapter Two

"Any more beer?"

Aidan's voice rose above the already loud voices of the guys currently playing gin rummy at his kitchen table. Adam pulled another six-pack from the cooler and walked back with them in one hand and another platter with nachos and cheese dip in the other.

"You rang?" he quipped, setting the beers down by his twin and holding the platter above their heads.

Five pairs of eyes looked up at him. "More nachos and cheese?" Bennett asked.

Adam nodded. "You got it. The wings are almost ready. Five minutes."

The guys fell to with a will, and the plate of nachos was soon empty. Adam had been smart enough to leave a portion for himself in the kitchen, so he wasn't mad at them for finishing it. He was happy he could actually spend a lazy evening with his siblings and in-laws...well, almost-in-law, in the case of Bennett's guy, Jordan. They hadn't decided on a date as yet, though they already knew where they were going for their honeymoon.

What he wouldn't give for a person of his own. If only his schedule was as cooperative as it had been these last two weeks. He knew the respite wouldn't last, and almost wished he had decided to take his colleague up on the offer to go spend a weekend hidden away in the woods, fishing and swimming. But he didn't, mostly because he didn't want to give the man any mixed messages.

He and Rob McIntyre — a trauma surgeon at the hospital — had been amicable colleagues for three years, and while Rob had never said anything, Adam knew the man was attracted to him. He did a good job of hiding it, of course, disguising his attention as merely friendly as often as he could. But every now and again, he let some of the emotion he was feeling slip into his eyes, and Adam had seen that certain look when he'd invited him to share his cabin in the woods outside of town.

It would have been nice to go with the flow, to take what was on offer and release the tension that his good left hand didn't seem able to deal with adequately any longer. But he wasn't that guy, and he knew it. He couldn't lead the man on. He was cowardly enough not to want to actually say the words, but he figured refusing the invitation would be clue enough. He sure as hell hoped it would be. The last thing he wanted was any drama on the job, or hard feelings between him and anyone he worked with. He'd managed to avoid that trap all his working life, and he wasn't going to mess up his perfect record now.

The timer dinged on the oven and he went to get the spicy barbecued wings he had made earlier. He also pulled the blue cheese and ranch dressings from the refrigerator and took the food back out to the waiting men. Aidan had already taken in the French fries he had contributed to the evening's meal, and Adam knew everyone was eager to demolish Bennett's brownies, which would top off the evening's fare.

"So, DanDan," Adam began, and chuckled when Aidan rolled his eyes and gave his twin the middle finger at his use of the childhood nickname that Bennett had used with him when he was little. Now, they used it to tease him. "How's the detecting work going these days? Business must be slow if you actually have a whole weekend off, dude! What, no one murdered in their sleep recently?"

Aidan chuckled. "It's as slow as your hospital gig, I imagine," he retorted, "since there haven't been any pile-ups on the highway recently!"

Adam knew it was black humor, but in a way, it was a relief to joke about the fact that there were no terrible cases filling the ER to keep him at work when he should be off. He hadn't had more than one day off each week in the last three, and he was glad for the chance to just kick back and chill with his brothers and their significant others.

Was it terrible that he didn't have any real friends? He got along well with everyone at work, and aside from Rob, who had a thing for him that he was trying to keep in check, there was no one who stood out as especially important in his life. No one outside of family that he turned to when he had problems. What the hell would he do if he didn't have his brothers? And that wasn't healthy, not having friends.

Aidan had his partner, a kickass woman who complemented his own snips and snails and puppy dogs' tails badassery with a side of sugar and spice and everything nice. It was the cutest thing to see them together. Her baby face and diminutive size next to Aidan's rugged features and hulking form surely confused a lot of perps. Adam smiled at the thought of her sweet smile and snarky mouth, and those Kung Fu moves. Her husband had become fast friends with Aidan over the years, and they had been nicknamed the Three Musketeers by the Kincaid family.

Even Benny, who was arguably the most reserved of the three Kincaid boys, had always had Ryland Tucker, III as his best friend. They had practically grown up together, and their two families had become extensions of each other. Adam had always loved watching his little brother engage with his bestie, and he was thrilled that Benny had found someone who loved him with the kind of single-minded focus that Jordan O'Leary showed him.

Adam had no one. As he watched his brothers argue over who had really won the last game, he wondered what had happened to him. Technically, he was the oldest brother, having been born an hour and twelve minutes before Aidan. Aside from that accident of birth, though, nothing marked him as older than Aidan. He was shorter by a couple of inches, slighter of build, though he was wide enough, and generally far less brash than his younger twin.

Maybe that's what his trouble was. He didn't lack self-confidence, he just didn't exude it as well as Aidan did. Where his twin was in-your-face bold, bordering on arrogant — which suited the career path he'd chosen — Adam was quiet, composed, calm. He'd never been one to push himself forward, which meant he'd often not gotten the thing he wanted, or the person. And if he wasn't exactly a wallflower, he wasn't the center of attention, either.

When had he decided to be an observer rather than a participant in life? When had he decided it was just easier to let things slide, let the world go by? Maybe it had been in those undergraduate years, after he decided he wanted to be a doctor, not a nurse, and during all the years of his medical training. Life was just easier if he focused on his studies and his career goals. He marveled at how he'd managed to find time to have a friends-with-benefits relationship with Cheryl.

She had been his friend. And he'd lost her to the one thing neither of them had seen coming. His thoughts went to Nova, all that was left of the friend he had treasured and would have married if she had lived for him to change her mind. Only his mother knew how deeply Cheryl's death had scarred him, because only his mother knew what he had been planning for after their baby was born.

"Hey, bro, snap out of it! Where the hell did you go just now?"

Aidan's voice in his ear jerked Adam back into his living room, to the place where everyone was watching him with concern. Shit! Not what he wanted. Not the center of attention, remember? What the hell could he say to get them off his back? Especially Aidan, who wasn't his twin for nothing. He could read Adam like a book, and sometimes he even knew what he was thinking before he said it. Like now.

"Don't go there, Adam! Just don't!" Aidan's voice was stern, his expression fierce and protective all at once. "We've got you."

"What?"

Adam felt panic rising inside him at the thought that anyone other than Aidan might have guessed what he'd been thinking about. He really didn't need anyone else knowing how inadequate and empty he felt because he didn't have a bestie. That just sounded downright juvenile, and he was a man, not a boy, for crying out loud!

"Don't go getting lost in your head. Nothing good lives there. We all know this, don't we?"

Aidan's words were teasing, and the others laughed at them, but Adam could see the concern in his eyes when he looked at him. At the end of the day, his twin was his best friend and had always been. He was the one who should be pulling Aidan along, not the other way around. He should be the one to have his brother's back. He should be the one with the strength, the power, the personality. Yet here he was getting maudlin on his own game night with the boys and needing Aidan to pull his head out of his ass for him.

"Sorry! Just a thought." Lame, Adam!

"Cut it out! You're off duty. Let it go, dude!"

Adam stretched his lips in a strained smile. "You're right. Sorry, guys."

"Is that an occupational hazard with you essential workers?" Benny asked, casting an accusatory eye at his fiancé.

Jordan laughed, and Adam sighed with relief. The focus turned to Jordan, who tried to defend his occasional lapses in attention when they were together without any success at all. They played a few more rounds of gin, won and lost the five-dollar bets and at the end of the night, Chandler, Ryland's husband, went home with twenty-five dollars. When only Aidan remained in the apartment, helping Adam clean up, he asked the question Adam had been dreading since his momentary lapse earlier.

"What's going on, bro? Why the space out earlier? What gives?"

Adam didn't know how to answer the question without sounding like a loser, but this was Aidan. If he could trust anyone not to judge him, it would be his twin.

"I don't know, man. I was just thinking about how…" The word hit him as soon as he began to speak, and it shocked him with its absolute truth.

"How…what?" Aidan eyed him keenly. "I can't help you if you don't level with me."

Adam swallowed the lump that choked him suddenly. "Hell! I'm lonely. You guys all have people you can turn to outside of your family for support, for encouragement, for companionship. Who have I got?"

Jeez! He sounded even more whiny than Nova did when she couldn't get the treat she wanted. Rolling his eyes, he turned away to tie off the garbage bag and pull it from the bin it sat in. Placing another in it quickly, he took the bag out to the trash bin in the garage. Aidan was waiting for him when he walked back in.

"Beer?"

"Sure." He went to wash his hands and took the can Aidan offered him once he dried them.

Aidan led the way into the living room, once again set to rights, and sprawled on the sofa recently vacated by their friends. Adam sat in the recliner and pulled the leg rest up so he could lie back, eyes closed. How hadn't he realized he was lonely until now? He'd been so busy working and caring for Nova that he hadn't had time to think about much else. That's how that happened, he supposed.

"You never really give anyone a chance to get close to you, bro. You know that, right? Especially not since Cheryl…"

Aidan let his words trail off. Adam knew he didn't like to speak of Nova's mother because he thought it would hurt him. But it didn't hurt to hear her name for the reasons most people assumed it did. What hurt was that he hadn't been able to help her, that he hadn't known she needed help until she presented in his ER with all the classic signs of eclampsia. Until she died shortly after they took Nova from her.

Fuck! He wasn't a crier, but the tears pricking at his eyelids were as hot and real as they'd been the night she'd died. Had it really been four years? It felt like yesterday. All the feelings of inadequacy, of guilt, of rage and bitterness and sorrow welled up again, washing over him like acid. He burned with them but he refused to succumb to them. His therapist had reminded him over and over that he knew he had nothing to be guilty about. He knew there had been nothing he could do. He knew the stroke would kill her.

Taking on the weight of a guilt that wasn't his was a kind of arrogance that he had learned to suppress. It wasn't about him. It had never been about him. But Cheryl had been his person and his sometime lover, even if she hadn't been his soulmate, his one and only. He had been prepared to marry her when she'd told him she was pregnant, but she had adamantly refused.

"I won't be party to a shotgun wedding," she had said angrily, "just because you and your family think it's 'the right thing to do'." She had put air quotes around that last bit. "It may be the right thing for the reverend and his missus, but it's not what I want. I don't love you, Adam," she'd said, almost desperately, holding him by the arm as if to imprint her sincerity on him. "And I don't plan to marry anyone I don't love. Neither should you."

"Hey!" Aidan's voice broke into his memories again. "I know how hard your job is. And I know how hard it is to find time to be part of something outside of work. But you have to try, big brother. I know I'm not the best one to give you advice about that, but once in a while Lana and Gage manage to get me away from work and into something mindless with other people so I remember what it's like to be human. You should try it some time. When was the last time you accepted an invitation to do something fun with people other than us?"

Adam's mind went immediately to Rob's invitation to spend a couple of days in his cabin in the woods. That would definitely have been fun. He loved to fish and swim and hike, and there would have been more than enough of that to last him a little while when he returned to work. But he had let fear of confrontation stop him from doing something he might have enjoyed.

It's been a while," he admitted. "In fact..."

"In fact...?" Aidan prodded.

"Rob invited me to go up to his cabin for some fishing this weekend. You know the place...it's close to where the Tuckers live, on the river."

"Isn't he the guy who has the hots for you?"

Adam felt his cheeks heat. "Yeah. So, you see why I couldn't go."

Aidan looked at him long and hard, unblinking, and then said, "Well, on the one hand, if you're scared you might actually like him in return and don't want to admit it for fear you break whatever promise you've made about being celibate or something, I suppose I can see why. But honestly, he seems like a cool enough guy, levelheaded. I checked him out the first time you told me he was giving off those come-do-me vibes."

This time a full-fledged blush stained his cheeks as Adam glared at his twin. Not that Aidan was wrong, because the first time he'd realized the other doctor was harboring less than innocent thoughts about him, they'd been at a barbecue he'd held at his riverside cabin for his friends to celebrate his dad's seventy-fifth birthday. The older man had just recovered from a heart attack and Rob had been eager to get him out to the cabin for some fishing and rest.

Rob had gotten tipsy enough to lose the strict control he normally kept on himself and had admitted that he wondered what it'd be like to take Adam up against a wall. Even now, the memory of that moment still made him uncomfortable. He'd made light of it, needing to give the man an out so that when he was sober again he wouldn't cringe too much at having made a fool of himself.

"Don't do it, man! The last time a date tried that, we both fell flat on our faces instead. It wasn't pretty," he'd quipped, pushing amusement into his voice. "And since you don't look too steady on your feet right now and I'm not eager for a repeat, how about you just forget it, huh?"

"Have you ever even given him the time of day? Tried a date to see if anything would come of it? In other words, do you have any real reason for not going this weekend?" Aidan asked him now.

"Come on, Aid, what would be the point? I'd only be getting his hopes up."

"Bullshit, bro! D'you think the guy would rape you or something if you said no to his advances? Assuming he'd even be bold enough to make any? And if he did, and you were uncomfortable, you could just drive home. Or, to avoid awkwardness at work after, maybe you could have just told him point blank you were only going as a friend not as a potential hookup. Ever thought of that?"

Adam hated it when Aidan was reasonable and no-nonsense. But to be that logical, he'd also have to be brave enough to talk to Rob, instead of merely hinting or avoiding him or making excuses.

"Have you even told him you're not interested?"

It's like he's reading my mind, damn him! "Not in so many words, no." Way to sound like a dumbass, Adam.

"And that right there is your problem, big brother. You have a really bad habit of getting lost in your head, and since I'm the only one who can read your mind, you're shit out of luck if you think he's gonna get the message clearly without you telling him. Maybe you should try using your words, bro."

"Shut up!" Adam said without heat. Because Aidan was right. "Who died and made you so damn smart?" he groused.

Aidan chuckled. "I'm not all that smart," he demurred. "I'm just not afraid to speak my mind and I don't care if it upsets people when I do."

Which was very true. That was one of the ways in which they weren't at all identical. Aidan didn't suffer fools gladly while Adam was all about being conciliatory.

"He's a nice guy, really…"

"And he'll survive when you just say no. Out loud!"

Adam laughed. Despite the awkward subject, he loved that his brother knew how to lighten the mood.

"So, now that we've solved your latest existential crisis, and while we're on the subject, has anyone other than Dr. Boner asked you out or even sparked your interest?"

Adam chuckled at Aidan's wry nickname for Rob, then sobered as an image of Isaac Hamilton flashed into his mind. He wasn't quick enough at hiding his expression, so he wasn't at all surprised when Aidan continued,

"Go on! Spit it out! Who's got you looking so...confused?"

"Dammit, stop watching me like a hawk, will you?"

"How else am I ever gonna get anything juicy out of you?" Aidan asked with a wide, unapologetic grin. "You've decided you need to keep secrets from me. We're twins, so that's not gonna fly, even if you are older than me by seventy-two minutes. You don't get to be the strong, silent type in this relationship. That's my job! I'm the cop."

More amusement accompanied this outburst, making Adam's smile return.

"It's just...weird, is all."

"Come on, Adam, you're killing me here. What's weird?"

Adam sighed. He may as well get it over with. "You know the guy who did the flowers for Benny's party? He has a contract to provide flowers for the sanctuary on Sundays."

"Yeah. He runs that cool flower and gift shop on Mulberry. Hamilton, I think his name is."

"Yes, Isaac Hamilton."

Adam stopped speaking because how did he say the rest of what was on his mind, which was that he was unaccountably attracted to the big man? So, not unexpectedly, Aidan made the leap and said it for him.

"You like the dude?"

Adam sighed again, then nodded, then spoke. Because he did know how to use his words, dammit!

"Yeah. I don't know anything about him, but I can't get him out of my mind. He's...I guess charismatic is a good word for him. Compelling. Fascinating. Dazzling. Captivating."

"Hmm. Sounds like you've got it bad for a guy you don't know if you're waxing poetic about him."

Aidan was teasing him, but he deserved it, because once again his little brother was spot on.

"Which is why I said it's weird. How can I be so...taken with this guy I don't know?"

Aidan shrugged. "Don't make me lie," he answered. "I've never felt anything like it." A pause, then he asked, "So, what are you gonna do about it?"

And that right there was the sixty-four-million-dollar question, wasn't it? It was a question for which he had absolutely no answer or even any idea of how to begin to answer it. The only thing he knew for sure was that despite his dismal record in talking with people about his feelings, he wanted to get up close and personal with the silver fox...really, really up close and personal. And he had no idea how to get what he wanted without doing what he was so bad at doing…using his words.

"I don't know," he told his twin. "I don't know."

Chapter Three

Isaac yawned and stretched. It was raining and the gray morning was cool and foggy. He snuggled deeper under his blanket and sighed. He should be getting ready for church, but he was reluctant to get out of bed. Mornings like these were meant for snuggling in bed with a sweetheart, making slow love, having multiple orgasms...though at his age, they wouldn't be that multiple or that frequent. Getting older meant slowing down all over, or at least that's what he'd heard. He had no personal experience to support the claim.

Unbidden, Adam Kincaid rose up before him, all blond and gray-eyed and sexy. What the hell? Why was he thinking about this man again? And why was his body waking up in a whole new way, for fuck's sake? He chuckled at the thought.

"Because that's what it's craving, fool," he told himself out loud. "A good, hard fuck."

But with the reverend's son? A doctor, a white boy, and a dude, no less? What in the entire hell is wrong with you?

The rest of that little diatribe was too...uncomfortable for him to say it out loud, but even thinking it made him almost queasy. He hadn't had any relationships since Rowena's death, not even the odd hookup he'd been offered a time or two by horny little dudes who were turned on by his age and size. His left hand had been his only consolation in those times when his body demanded some kind of relief from the sexual frustration he felt once in a while.

But a week after handing off the flowers for the church to Adam Kincaid, he had reluctantly concluded that he was more than passingly attracted to the young doctor, and ignoring it wasn't going to make it go away. Which meant he'd need to figure out how to handle it properly, especially since it also meant he was not straight, at least not where Adam was concerned. He'd have to do a little research.

His knowledge of life on the Kinsey scale (which he only knew about through the sex education pamphlets David had brought home from school) was slim to none. Straight and gay were all he knew and understood, and he had more or less discounted 'gay' since Adam was the only man he seemed to have any interest in as more than a customer or friend.

Sighing, he pulled back the covers and sat up, letting his hands hang between his spread legs. The room was chilly, but he needed that just now to tamp down the interest his dick seemed ready to pay to the direction of his thoughts. This past month, and especially this past week, he only had to think about the good doctor to send his ball sac tingling. And if he didn't stop his train of thought, he'd plump up, something that had not happened much since Rowena's death, and never at all for any other man.

He needed to shower and get ready for church. If he didn't get a move on, David would sleep in, and one of the promises he had made to himself, after his wife's death, was that he would keep his son in the church. Being spiritual was as much a part of him as his DNA, and he wanted to ensure that David had the same source of strength for the hard times he would no doubt face as he grew older. He wouldn't let him slack off church attendance just because his dad was pining over some dude he didn't really know well at all.

Dragging on the ratty cotton robe from the end of his bed, he left his bedroom to go down the hall to his son's and knocked. Hearing no answer, he opened the door cautiously and peered around it. He never, ever wanted to surprise his son as he had once been by his father in flagrante delicto, cock in hand in the midst of a hard orgasm. Masturbation, according to his conservative father, was a sin, and he had not heard the end of it for months. He didn't need to subject his son to that kind of humiliation. Besides which, even though he knew the boy was at the age where exploring his sexuality was normal and healthy, he really didn't want to see him at it.

"David?" he said softly, shaking the boy's t-shirt-clad shoulder gently. "Time to wake up, son. We have church this morning."

David dragged an eye open and looked fuzzily at him. "It's raining, Dad!" he protested, covering his head with his pillow.

"That's what cars are for bud. Come on, chop, chop! I'm leaving in an hour."

Showered and dressed in a dark brown suit, his boots shiny, his beard neatly trimmed, he went down to make himself some coffee and toast a bagel for David. Knowing the boy couldn't manage without some sustenance before the usual Sunday brunch after the youth hour, he always made sure to have something for him to munch on before service. He was just pouring his coffee into his to go mug when David walked in, dressed as he was in a nice suit and tie.

"You look good, son." he said, handing him the bagel, which he had spread with cream cheese, in a plastic sandwich bag. "Get something to drink and let's go. We don't wanna be late."

He got their coats out of the hall closet and they put them on before they left. By the time they got to the graceful old church on the outskirts of town, David had wolfed down his sandwich and was draining the last of the apple juice he had poured for himself. Isaac's coffee was also gone. The rain had eased, but the ground was still a little slippery. He stepped into the brightly lit sanctuary, pleased as he always was to see his floral arrangements adorning the space. The organist was playing a hymn softly, and the pews were filling up.

"Good morning, Isaac, David. Happy Sunday! It's good to see you today."

Isaac smiled at the greeter, a sweet old lady with a shock of white hair and a beatific smile and shook the proffered hand gently.

"Thank you, Emmeline. I wish you the same."

David murmured something indistinguishable as he shook hands and smiled at the woman who patted him on the arm.

"Such lovely manners," Isaac heard her say as David walked away.

Isaac sat in his usual seat on the far right, three pews from the back of the church. He closed his eyes and just listened to the quiet whisperings around him, to the organ humming in the background, and when a silence settled, he looked up to see that the service was about to begin. From the opening hymn, through the bible readings and prayers to the sermon, communion and closing, Isaac felt a peace steal over him, a quietness of spirit that he had needed so much in the early days of his bereavement.

Back then, those feelings had been his crutch, the healing salve to the deep wounds in his soul. Nowadays, they were his trusted boon companions, keeping his emotions on an even keel, filling up the empty spaces in his heart with warmth. He may not have a special someone anymore, but his spirituality did a fair job of keeping him settled.

After the service, as Reverend Kincaid stood just outside the door to greet his parishioners and any visitors, Isaac noticed a flash of blue-gray heading his way. It reminded him immediately of Adam, and he looked up, unprepared for the sight of the man himself moving toward him. The color of his suit matched the color of his eyes. What a powerful thing it was to see that his eyes looked a darker version of themselves as they reflected the light from his suit.

David had disappeared around the side of the church to the room where his youth meeting was being held. Isaac had decided that today he'd wait quietly in the sanctuary, which remained open for anyone who needed a place to wait for their children. He preferred that to waiting in the church hall where brunch was being set up, because he didn't want to look like a starving man at the soup kitchen on Christmas Day.

Now, though, he found himself smiling at the younger man as he approached.

"Good morning, Dr. Kincaid. Happy Sunday!"

Adam smiled and extended his hand. "It's Adam. And happy Sunday to you, too, Isaac."

"I don't believe I've ever noticed you in service before," he continued. What the hell is with you running off at the mouth like this, Zac?

"I don't usually come to this service, when I come," Adam explained. "But I woke up late and didn't want to miss out all day."

"I have a teenager," Isaac said with a chuckle. "It's hard enough getting him out of bed for this service."

"Where is your son?" Adam asked next, looking around him.

"Gone to youth meeting."

He had managed to release Adam's hand by this point, but his fingers felt the immediate loss of Adam's firm grip.

"I remember those," the doctor said wistfully. "Oh, for the simplicity of my youth."

"One thing the Major drummed into me that I have never forgotten. It's one of the few things we agree on. He told me the older you get the harder life gets."

Adam looked at him inquiringly. "The Major?"

"My father."

Isaac could see the question in Adam's eyes and was grateful that he didn't ask it, but only said, "Well, I have to head home now. Work this evening, and I have some chores to complete before I go. It's nice to see you again."

He stepped past Isaac, reached in to hug his dad, and then walked away to where his vehicle was parked. Isaac tore his gaze away from the enticing man, not needing anyone to take note of his interest. He stepped up to shake the rector's hands and found Reverend Kincaid's shrewd eyes on him with a speculative gleam in them.

"A blessed Sunday to you, Isaac," he said with a genuine smile. "How are you and David?"

"We're well, thanks, Rev."

No matter how often his rector had told him to call him by his name, Isaac didn't have it in him to do so. His mother may not have been with them long, but while she was there, and after she was gone and it was just him and the Major, he'd learned too well the lesson of respect for those in authority. And a priest had a kind of divine authority that just wouldn't permit that kind of liberty to be taken, even if it were allowed. So, he'd settled on 'Rev' as a compromise. And now, given the way the man had looked at him when he'd caught him watching his son, maybe it was a good thing he hadn't caved on that request.

"We missed you in church last Sunday," the priest continued. "The men could have used your help in the worship sing-off."

Isaac laughed. "I am sorry I missed that but I wasn't feeling too well."

"I'm glad you're feeling better now, my friend. I think, if you're like me, maybe you overdo it a little bit sometimes and then the old body complains."

"You may be right about that, sir," he agreed as he stepped away to let the next person have a turn with the priest.

Isaac was unsurprised by the minister's use of the word 'friend'. He knew he could have a good friend in his rector if he let himself go there, but he just wasn't sure how to do that. He had always been a loner, probably because he was an only child whose father didn't understand the need for children to socialize with others their own age. And his natural inclination to separate himself from others was fed by that lack of companionship.

Maybe that's what he needed…a real friend. He had never really had one of those, though he'd been friendly enough in school. But those companions had never gone home with him, and he had never been allowed to hang out at their houses. The boy he had been closest to had left right after high school and joined the Navy. He himself had left his hometown for a college on the other side of the country, and when he returned four years later, he had kept to himself as much as he could because none of the few companions he knew from school were still there.

As he sat in the pew listening through his bluetooth earphones to jazz on his phone, he considered that perhaps he was not doing himself any favors by working all day every day except Sundays and not having any time to call his own. He had known he wouldn't raise David the way he had been raised, but it seemed he was living his own life the way his father had lived his...all work and no play. Maybe it was time to change that.

After brunch, once they were back at home, he left David watching a spy movie on the television while he figured out dinner. As he prepped the fish he'd be roasting and peeled the potatoes for the potato salad that David demanded for dinner every Sunday — no matter what else was on the menu — he thought about how he could start to make a life for himself that wasn't only about his son and his store.

He'd been invited more than once to be part of the men's choir at church. He could definitely find at least one friend there. And maybe he could look up the few guys he'd hung out with in school to see if any of them were back in town. He doubted that, but it was worth a try. Also, he could host a barbecue for David and his friends and invite their parents. Who knew, maybe one of those dads would make a good friend as well. He knew for a fact that John Mansfield,

David's best friend's dad, was a funny, friendly guy with a warm heart for kids. They got along on the few occasions when they were together.

"Dad, what are we gonna do for Christmas this year?"

David's voice interrupted his musings and Isaac turned to find his son sitting at the kitchen table regarding him curiously.

"I don't know. Do you have something in mind?"

Because usually, when David asked a question like that, he already had some idea of the answer he would like to hear. Every year they did something different for the holiday, which was their favorite one. The tradition had begun while Rowena had still been alive. They were never at home for the holiday, either going away for a couple of days or out on the day itself.

"Can we go with Alex's family to Daytona Beach? His dad said we could if you said it was okay."

The one thing they had never done was spend time with anyone outside of the family. Isaac hid a smile. David knew what his main concern would be and he'd addressed it right out of the gate. He pretended to think it through, as though it were a thorny problem. He would definitely call John later to verify that a conversation had been had before confirming or denying the request.

"I'll let you know, son. In the meantime, is there a second option on the table?"

David nodded. He'd clearly been thinking hard about this and since Isaac usually let him decide on their Christmas adventure, he waited with interest to hear the alternative plan.

"Can we go cabin camping again?"

They'd done that once a couple of years before and David had thoroughly enjoyed 'roughing it', by which he meant not having a television, needing to build a fire in the fireplace to stay warm, taking a bath instead of a shower if he wanted to bathe in warm water — which he had to boil on the stove — and going for long hikes in the snow. It had been a great three days away, and Isaac had returned to the store feeling refreshed and almost happy. Frankly, he'd much prefer to do that than to go hang out in someone else's place for three days.

But Christmas was for his son. It was their way of keeping Rowena's memory close. Christmas had been the one holiday that they had all loved. And she had died on Christmas Eve, on her way home from a last-minute shopping run. That's why Isaac couldn't bear to be at home and why he needed to make each year special...to honor her memory and keep her close in their hearts. So, he'd do whatever it would take to make David's memory of the holiday a happy one, even if it meant spending time with another family.

"Are we going to visit Maje on Christmas Eve? Because if we are, I haven't bought him a gift as yet. And I think I know what he'd like for Christmas this year."

"Oh? And what's that?"

Isaac always gave his father a card and a bottle of some favorite liquor. He didn't have to think much beyond that. At most, he'd spare a thought to which new brand he'd introduced him to.

"I know he likes to play gin, and there's a pack of playing cards in the shop that have Braille markings on them. I know he wants to play with the new blind guy who's come to live there. They were in the same platoon or something."

Isaac's heart clenched with love and guilt. He had raised a compassionate and loving son, and by his example, he was showing Isaac up as being less than that to his own father. How the hell had he gotten so lucky? And how could he make sure that David stayed the same sweet kid with the heart of gold that he was? And more, why was he still holding on to hurts from his childhood? He knew his father was a hard man but seeing him with David when they went to visit had shown him a whole other side to the man, a softer, gentler side, if you will.

"That sounds like a great gift, son. Your grandfather will love that you thought of it."

And he would. Isaac knew his father would appreciate the thought that had gone into the gift, and would understand how much his grandson loved him, enough to want him to have friends where he was, friends he could engage with in ways that they would both enjoy. He had no doubt his father would see immediately how different Isaac's own gift was, and how much it spoke volumes as well about their own relationship.

Something like shame curled in his gut, but he stifled it. He had nothing to be ashamed of. Maybe he'd been too hard on his father for too long, but he couldn't find it in himself to be sorry about that. Still, he could stand to change that as well, just like he was thinking about changing how he lived the rest of his life. It couldn't hurt to be more than merely cordial with his own father. His son was managing that just fine. If a fifteen-year-old could manage to show love for his eighty-year-old grandparent, surely his forty-seven-year-old son could make the effort to get along better with him?

"I'll make sure to put a pack aside for you. Do you have the money to pay for the one you want?"

"Yeah. I want the one that costs twenty bucks. The black ones with the wolf pack on it. Maje likes wolves."

"I'll set that one aside tomorrow."

Isaac didn't betray his astonishment at that tidbit. Apparently there was a great deal that he didn't know about his father. He didn't want to dwell on any of that, so he concentrated on seasoning the fish cutlets, and had David cut the potatoes and put them in the boiling water when it was ready.

"Fish the eggs out of the water in another five minutes, will you, son?" he instructed him. "And while you're waiting, how about you add the corn and peas to the other pot there? Thanks."

They worked quietly together getting dinner ready, and once the potatoes were ready, David made the potato salad and put it in a covered dish in the refrigerator. Isaac loved Sunday afternoons. It was the one time when he was with David and it wasn't about school or work. It was just the two of them, cooking together, talking, settling into the bond between them even more deeply. He was more grateful than he could say that his son was amiable and not inclined to rebellion. He didn't know how he would have managed if David had decided to be anyone other than the strong and charming kid that he was.

"Dad, how did you know you loved Mom?"

The question floored Isaac because he hadn't expected ever to be asked that. They rarely talked about his mother these days. When she had first passed away, David was inconsolable. Then, once he reconciled himself to the fact that she wasn't going to wake up from her long sleep, he began to ask questions. Where had she gone? Who was with her? Was she lonely? Could she see them? Did she still love them? Did she miss them? Would they ever go where she was?

They had never talked about love, either his or David's love for her. It was a huge question and it raised one he hadn't ever thought he'd ask himself again in this lifetime. Could he ever love anyone again like he had loved her? He didn't know. He didn't want to think about it. So why, instead of thinking about how to answer his son's question, instead of trying to find out why he was asking it at this point, was his mind recalling the tall, sexy doctor in the blue-gray suit striding away to his car after service that morning? What did Adam Kincaid have to do with anything in his life?

Chapter Four

Adam pushed open the door to Wine and Roses Flower and Gift Shop and searched immediately for its owner. He wasn't standing behind the counter. Instead, a smiling middle-aged woman looked up from whatever she'd been doing and greeted him.

"Good afternoon, sir. How may I help you today?"

Adam returned her smile. She wore a black plastic name pin with the word 'Peaches' engraved on it in white. Amused by the name, he walked over and said, "I'm interested in a music box for my daughter."

"Right this way, sir." She led him out of the flower section into the part with the gifts. "We just got in a new consignment a few days ago. How old is your daughter, sir?"

"She's four."

Peaches smiled. "They're so precious at that age, especially if they weren't too terrible at two."

Adam laughed. "You're not wrong about that," he agreed. "She's very independent and opinionated, but otherwise, she's a sweetheart."

They came to a stop in front of a larger display of music boxes than there had been the last time he'd been shopping in the store. He noted the range in prices and materials and tried to decide which one Nova would like the look of best. Maybe that shell pink lacquered one...

"What's your daughter's name, sir?" Peaches asked, "and what's her favorite color?"

"Her name is Nova and at the moment her favorite color is pink."

"At the moment?" Peaches tilted her head like a bird.

"Yes, at the moment." He chuckled. "Last year it was lavender."

Peaches echoed his chuckles. "Well, at least she's color coordinated."

Adam cracked up at that, only managing to sober up when Peaches handed him the pink music box he'd been eyeing.

"Have a listen. This tune is especially sweet for the time of year."

Peaches had wound it up before handing it to him and when he opened it, a tiny ballerina rose up, twirling to the Dance of the Sugar Plum Fairy. The little miniature was dressed in delicate ice pink, her limbs and hair glittering with sparkling snowflakes. It was gorgeous and Adam knew Nova would love it. And it would be the perfect gift to remind her of this year's family outing. After Christmas dinner, the family always participated in a public activity, usually taking in a show at their local theater. This year's offering was from a ballet troupe visiting from New York City performing The Nutcracker.

"I'll take this," he said. "May I have it gift wrapped, please?"

"Certainly, sir. Will there be anything else?"

"I'll have a browse in your LP collection. I'll be there, soon."

He would treat himself this year. He hadn't added to his LP collection in a few years, not since Nova's birth, in fact. But for some reason, he was feeling more himself again, not grieving her mother's death as deeply as before. And he felt buoyed up, almost optimistic, as though something good were waiting in the wings to surprise him. He didn't have a clue what that might be, though he did know when the feeling started...after service on Sunday morning, when he'd bumped into Isaac Hamilton again looking as fine as wine in his brown suit and shiny boots.

Peaches left to wrap his daughter's gift and he breathed a sigh of relief. She was a lovely woman, but he wanted to see Isaac, and he hoped if he lingered in the shop a bit more, the man himself would appear and he could find some pretext to speak with him. To that end, he looked over the selection of albums, pulling one or two from the shelf to examine more closely. His eye caught an album by Ella Fitzgerald and he pulled it to have a look at the tunes included. He found himself wishing he could hear the songs and was listening on his cellphone to one of them when Isaac said behind him,

"Good choice. The lady's got a sweet, crisp, clean voice...emotive and compelling."

Adam shivered. He hadn't heard him approach, because as always happens, he got lost in the music. Isaac's voice was deep and as captivating as the music he was describing.

"I thought I'd treat myself," Adam said, hearing the huskiness in his voice and wishing he could better hide his reaction to the man now standing next to him.

"Good treat," Isaac said. "Great Christmas gift for a slow night at home. Sing your little one to sleep with Ella."

"Not a bad idea," Adam replied. "I've just bought her a music box for when I can't do that, though. She likes to go to sleep with music."

He turned to look at Isaac. "So, you recommend this as a self-care treat for a tired ER doctor?"

"Absolutely. Maybe you can download it on your music app and play it when you're on a break. It's good for the soul."

"Yeah...jazz and gospel music do that for me. They refresh me."

"Do you have any particular jazz musicians that you favor?"

Adam considered for a moment, needing the time to settle his nerves and steady his breathing. Why Isaac made him feel like a teenager he couldn't say, but it wasn't a bad feeling, just one he had left behind him decades ago and had never expected to feel again. It took a little getting used to.

"I discovered I liked jazz by accident a few years ago, so I'm still refining my tastes, I guess."

Isaac's smile lit up his whole face, making his light eyes sparkle. "I could go on and on about the ones I most enjoy, but I'll say you can't go wrong with the female vocalists. Let me know what you think about this lady, and then I'll introduce you to another one. When can you come by again?"

This isn't a date, you idiot! Stop doing the mental happy dance! "I have to work on Christmas day, but I'm off the day after."

"I'll be out of town. How about the day after tomorrow? I'll be open late, since I won't be here for the three days following that."

"Going out of town for the holiday?" Way to be a nosy bastard, Adam. It's none of your business what he's doing for Christmas.

"Yeah. David and I are going to Florida for a few days."

I'll miss you. Thankfully, he managed to keep those three words buried in his gut. You barely know the guy, Adam. How are you going to miss someone you've never been with? It didn't feel like only six weeks since they'd first met each other. And it sure as hell didn't feel like brief meetings each time since, either. Each had had some kind of significance, something he didn't fully understand but knew instinctively was important. So, while he couldn't ever admit it, he would certainly miss the man.

"Well, I hope you'll have a great time," he said. An appropriate answer well received. Job done. Time to move on. "I'd better get going. Peaches is wrapping the music box for me. I don't want to keep her waiting."

Isaac turned with him and Adam felt the touch of his broad hand at the small of his back as he shepherded him back into the main shop. The touch sent fresh shivers up his spine. He tried to hide his reaction but knew Isaac had noticed it because he moved his hand away immediately. Adam felt the loss keenly. What would it be like to have Isaac hold him there, use that hand to pull him into a tight embrace?

"Will that be all, sir?"

Peaches was speaking to him. He blinked, probably looking as clueless as he felt, because he'd been so lost in that fantasy, based solely on a simple touch, that he hadn't heard a word she'd said. He could feel the color of his embarrassment rising in his cheeks. The bell over the door dinged and Isaac said,

"Peaches, I'll finish this. Can you help the lady, please?"

"Sure, Boss." She smiled at Adam as she moved away to do as Isaac told her, saying as she went, "I hope your little one enjoys the music box, sir."

"Thank you."

Adam returned her smile and then turned his eyes to Isaac's face, surprising a look of yearning on it an instant before the older man shuttered his gaze and finished ringing up the sale. Isaac handed him the receipt to sign, put the music box and the LP into a cheerful Christmas-colored shopping bag, and handed it to him with the customer copy inside.

"Thank you," he said again. "I hope you have a happy Christmas. Will you be gone for the New Year as well?"

Apparently his mouth had declared its independence over his brain because the question flew past his lips without any conscious thought on his part. He cringed inwardly and opened his mouth to apologize for the intrusive question when Isaac answered with a smile.

"No. David and I usually just hang out at home doing nothing much."

"Our family has a big backyard party, weather permitting, on New Year's Day. If the weather's bad, or there's too much snow on the ground, we take it indoors. Why don't you come over? I'm sure David would like hanging out with the younger set, and if you don't mind hanging out with a loud and sometimes obnoxious bunch, you might have some fun, too."

Good grief! What the hell was he thinking, inviting this man to their family day? True, it was the tradition for the Kincaid boys to invite a friend or two over on New Year's Day to share the Family Day with them. But after having that come-to-Jesus conversation with Rob about their friendship, he had invited him to share the day with them. So why ask Isaac, whom he didn't know nearly as well? He didn't seem lonely or anything, but Adam felt compelled to reach out and draw him closer. For now, the only way he could do that was to have him come over. But really, was there even any other reason than his need to connect with him? He couldn't think of one. He hurried to provide some kind of excuse for his impromptu invitation that wouldn't seem creepy.

"Jordan has mentioned your son once or twice. I didn't know who he meant at first, and then I met you. He loves your son."

Isaac's eyes widened in surprise. "That's nice of him. I know that David loves him, too. I think Mr. O'Leary is probably his favorite teacher. He's certainly been very kind to David and has worked wonders with him in math."

"Jordan is really proud of how well your son is doing."

Adam felt a moment of disquiet at the thought that perhaps Isaac would be offended that Jordan was talking about his son's dysfunction with strangers and he wanted to assure him that no confidences had been shared.

"Jordan doesn't share any confidential information about any of his students, but we were talking about having kids one night and he and Bennett said they wanted to adopt. We asked them what age they wanted to adopt, and they both said older kids, and then Jordan added, a kid like David. We asked him what made David so special and he said he admired the way he didn't allow his disability to affect his personality. That he was the sweetest kid he knew."

Shut up! Shut up! Stop running off at the mouth, moron! Adam closed his eyes briefly, then looked down at the bag in his hand before looking up again.

"Anyway, sorry to talk your ear off. I'd better get going. Let me know if you'd like to join us on New Year's Day."

He put the bag down for a moment to fish a business card from his wallet. Isaac took it from him with a smile before he could put it on the counter.

"Have a happy Christmas," he ended, taking his bag and walking out, steeling himself not to look back.

But when he got outside and turned to walk toward where he'd parked his car, he couldn't stop his gaze from swinging back through the plate glass window. Isaac was watching him, but Adam was too far away to read his expression. He raised a hand in farewell and felt his heart rate kick up when Isaac returned the wave with a smile.

All the way back to his parents' home, he tried to control his breathing. He couldn't believe how deeply affected he was by Isaac's mere presence. He still felt faintly breathless when he parked and went inside to get his daughter. She had just woken up from her nap, and Adam gathered her warm body against him, loving the way her arms encircled his neck and her pink lips kissed his cheeks.

"Daddy!" She always exclaimed when he came to get her, as though she were surprised that he had come back, after all.

"Nova!" He echoed her tone, as he always did, and they both giggled.

"Did you have a good day, Daddy?" she asked before he could ask her the same thing. "Because Nova Madeleine did."

Adam chuckled. It amused him that she sometimes spoke about herself in the third person.

"Daddy had a very good day, Nova Madeleine. Thank you for asking," he replied, kissing her temple as he remembered how his day had just ended. "And he's glad you had a good day, too. Are you ready to go home?"

"Yes, please. Nana says when I come back tomorrow, we're going to make Christmas cakes. So, I have to get a good night's sleep, she said."

As though she had been summoned, Mrs. Kincaid walked into the room carrying Nova's backpack and a shopping bag.

"She didn't sleep for long," his mother said, reaching over to hug him. "I've washed everything in the bag, and I've packed your dinner so you don't have to go home to cook today."

"Thanks, Mom. You're the best."

Mrs. Kincaid smiled and kissed his cheek. "I need to know how many people are coming for Family Day, honey," she said, "and I need to know what you'll be bringing."

It was as though his mother knew he had just invited Isaac, as though she had some special Spidey sense and knew the optimal time to ask about guests. Did she notice something different about him? Was he smiling too much? Glowing? Because he sure as hell felt lit up, despite having left Isaac's store half an hour ago.

"I've invited two people, actually. Well, three if you count Isaac's son, David."

His mother turned her sharp gaze to his face. "Isaac? The flower shop owner?"

"Yes. I sort of sprang it on him at the last minute, but I'll let you know as soon as he tells me what he's doing. My other guest is definitely coming. It's Rob McIntyre."

"The boy who has taken a shine to you, you mean? Is that wise, son?"

Adam smiled. "We've had a talk, Mom. He understands I don't feel that way about him, and we've agreed to be just friends."

She looked doubtful. "And you trust him?"

Adam thought for a moment, then nodded. "Yeah, I do. He's a really cool guy. I think he was just focused on me because I never gave him any reason not to hope, which for him meant he could hope. Now that I've cut him off, he can open his eyes again and look around at all the other great guys out there."

"Well, if you're sure, I'll be happy to welcome him. You do need friends, honey…you work too hard and don't take care of yourself."

Adam smiled at his mother. "I know. I'll do better, I promise."

She rolled her eyes at him, making him laugh. "You make that promise to me at least once a month," she grumbled. "So, pardon me if I am skeptical. I'll believe that when I see it."

Then she turned to Nova, who had put her head down on Adam's shoulder and was watching them sleepily.

"Give Nana some sugar, baby," she said and pouted her lips for Nova to kiss.

Once kisses and sweet hugs had been exchanged, and Nova had promised to make sure Daddy went to bed on time — much to Adam's amusement — Adam took her home. He would have to struggle to keep her awake long enough to have dinner. When she was this sleepy, the last thing she cared about was food. Maybe he'd visit his brother so she could play with Claus. That would perk her up some.

Thankfully, Benny was home, but so was Jordan. Maybe he wouldn't visit his little brother after all. The last thing he wanted to do was interrupt sexy times between the engaged men. He felt sadness tug at his heart at the thought that he didn't have anyone to call his own. If it weren't for Nova, he'd be alone in his apartment. And she didn't count in this equation. He had just rounded the corner from the elevator to his apartment when Benny opened his front door.

"Hey!" He reached out to hug Adam and then picked Nova up and kissed her. "How's my favorite niece today?" he asked.

Nova laughed in delight. "Nova Madeleine is very well, thank you, Uncle Benny."

"Uncle Benny is very glad to hear it," Benny said with a chuckle. "Would you like to come over for some ice cream?"

Nova clapped and grinned at him. "Yes, please!" Then she turned to Adam and added, with the biggest puppy dog eyes Adam had ever seen, "Please, Daddy?"

Benny chuckled and Adam rolled his eyes. "Sure, baby. You go with Uncle Benny while I put stuff away."

"We were waiting for you. We've made dinner, so you don't have to. We need to talk about the Family Day."

"Okay. Give me a few. I need to change and put Mom's dinner in the freezer."

Ten minutes later, he walked into Benny's condo to find Nova ensconced on the rug in front of the fireplace in the living room rubbing Claus's belly. The cat's purrs were loud in the silence. Jordan was nowhere to be seen, and Benny was in the kitchen dishing up dinner. he took the juice he'd brought for his daughter and the beers he'd brought for them into the kitchen and helped Benny put things on the table.

"Where's Jordan?" he asked.

"In the office. He's grading some tests to give back tomorrow. But he said to interrupt him when you got here for dinner. He's been at it for almost two hours already."

Adam tsked. "Education was never supposed to be a hindrance, was it?" he asked, sighing dramatically.

It took Benny a second to get his meaning and then he laughed and flipped him the bird.

"Fuck off!" he said without heat. "That's for later. After dessert."

Adam kept his face clear of any expression, but inside, something tore at him. How had he not realized in all this time how very lonely he was, how very much he wanted a love of his own? And why, now that he recognized it, did it seem like every time he thought about it, Isaac Hamilton was at the top of his list of prospects? Hell, the man was the only one on his list. This was new territory for him. He'd never felt this kind off connection with anyone before, and he hadn't exactly been a monk all his life.

He didn't know how to respond to his brother's comment. Good for you, bro! sounded downright cheesy and nothing else came to mind that wasn't an idiotic or whiny response. He was the oldest brother. He didn't need to burden his youngest sibling with his emotional drama. It'd be fine. He just had to focus on things other than himself. Like the food Benny had set out.

"Is this Jamaican jerk pork?"

"Yeah. Jay wanted some for dinner, so I ordered it to pick up on the way home. I bought just regular fried chicken wings for the munchkin."

"Thanks, bro."

"Lemme just go get Jay. You can wrangle Nova for the hand washing."

Adam chuckled. "You just don't wanna have to drag her away from Claus."

"You're her father. That's your job," Benny said as he walked away grinning.

But the time the two men walked into the kitchen, Adam was drying Nova's hands and setting her on the cushion that Benny had for her to use when she stayed over.

"Wings, Daddy!" she exclaimed as he settled her properly on it. "Nova loves wings!"

"So that means Nova loves Uncle Benny, right? Because I got them for you," Benny chimed in, passing by her chair to ruffle her hair.

Nova giggled and turned her face up for kisses. Benny obliged, followed closely by Jordan, whose neck she hung on to for a second.

"Hey there, Princess," he said hugging her back. "How are you?" He looked over at Adam and added, "When did you get here?"

"About fifteen minutes ago. But she's been with Claus."

Jordan chuckled, planting another kiss on her cheek before taking his seat at the table.

"Is it my turn to say grace, Uncle Benny?" Nova piped up.

"It's always your turn when you come over, baby girl," Benny said, closing his eyes dutifully.

After she said grace, Nova dug into her food, and Adam was grateful for the distraction that her visit to her uncle's apartment caused. It meant she would sleep like a log when he took her home. In fact, she might even fall asleep before he got her next door. Which would be even better.

"So, what did you want to talk about?" he said, slicing into the juicy cut of meat on his plate.

"I've never been to a Kincaid Family Day," Jordan said. "Benny just keeps telling me it'll be like Sunday dinner, which I've been to quite number of. But if it's going to be more than just the family and more than just dinner, I'd prefer to know everything going in. For example," he gestured with his knife, "am I supposed to cook something to take to the event? Or will all the cooking be done there?"

"Well, you can choose to make it there, if it's easy to make and doesn't involve a lot of stove time. Or you can prepare it and bring it. Or, if you can't cook, you can buy it." Adam grinned as he made the last statement, pointing to his plate. "I'm sure no one will complain if you bring some Jamaican jerk to the feast."

They kept talking about the day, the games, the reason they made a day of it. Adam knew they'd eventually get to the question of who would be invited, and at that point he'd have to say whom he'd invited. He knew he could expect a grilling from Benny, but maybe, if he could manage it, he could talk about why he'd invited Isaac. Maybe…he'd have to wait and see if he had the balls to talk about his feelings.

"When we were much younger, we lived in a small house in the city. Dad was working in a small church, assisting the rector who was to retire at the end of the year. Dad was being groomed to take his place. The rector had a heart attack on Christmas Day, and before he died, he made Dad promise to carry on the tradition that he had started of having guests over to begin the new year with his family."

"Why?" Jordan asked. "Most people are hung over and want nothing to do with anything other than their beds on New Year's Day."

"Dad said the rector felt it was important for him to show his parishioners that he was invested in his community and that his home and heart would be open to them for the rest of the year. So, each year, it became a kind of unofficial pledge between the rector and the people in his parish."

"When Aidan and I started high school, Dad asked if we'd like to be the ones to invite people over for the Family Day. He wanted to grow the youth arm of the church, and what better way to do that than to get his sons' friends over for dinner and games? Family time with more than just blood relatives."

"That's pretty radical thinking," Jordan murmured. "But didn't you guys invite the same people every year?"

Benny chuckled. "You'd think we could, right? But no! Dad insisted we invite different people every year."

Adam chimed in with a chuckle. "I remember when we protested, Dad told us if we wanted to hang out with the same people, we could do that on our own time, but that New Year's Day was his time."

"I'm guessing you guys had a lot of sleepovers and cookouts, huh?"

Both Benny and Adam nodded. "Up to this point, it'd been pretty neat to bring new people in to hang with the family, though over the years, the 'family'," Adam made air quotes around the word, "has been enlarged by longstanding friendship and marriage. So now it includes the Tuckers and McKenzies."

"And as of this year, it'll also include you," Benny said, winking at his man.

"We're not married yet," Jordan protested teasingly. "What if I change my mind?"

Benny mock-glared at him. "Try it, buddy. Just you try it. You'll get what's coming to you!"

Adam watched as color bloomed in Jordan's cheeks and he felt left out in a painful way. Dragging his eyes off his brother's lover, he turned his attention to Nova, catching it just before the bone she was sucking on fell to the floor. He cleaned her up a bit with a napkin and then let her get back to her meal. Turning to his own plate, he cut another piece of meat and put it, with some rice, into his mouth. Maybe they could move on to other topics now that Jordan's questions had been answered.

"So, we both know who I'm bringing this year. Who are you bringing?"

Apparently he wasn't going to escape today. "I've invited Rob." He held up a hand before Benny could speak. "Yes, I've talked to him, and yes he gets that we're never going to be a thing."

Benny looked dubious. "Okay…if you're sure it won't be awkward."

"It won't." He took a breath, praying that they'd move on now.

"So, just one guest? You know we're each allowed more, right?"

Dammit! The only thing that could make this seem less random is what Adam decided to say as a prelude to his revelation.

"Well, my second and third guests are actually bona fide members of Dad's congregation." He paused, taking another slow breath. "I invited Isaac Hamilton and his son."

"Hey! That's great. David's such a cool kid!" Jordan exclaimed.

"Yes, I know. I told him you said as much."

Adam smiled at Jordan's enthusiastic reaction. Then he glanced at his little brother and groaned inwardly. Benny's gaze was fixed on him in deep concentration, as though he were calculating some thorny mathematical problem. He dreaded what Benny was going to ask or say, but there was really very little he could do to stop the train he saw coming when Benny opened his mouth to speak.

"I thought you said you didn't know him?" he asked suspiciously.

"When did I say that?" Adam asked defensively.

"As he was leaving Jordan's party in November. I asked you if you knew each other and you said no." Adam could almost hear Benny's unspoken challenge: Get out of that one if you can!

He sighed. There was nothing for it but to come clean with the whole story.

"I didn't know him back then," he began. "But I've seen him a few times since then, mostly in his store and once at church."

"Only seen?" his brother asked, still dubious.

"And talked to, of course."

Now even Jordan was eyeing him questioningly. "What?" he asked again, still feeling defensive.

"What else should we know about you and the good florist?"

Benny was going to be an asshole; Adam could see that clearly now. He wasn't going to let this go at all, or at least not until Adam had spilled all his secrets. The brothers didn't make a habit of keeping each other in the dark about anything outside of their work. But Adam had hoped he could weather this storm of feeling on his own. No such luck...but maybe that was a good thing.

"There's really nothing else to tell," he said, which was true, though it didn't give the fullest picture of what was happening between them on his end.

"Well, I'm just curious about why you chose him, is all," Benny said. "I mean, what is it about him that makes him worth an invitation to join the family for that day? Aside from him being a congregant?" he added, forestalling Adam.

Just like I thought it would be. Maybe Benny should have been the detective.

"He's a nice guy," Adam said lamely. "And I like his store. He's got some cool gifts in the gift shop."

"Yes, he does," Jordan said, giving him an assessing look. "He likes jazz music just like you do," he added.

"I know," Adam answered without thinking, then looked up to find amusement flashing in Jordan's eyes. Amusement and certainty. Damn! He'd just gone and given himself away.

"He's charming," he admitted.

Might as well be hanged for a sheep as a lamb. It wouldn't hurt him too much to admit being intrigued, but anything else would be tantamount to admitting a crush. And he was definitely not going to admit that he was more than just interested, that he was aroused by thoughts of the man.

Chapter Five

When Adam walked into Wine and Roses Flower and Gift Shop on the day before Christmas Eve, he was exhausted. It had been a long double shift, and in the second shift, one of the patients had coded twice before they had managed to stabilize her. That she had only been nine years old had not helped his mood or his emotions. He stepped into the warmth of the open space and inhaled the fragrance of the scented candles. He could make out vanilla, apple, cinnamon, pumpkin spice, and altogether, they reminded him that he was starving.

He hadn't taken more than potty breaks for the entire second shift, scarfing down a protein bar from the break room machine and swallowing a bottle of water when his stomach had complained. But that had been hours ago, and before that, he had only had a spare breakfast of a toasted bagel with cream cheese and a large mug of coffee. He walked past the counter, where Peaches was serving a customer and saw that Isaac, who had caught his eye as he stepped inside, was just going into the back behind the saloon doors.

Adam headed into the gift shop, hoping that there would be a display of snacks so he could find something to munch on while he waited for the older man to get to him.

"Hey there!"

The man himself spoke behind him and Adam whirled around, feeling unsteady and certain it wasn't just from a lack of food.

"Hi. I wanted to stop by to let you know I loved the LP. You said you had other female artists you could introduce me to."

"I did," Isaac said, smiling at him. "I'm glad you're back."

His heart skipped a beat at the possibility that Isaac might mean more than just being pleased that he'd come back to spend more money in his shop. That would be a great way to end a shitty day. His stomach chose that moment to growl and Adam cringed. It had been loud enough that Isaac could not possibly have missed hearing it. He glanced up and found the older man eyeing him appraisingly.

"When was the last time you ate?" he asked.

Adam blinked. "Not sure. A few hours ago." It had been maybe six hours ago, and it hadn't really been eating, but he wasn't going to share that. Isaac didn't need to know the details.

"I just ordered dinner for myself and David. You're welcome to share it with us. He'll be here in another few minutes. He had a tutoring session with Mr. O'Leary after school."

"It's okay," Adam said. "You don't have to…"

"I know I don't. But I ordered a lot of his favorite food, more than we would have been able to eat at one sitting. If you don't object to mac and cheese done in some innovative ways, it'll be my pleasure to share it with you."

Everything in Adam froze for one long moment of indecision before he relaxed and said,

"Okay. Thanks. I appreciate the offer."

"No problem."

Isaac turned away and headed toward the section housing the LP collection. Adam followed, enjoying the view of the big man's confident stride and broad shoulders.

"I have a number of other Ella Fitzgerald albums, if you'd like to stay with her a while. We can always come back to the others later. Or, if you prefer, I can show you another favorite of mine and we can listen to her while we eat."

Damn! This wasn't a date, and really could never be considered as one because there'd be a teenager present at dinner. But the glow that Adam felt from being invited not just to share a meal but also to enjoy something that Isaac loved with him, was the kind of thing he had only experienced when he was out on a date with someone he was really very attracted to. Someone who made him feel special, who made him feel that they valued the time they spent with him.

He smiled slowly, happy to accept whatever Isaac was prepared to share with him and willing to keep his foolish fantasies to himself. What Isaac didn't know wouldn't hurt him, and Adam could have another special time to store in his memory bank. If he and Isaac were an item, this could almost be labeled romantic. But they weren't, and no matter how attractive he found the big guy, he would not allow himself to show any of it. Mild flirting he could handle...it would be a lie to pretend otherwise. But that was all they could have.

"I can always come back to Ella. I prefer to sample a variety. So, who's next on your list?"

"I love Billie Holliday," Isaac said at once.

"Oh, me, too," Adam said. "I started a collection of her music about a year ago."

"Maybe share with me what you've already got and I'll see if I can help you find the rest?"

"Deal!" Adam returned Isaac's smile.

"So, let's see," Isaac continued, trailing his fingers along the spines of the LPs. "How about Sarah Vaughn? Have anything by her?"

"No, I don't. I've heard a song or two of hers, but I've been concentrating on the instrumental pieces for a while. I only stopped for Billie Holliday, but other than her, I've been doing the band scene."

"Well, I can promise you won't be disappointed by her. We'll listen to her over dinner. Right this way."

Excitement churned in Adam's gut at the thought of sitting down to a meal with the man leading him back through the shop. All his earlier exhaustion and the sorrow that was waiting in the wings to swamp him were pushed to the far corners of his mind as he went through the swinging doors to what was clearly the workspace where Isaac made the bouquets and other floral arrangements. They went through another smaller door on the left into what turned out to be a break room, complete with a small refrigerator, a microwave and a table just able to seat more than two at a time.

"Have a seat," Isaac invited him. "I'll just get things warmed up. David will be here in a minute."

Adam sat down on one of the sturdy chairs at the table, glad that there was at least enough seating for four, so no one would be left standing to eat. Not wanting the silence to stretch too long between them, he asked,

"So, what flavor mac and cheese will we be enjoying today?"

Isaac chuckled. "I ordered three kinds. David's favorite is bacon mac and cheese. So, there's a pot of that. I also ordered a pizza mac and cheese, in case he's feeling a need for something different, and last there's my old favorite, homestyle baked mac and cheese. I also ordered a salad, which I can almost guarantee my son will not touch."

Adam laughed and looked up as David walked into the break room. He paused on seeing Adam at the table, then smiled and said,

"Hi!" Then he walked over to his dad and gave him a one-armed back hug. "Hey, Dad!"

Isaac turned to hug his son back and asked, "How was tutoring?"

"It was okay," he said. "Mr. O'Leary helped me with some classwork that I needed to finish and submit, and helped me prep for the test we'll have our first day back after the Christmas break."

"Dr. Kincaid is joining us for dinner this evening and we'll be listening to some jazz. Just warning you before you whine at me about my music selection. Dr. Kincaid is a lover of jazz, like I am."

David made a disbelieving face. "Sure," he said, and Adam smirked. Poor kid! At least he was being polite about having his time with his father invaded by a virtual stranger. Not that they would be for much longer if Isaac accepted his invitation to their Family Day. He was tempted to ask what the big man had decided to do, but he didn't even know if he had told his son about the invitation or not. He figured the boy would be thrilled to spend some time with his favorite teacher, but it wasn't his place to push.

"David, get plates and cutlery from the cupboard, please."

Isaac placed the ceramic pots of food on the table and then went to get drinks from the refrigerator. He set everything on the table; there were two beers and a bottle of soda.

"Help yourself," Isaac invited him. "David, what would you like?"

"The usual," the boy said without looking up from the phone in his hand. "Thanks, Dad."

Isaac shared a plate for his son, sneaking a bit of the salad onto it. Adam smiled, amused by the move. It was such a parent thing to do. He did that to Nova every once in a while when she got ornery about eating certain foods. He helped himself to a little of each choice and sat back, pulling the beer toward him.

"Thanks again for inviting me to dinner," he said as Isaac sat down across from him.

"Physician, heal thyself!" Isaac said. "It's not good for you to miss meals."

David chuckled behind Adam, who looked over his shoulder to find that the boy had opened up a card table by the window and had placed his food and drink on it. The phone was open to some kind of game which he was playing even as he speared the first forkful of food. Adam turned his attention back to his own food.

"I hope you're not going to channel my son," Isaac said sardonically, eyeing the salad bowl with more than half the contents still in it.

Adam chuckled again. "I love salad," he told him, "so you don't have to worry about that. I just feel the need for some warm food, first."

"Okay. Let me cue up some music."

Isaac took out his phone and fiddled with it for a bit. Then the sultry sounds of a female voice, smoky and sexy, floated into the room. Adam ate everything on his plate while he listened, loving the way her voice seemed to make love to the words as she sang. The songs made Adam wonder what it must have been like to hear her in concert way back when his parents were kids. He loved the songs Isaac had on his playlist, but he was drawn to a couple of them that he would make sure were on whichever album he bought before he left.

"How did you get turned on to jazz?" Isaac asked as they were finishing up the meal.

"My dad is a great lover of all things jazz," he replied. "When we were still very young, he used to play jazz and gospel music on Sunday evenings at dinnertime."

"I knew there was a reason I liked him," Isaac said with a chuckle. "He's got good taste."

"He'd agree with you there," Adam said, grinning. "But he didn't play the hardcore stuff at dinner. He saved that for when he was working in his study, or when he was helping Mom in the kitchen or when he was doing yard work."

"Is he still an enthusiast these days?"

"Oh, for sure! And now with Nova, he's back to playing the easy stuff. He's the reason I discovered Billie Holliday. He was playing an album of hers one evening when I went to pick Nova up after work. I ended up listening to the entire album before I left."

"Hey, Dad?" Isaac looked over at his son, who continued, "Sorry to disturb you, but what time are we leaving tonight?"

Isaac looked up at the big analog clock on the wall over the door and shrugged. "Maybe another couple of hours. Why?"

"Alex just asked if I could hang out with him at Strike Kings."

Adam smiled. He remembered spending a lot of his teenage years at the town's most popular bowling alley that was open to kids as well as grownups.

"How are you going to get there?" Isaac asked him. "I'll come get you when I leave here, but you're on your own to find your way there."

"Alex's mom has a meeting in town and she'll bring him. He's almost here. So that's a yes, right?"

Isaac nodded. "That's a yes. Just remember, we're leaving early so we can go visit the Major before our flight."

"I know," David said. "I'm already packed."

"Okay, then have fun, son."

The boy stood up, gathered his dinner things, and dumped the paper plate and napkin in the trash. Then he washed the fork he'd used in the small sink, dried it and returned it the drawer he'd taken it from.

"See you later, Dad," he said as he walked out. "Bye, Dr. Kincaid."

"Bye, David."

Adam watched him leave and turned back to Isaac, who was packing away the remains of their meal. He cleared away the paper plates and beer bottles and washed the forks they'd used. He was full, the meal had been pleasant, and the company had been great, even if it included a fifteen-year-old boy.

"You've raised a good son," he said, turning from putting the forks away to speak. "You should be proud of him."

Isaac's eyes met his for a moment as he dried the small ceramic bowls that the food had been reheated in.

"I am, thanks."

Adam knew it was time to go. He wished he could stay, but he had to go get his own child and get her home and ready for bed. She'd be staying over at his parents' place until the day after Christmas, so he'd also have to pack her a bag. And then there were the gifts to pack after she was asleep. He'd need to get those to his mom secretly so she could place them under the big tree with all the other gifts that would be opened on Christmas Day.

"I'd better be going as well," he said.

"Okay. Let's go see which Sarah Vaughn album you want to buy."

They left the break room as tidy as they'd found it and walked back into the gift shop where Isaac searched through the LP stack until he found the ones he wanted.

"Which of these would you like to try first?"

Adam looked for any that had the two songs he had liked and when he found one that had the two tunes he especially liked; he chose that one.

"I'll start here," he said, pulling out the album and heading to the cash register.

Peaches was tending to another customer. Isaac stood next to him, his hand once again at the small of his back, and for a moment Adam couldn't hear the words he was saying over the roaring in his ears. The touch was gentle, almost ghostly, barely there, but it was driving him insane with desire for things he had no business wanting from a man who was most likely straight. Straight men sometimes flirted with gay men, but they didn't mean anything by it. They were just being friendly.

Touching you like that is more than just friendly. How was Isaac touching him, though? He wasn't doing anything remotely sensual or sexual, yet Adam's reaction to him was hypersensitive. He was probably reading way more into the touch than he should.

"Will this be all, sir?" Peaches asked him when he stood before her with his LP.

"For now, yes, thank you."

He handed over the album, signed for it after she rang it up, then waited while she bagged it and gave it back to him before moving away.

"Have a happy Christmas, Peaches," he told her, loving the smile that brightened her features even more.

"You, too, Dr. Kincaid," she replied.

Then he moved to leave, the Christmas-themed fairy lights twinkling warmly over the entrance, when Isaac said,

"Rest and enjoy Christmas with your family, Adam," he said. "And thanks for your business."

"Enjoy your stay in Florida. Maybe we'll see each other when you get back?" He could ask without being pushy about it.

"I'll let you know in good time," Isaac promised with a smile.

If Adam weren't mistaken, those light eyes landed and lingered on his lips, making him wonder if Isaac was needing to kiss them as much as Adam discovered he wanted to kiss the big man's pretty, lush brown lips. He raised his eyes to Isaac's and saw a mix of emotions in them for a moment before he looked away, opening the door for Adam.

"Thanks," Adam said, his voice low and husky.

"Maybe we can have dinner again some time?"

Adam nodded, trying to form the right words. Dinner, a movie, whatever he wanted, Adam would give him, even if he wasn't gay and didn't want to jump his bones the way Adam was beginning to want to do to him.

"I'd like that a lot," he finally said.

Isaac's smile did something inexplicable to him, but its effect was electrifying, nevertheless. He returned the smile helplessly and then headed out the door before he did something stupid. He didn't feel completely in control of his limbs, which were trembling like jello when shook. He put his purchase in the passenger seat of his car when he got to it and leaned his head against the head rest, trying to bring his body back under his control.

There had been nothing remotely romantic about his evening, at least nothing any outside observer could put a finger on. But as far as Adam was concerned, this had been one of the sweetest evenings he had ever spent in another man's company. And if he had his druthers, he'd do it again in a flash. Isaac Hamilton was ticking all his boxes, and the part of him that wasn't practical and seeing all the drawbacks to starting anything with him was elated that a man such as he existed in Adam's world.

He drove to his parents' home so he could spend some time with Nova before he went to his own place to a lonely bed and insufficient sleep. He was working the next two days and wanted Nova to enjoy some quality time with her grandparents. But he was determined to see her at least at dinner time and to spend time strengthening their bond. He was glad he'd be off for New Year's Day so he could start the year off on the right note with her.

"Hey Mom," he said, hugging his mother who had come to the door to greet him when he walked in. "Everything okay?"

"Everything's peachy, son!" His mother kissed his cheeks and added, "You look exhausted."

"It's been a very, very long day." And that isn't the half of it.

"Come through to the kitchen. Your dad is in his study. He'll take a break when I call. Nova is watching a kiddie show on the television. She's ready for bed, but she wanted to wait for her daddy."

Adam felt a stab of guilt at the thought that he had put himself before his daughter, choosing to spend time with a man he was most likely never going to have instead of hurrying home to be with his daughter whom he wouldn't be with for the next two days. The urge to apologize to his mom overwhelmed him and he gave in to it.

"Sorry I'm late, Mom. I had a stop to make and had dinner with a friend. It wasn't planned..."

He trailed off, wondering suddenly why he had told his mother any of that. As excuses went, it was pretty flimsy. Still, there was little he could do about that now, so he followed her into the kitchen, waiting to hear what she'd say.

"Who was the friend?" she began her interrogation.

"Isaac Hamilton." The less he said, the better, he figured.

"Lovely man," she enthused, reaching into a cupboard and pulling out two covered glass containers. "Why didn't you tell me you had a dinner date?"

Adam huffed out a laugh. "It wasn't a date, Mom." he protested. "I stopped by the store to pick up an item I had asked for and he invited me to share dinner with him and his son."

"Just like that?" she wanted to know, dishing up some potato salad into one of the bowls.

Adam felt his cheeks heat when she looked up from what she was doing to spear him with a knowing glance. He knew what she was thinking, and though he wished that that were the case, he knew his having been invited to dinner had had nothing to do with anything even remotely romantic, no matter how he might wish it to be so.

"I was hungry and he could tell."

His mother's laughter didn't surprise him. He was notorious for not eating and then having his stomach growl loudly enough for people around to hear it. His brothers teased him mercilessly every time it happened and had done so ever since they were young boys.

"Oh, Adam! Now your secret's out."

Adam laughed ruefully. "I told him he didn't have to, but he insisted. What was it he said?" He thought for a second, then continued, "Physician, heal thyself. It's not good for you to miss meals."

Mrs. Kincaid finished adding meat to the second glass bowl, closed it and walked with both of them over to the table where he was seated. Placing them before him she remarked, before moving away.

"Spoken like a true dad. And he's not wrong, either. Now, will you make your own salad, or do you want what's left of mine?"

Adam knew he wasn't going to go home to fix anything for lunch the next day, so he opted for the easiest route.

"Yours, please," he said. "I have to be up again to start work at the hospital by seven."

"You work too hard, honey," she told him, pulling the salad bowl from the refrigerator and filling a third glass bowl. "How was work today?"

Adam sighed heavily. "Pretty bad in the second shift."

'Pretty bad' was code for 'really awful and/or life threatening', and his family knew not to ask for more information. He leaned in when his mother came around to hug him and let his body sag into her warm embrace for a long moment. then he leaned away to return her hug and said,

"Thanks, Mom. I'll just go sit with Nova a while. And I'll put her to bed. You've done enough for the day."

"No. It's fine. I can put her to bed. You go and say goodnight and get on home. You look positively wiped out."

Mrs. Kincaid shooed him out of the kitchen to the family room where Nova was giggling at something that Bugs Bunny was doing on the screen. He loved that she enjoyed watching the old cartoons, since some of the newer ones seemed a little bit too 'old' for a toddler in his opinion. She looked up as they walked in and jumped up at once, flinging her warm body at him with a delighted cry.

"Daddy!"

Her arms around his neck were his most favorite thing to feel in the whole world, even more so than his mother's hugs. He squeezed her tightly to his chest and kissed her on the top of her head as well as on her cheeks.

"How is my lovely Nova this evening?"

"Your lovely Nova is fine, Daddy. Are you going to stay for Christmas?

"No, baby," Adam said, chuckling at her repetition of his words. "Remember I told you that you were spending Christmas Eve and Christmas Day at Nana's?"

Nova nodded sagely. "Yes, Daddy."

"Well, tomorrow is Christmas Eve, so you're sleeping over these next two nights."

"Okay, Daddy!"

Adam loved her innocent acceptance of his words. He could only hope she'd remain as acquiescent when she became a teenager, but he doubted it. He chuckled at the thought and then spent the next half hour watching another Bugs Bunny cartoon with her before he took himself home. Tomorrow was another day...another day closer to hopefully seeing Isaac Hamilton again.

Please let him say yes. If only God could be coerced into granting selfish wishes.

Chapter Six

Early morning found Isaac on the beach outside his hotel, his sandals in one hand, wading in the warm waters of the Atlantic at Daytona Beach. The sand stretched on, as far as the eye could see, bordered on one side by the sun-kissed ocean and on the other by one hotel after another down the stretch. There were no cars as yet and hardly any people. It was quiet and peaceful, and the cool morning air was refreshing.

Isaac paused in his morning ramble to watch the seabirds play. The smallest among them waddled from one pool to another on the beach, searching the sand for God knew what. He couldn't imagine what food they would find beneath the saltwater-soaked sand. The larger birds wheeled and screeched above the rolling water or dive-bombed fish beneath its surface or rode the waves.

The last time he had been on a holiday that wasn't in-state had been…he realized with a start that it had been the year of Rowena's death. Every Christmas since then, he'd taken his son and gone cabin camping or been to a house on a lake or riverside close by. David hadn't minded where they went, as long as they left home. And Isaac hadn't been interested in going out of state because that took more time to organize than he was willing to spend on it.

Rowena had been the vacation planner in their family, and he had loved every place she'd taken them at Christmas and July 4th, which was their wedding anniversary. They'd never been to Daytona Beach. He loved the feel of the sand under his feet…silky soft and fine, like confectioner's sugar before the shoreline, where it was compacted by the action of the surf. He moved again after taking a few shots of the birds and the rising sun reflected on the water and in the sky.

He and David had arrived the evening before in time for dinner, and after spending the rest of night with his hosts and their two kids, he had happily hauled his tired ass to bed. It had been an emotional day all around. They'd visited the Major that morning, given him his gifts, and David had spent a pleasant hour with his grandfather bringing him up to speed on the happenings in his life, including the upcoming trip to Daytona Beach for the next three days. Isaac had sat quietly by and watched and listened, only participating in the conversation if David asked a question. The Major didn't speak to him, which was par for the course, except when he said,

"Rowena would have loved to spend a few days at the beach in December. That girl loved her some sunshine."

He hadn't exactly spoken to Isaac, but the words were clearly meant for him as much as for David. Isaac's eyes had collided with his father's over David's head, and a flash of pain had spent a moment in the Major's eyes before he looked back to his grandson and asked him a question about what he was going to be doing on New Year's Day. Which had reminded Isaac that he needed to talk to David, to see if he'd mind spending their day with the Kincaid family and their friends.

Now, as he turned to walk back to the hotel, he figured he'd better call Adam and let him know he had decided to accept his invitation. After all, what did he have to lose? Exactly nothing. But he had so much to gain…companionship for himself and his son for another day, which would become another great memory for David of an exceptional Christmas vacation. And if there were other kids David's age or close to it there, it would be another way to help his son socialize outside of school and meet new people.

He wasn't necessarily eager for David to start dating, but he knew the boy was at the age where he would at least be thinking about it. So, if there was anything he could do to facilitate that natural progression in his son's growth as an independent person, he'd grab it with both hands. David didn't ever have to know his dad had — and usually always had — an ulterior motive for everything he did. There was always an agenda with him, and it always had to do with David.

Except not this time. Don't even lie about that.

It was true and he conceded the point to his conscience. This time, his other ulterior motive was entirely about himself and his desire to see and spend time with the delectable younger doctor who had caught his imagination and wouldn't let go. He pulled the cellphone out of the pocket of his shorts and found Adam's number. He hoped it wasn't too early to be calling him. The phone rang a few times and he was just about to hang up when Adam's voice sounded in his ear.

"Adam Kincaid, good morning!"

Damn, he sounds sexy! "Morning, Doc. It's Isaac Hamilton. Merry Christmas!"

"Merry Christmas to you, too, Isaac. How's Daytona?"

"Cool and quiet," Isaac said. "I'm currently watching the sun rise over the ocean, standing ankle deep in the water."

"Mmm. Sounds wonderful. I hope you have a lovely holiday."

The pause that followed his comment was just about to get awkward when Isaac said, "I just wanted you to know I've decided to take you up on your invitation. David and I will be happy to spend New Year's Day with you and your family."

"That's great, Isaac. Thanks for letting me know."

Isaac got the impression that Adam wasn't alone and he realized suddenly that he'd called while Adam was at work. He was mortified...this was what he got for thinking with his gonads.

"Sh...oot!" He cut off the cuss word he'd been a millisecond from spouting, changing it to its far more innocent cousin. "I'm sorry I disturbed you while you're at work."

"It's not a problem. I do have to go, but I'll call back later, in case there's anything else you want to say."

"I'd like that." Isaac's reply was straightforward because it was exactly what he'd like.

All the way back to the condo, he couldn't pull the smile off his face. He walked in to find the place still quiet, though someone was up and taking a shower. He walked into the kitchen, determined to do his part for the family so they wouldn't be responsible for everything for the next three days. He checked out the refrigerator and saw there were enough eggs, cheese, onions, scallions, bacon, and butter to make omelets. He pulled out what he needed and set them on the counter. Not feeling especially industrious beyond that, he decided to toast bagels to go with it.

"Morning, Isaac."

Isaac turned to find his host standing by the breakfast counter in blue shorts and a tee shirt that said NOT a Captain of Industry. He grinned and said, gesturing at it with the knife he had been using to slice the onions,

"I take it one of the cops you supervise gave you that?"

"No, actually my wife gave this to me the year I thought we might be able to afford a boat. This was her not-so-subtle way of saying that a cop's salary, even when the cop is high ranking, does not spell the word 'yacht' in any way, shape, or form."

Isaac laughed along with him, then said, "So, I figured I'd make omelets for breakfast with toasted bagels and whatever else you all need."

John Mansfield stepped away from the island, going around till he was standing next to Isaac.

"You don't have to do that," he said. "You're our guest."

"It's not a problem, John, truly. I would have been doing this anyway if David and I had gone away by ourselves."

John smiled. "Seems like we have more in common than I thought. It's what I do whenever I'm home with the family for Christmas. So, how about I make my famous banana pancakes. I hope you and David like bananas, because that's what I bought the fixings for."

"We eat everything," Isaac assured him, "and that sounds great, actually. Sweet bananas and salty bacon should be a fabulous combination."

"I usually also have strawberries and whipped cream, in case anyone isn't feeling like having protein with their pancakes."

Isaac inclined his head with a chuckle. "I should have known that David liked spending time with you guys for more than Alex's company. You spoil them rotten, don't you?"

John laughed. "My job is hard, and it took me a while to realize that I needed to connect with my family in ways that made them happy and gave me some peace. Cooking for them is how I do that."

"So, what else do you cook?" Isaac asked as they worked around each other and prepared the breakfast feast.

"I don't mess about with much on a dinner menu. I'm the breakfast and lunch guy. The only dinner thing I do well, aside from making a mean chef's salad, is the turkey for Thanksgiving. I get that prepped and all Helen has to do is put it in the oven, baste it at timed intervals, and pull it out when it's done."

Isaac felt himself relax further as they finished up the breakfast prep. As they were putting things in the two ovens to keep warm, David showed up in the kitchen looking rumpled and still sleepy.

"Hey Dad," he began, noticing his father with the one eye he had open. Then John walked back in from where he'd gone out to the patio to set the table. "Morning, Cap."

Isaac looked over at John to see his reaction to the nickname. Nothing but a wide smile greeted his son's words.

"Morning, son. Did you sleep well?"

John walked over and hugged David and Isaac had a moment to wonder when David had become a person he didn't know as well as he thought he did. And another moment to feel ashamed and embarrassed that his relationship with John's son was nowhere near as close. What did that say about him, that he hadn't been able to open up to anyone other than his son in eleven years?

"Yes, sir! Dad didn't snore too loud last night."

Isaac's attention snapped back to his son, who was smirking at him. "I do not snore, boy!" he said, flicking water at him before stopping to wonder if he should be getting the floor of the condo wet.

"How would you know?" David asked, still smirking as he filled a glass with water from the tap and dodged his father's playful jab as he did so. "You were asleep."

"But as you know very well, I'm a light sleeper. If I snored, I'd probably wake myself up."

David nodded. "Okay, so maybe I was exaggerating a little bit." He chuckled and then downed the water in a few gulps.

"Thank you!" Isaac said, grinning at him in his turn.

"When's breakfast?" David asked next.

"As soon as you're dressed for company," Isaac said at once. "So please go wash up and dress like I taught you to."

David grinned at him, then turned to John and asked, "Do I have to dress up right now?"

"No, son. In fact, after breakfast, we'll open the gifts and then we're going down to the pool. There's a game arcade that you and Alex might enjoy. We'll dress up for dinner."

"Okay. Dad, did you bring the camera?"

Isaac smiled. "Yes, son. I'll have it ready for after breakfast and I'll take it down when we go to the pool."

John Mansfield's family all came out to the patio at the same time as David when he returned wearing board shorts and a t-shirt. Everyone exchanged Christmas greetings, including hugs and in the case of the Mansfield family, kisses as well. Helen Mansfield kissed David and hugged Isaac and thanked him profusely "for helping John make such a superlative breakfast."

Isaac smiled indulgently. The entire family was so easy to get along with, so natural in their show of affection, in their acceptance of him and his son. It floored him but he did his best to hide his surprise. They all helped themselves, no one standing on ceremony, and they ate mostly in silence, aside from the odd question that one of the Mansfield kids asked their parents.

Cleanup after breakfast went quickly as the younger set, including the Mansfield's eighteen-year-old daughter Haley, were clearly eager to get to the gift opening portion of the day. Everyone gathered around the table-top Christmas tree that John had brought down and decorated with his wife and kids by the time Isaac had arrived with David the day before. There were a lot of gifts for such a small group, but that was because, as Isaac discovered, he hadn't been the only one to think he needed to get gifts for the members of the family who had invited him to share their holiday with them.

"Okay, kids, you all go first, since you have the most gifts, anyway," Helen said, chuckling. "We grownups can wait."

Isaac sat back in the love seat he had chosen to occupy, watching the couple sitting across from him as they in their turn watched the three teenagers ripping through the beautifully wrapped presents to get at whatever was inside. For a long moment, he was lost to the sudden need to be with Adam like they were, arms around each other, Adam's head on his shoulder, enjoying being together with family.

"Wow, Dad, look what I got!"

David's excited voice broke into his thoughts and he looked over to where his son sat cross-legged, holding a brand-new zoom lens for his camera. Isaac knew how expensive those items could be, and he could only hope that they hadn't spent too much money on the gift, especially since what he had bought for their kids was nowhere near as expensive.

"I saw it on sale at Mancini's, and it was a steal, so I gave Dad all the money I'd been saving for it," Alex said, looking at his best friend, "and he and Mom made up the difference. I knew you'd love it. It was all you ever talked about."

Isaac wondered if Alex had seen the growing emotion that he saw as watched his son struggling to stem the tears building in his eyes. His own eyes tingled but he closed them and swallowed. This level of personal connection was not something Isaac had ever shared with anyone, and he would just have to get used to being part of a group where others cared about his son as much as he did.

"Thank you, Cap, Mrs. M." David's voice broke, but he managed to keep the tears at bay.

"It was our pleasure, son," Helen said, smiling at him. "You've been the best friend our Alex has ever had, and you're like our second son. We wouldn't have done anything different."

They both looked over at Isaac at the same time, and he could see them wondering how he would react to their very generous gift. He smiled, swallowing his own emotions.

"I appreciate you both for welcoming him into your family. It's important to me that he have friends his own age and that he learns what it means to be a good friend to others. You've helped him with that, and I'm very grateful to you all."

His words were heavy, despite the control he was holding over himself, and he knew he'd need to lighten the mood for the kids' sake. So, he turned to Alex and Haley and said,

"So, what did you guys get for Christmas this year?"

They each held up the gifts they'd been unwrapping while David had had his moment. Their parents had given Alex a telescope, and he was clearly as emotional about receiving it as David had been about the zoom lens. His sister had given him a bottle of cologne and from the expression on his face that was the best thing she could have given him.

"Thanks, Hay!"

"Now you can smell like your favorite teacher," she said, grinning at him. "I have to agree with you, it's a very manly scent, so you'll be getting all the girls."

Isaac chuckled. Alex's cheeks bloomed with color but he smiled happily and put a little bit on the back of his hand, sniffing appreciatively. His mother called him over to get a whiff and smiled.

"It's quite nice, son. If your dad weren't allergic to most colognes, I'd buy him one of these myself."

Alex grinned. "Mr. Hamilton bought me this."

Isaac tensed and hated the niggling dread that his son's best friend wouldn't like his gift as much as David liked the Mansfield's. He had never felt inadequate before, but this little vacation was bringing out insecurities he hadn't even realized he had. He shook himself mentally. Get over yourself, Zac. This isn't about you.

Alex held up a ukulele with a smile so broad it threatened to split his face in two. Amid the oohs and aahs, Alex looked over at Isaac. "Thank you, sir. This is way cool!"

"I'm glad you like it, son," Isaac said, relaxing finally.

Then Alex turned to his bestie and nudged him with his shoulder. "Thanks, Dave." David grinned and slung an arm across his friend's shoulders.

"Are we gonna get some ukulele music after dinner?" Helen asked teasingly.

Alex laughed. "We'll see. I have to learn how to play it first." Then turning to his friend, he asked, "So Dave, what else did you get?"

David unwrapped another box and then looked up at Isaac with fresh tears in his eyes. The magnetic wireless speakers that hovered just above the base projected different colors when it was activated. Isaac had overheard David talking to his bestie about it way back in the summer and had decided it would the perfect gift to surprise him with this Christmas.

"Wow! That's so cool, Dave," Alex said, going over to sit by his friend.

They checked out the specs together and Isaac's heart swelled with warmth at the way they looked, heads almost touching, completely captivated by the technology. David loved music as much as he did, and it pleased him to be able to give his son a new way to enjoy it.

"All right, Haley, your turn," Helen said, turning indulgent eyes to her daughter.

The young woman grinned and brandished the magenta eternity scarf that Isaac had bought for her on his and David's behalf, the black leather designer knee-high boots that her parents had bought for her, and the gift card to her favorite makeup store that Alex had bought her tucked inside a card that declared her the best sister in the world.

"I'm glad you kids like your gifts," John said. "I don't know about you, Isaac, but the older these two get, the more I fret about what to buy them. Somehow, I don't think the bonds we bought for them when they were born will impress them half as much."

Isaac laughed. "I hear you. I'm just grateful that my boy is easy to please. But the savings bond is a great idea. We have one for David as well."

We. The word stabbed him briefly, a sharp reminder that the woman of his heart was no longer there. He schooled his features not to show that the memory of his dead wife had snuck up on him. He was not about to spoil the positive energy flowing in the room, and he didn't want anyone's sympathy.

"So, Mom, Dad, what did you get?"

Helen reached for the remaining items under the tree and handed the two that belonged to Isaac to him, before carefully opening the wrapping paper on the first gift and showing them the crystal globe music box on a lighted stand that their children had given them. It had a picture of them engraved on it, and words which Helen read to them.

"I heard the bells on Christmas Day..." she began, then added, "Oh...it's the first stanza of the Christmas carol."

Turning the box in her hand, she worked the mechanism and then turned it back so they could hear the tune as it played while Christmas-colored lights flashed inside the globe.

"This is beautiful, children," Helen said. "Thank you."

"David helped us pick it out from his dad's shop," Alex announced.

Isaac was surprised by that. He must not have been around, or maybe he'd been working in the back when they'd done that bit of shopping. His own gift to the couple, also from his gift shop, was something he knew they would both appreciate, since he had seen the vintage record player they had and was adding to their R & B collection with the two LPs he had bought them. He hoped they'd like the Earth, Wind and Fire and the Sam Cooke albums.

"This is great, Isaac. Thank you." The smiles on their faces were as warm as John's words.

"You're very welcome. I figured you'd both like to add to your collection."

When Isaac unwrapped his gifts, his eyes lit up at the beautiful silver pocket watch that David had bought for him. He looked over at his son, hoping the love and pride he was feeling showed in his gaze.

"You're a sneaky kid, aren't you?" he said, chuckling.

"You do that to me all the time, Dad," David replied. "So, when I heard you telling Peaches about the watch, I asked her to help me get the right one for you."

"Ah! So you had an accomplice." He chuckled along with his son, then said, "Thanks, son. I love it."

Then he thanked the Mansfields for the beautiful hunter green and beige scarf and matching beanie and the leather driving gloves. It was a thoughtful and timely gift, one he knew he would always treasure. It seemed his decision to make new friends had been the right one to make. Now all he had to do was maintain the friendships.

They cleaned up the wrapping paper, took their gifts back to their rooms and all went down to the pool. Isaac pulled the t-shirt over his head and dove into the deep end of the pool when he saw that diving was permitted. He swam the length of the pool a few times, pausing to catch his breath once or twice before hauling his big body out at the shallow end and going back to lie on the lounger.

He hadn't had a holiday in a long while, at least, not one where he hadn't had to foot the bill and wasn't responsible for coming up with the entertainment and meals. He had brought a cake and wine, and the fixings for his special potato salad for Christmas dinner and had paid for everyone to go sailing the next day. It eased his mind to contribute to the holiday, especially after he saw how much money they had spent on him and his son.

He must have dozed off, because a cold drop of water on his skin woke him with a start. His eyes flew open and he looked up to find David reaching across him for his towel.

"Hey Dad, can I have a soda?"

Isaac sat up and reached for his wallet, which he had hidden under his t-shirt and towel.

"Get me a bottle of water while you're at it, please."

He watched his son walk away to the poolside bar and looked around him. Helen Mansfield was sitting at one corner of the shallow end of the pool watching her husband swim laps. Another couple was kissing at the other side. They were young, maybe newlyweds, since they couldn't seem to keep their mouths off each other. A couple of teenage boys were throwing a ball around at the deep end, two little boys and a little girl were playing in the shallow end and going to dive off the side into the middle of the pool, and an elderly couple floated on wide plastic beds, managing to avoid everyone else in the pool.

Where were all the little kiddies? Was everyone still asleep, or had they all gone out? Isaac was surprised at how few people there were at the pool. Maybe there'd be more families later. David came back with his water and his credit card and he drank thirstily. Maybe he'd do a few more laps and then go back up to the room. He had plans to make his famous potato salad but he needed to buy the potatoes and get that done before Helen needed the kitchen again.

Once he found the market and returned to the condo, he made quick work of peeling the potatoes while the water boiled and preparing the dressing. He was ready by the time the potatoes were cooked and put the salad into one of the large bowls he found in a cupboard. He basted the turkey that Helen had put into the oven after breakfast, went for another swim, and later, dressed carefully in faun-colored corduroy slacks and a burgundy button-down shirt for dinner. He hadn't looked forward to a meal more in a long time, and he knew it wasn't about the food, but about the companionship.

He could get used to this.

Chapter Seven

"Merry Christmas! Ho! Ho! Ho!"

Reverend Kincaid twirled Nova around as he spoke the famous words and then sat heavily in his favorite armchair with her in his lap as she giggled in delight. He was not wearing a Santa costume, but she knew he was channeling the Santa she had seen at the mall earlier the day before when her grandparents had taken her shopping.

"Merry Christmas, Papa. That was fun!"

"I'm glad you liked it, sweetie pie."

He kissed his granddaughter's cheeks and hugged her back when she wrapped her arms around his neck in joy. Adam watched them with a smile before turning his eyes to the rest of the family sitting in the living room. Dinner had been over for a while and they were now having seconds on dessert. They always left the gift opening until after dinner, a tradition that the boys had chosen way back when Bennett was still a toddler.

Their parents had given them three choices. First, they could open the gifts on Christmas Eve, but not before the Children's pageant at five and candlelight mass which began at nine at night. They were always ready for bed by the time they got home from that service, so that was a no go. Next, they could open them the following morning, but not until after the Christmas Day carol service which began at nine.

He remembered the lively discussion that he and Aidan had had about which to choose, and they had decided that it would be the coolest if they waited until after Christmas dinner, which was always early on Christmas Day, because no one else at school did that. They had wanted to stand out among their peers, and the only compromise they had been willing to entertain was that they could open the stockings in the morning before mass.

Now, he watched his little brother and Jordan settle Mrs. Salvietti, Jordan's landlady and foster mother, into the comfortable Queen Anne armchair, before helping their mother hand out the gifts. Since Nova's birth, she had always gone first, and her squeals of delight and tears of happiness at the gifts she'd been given melted Adam's heart. Next was Mrs. Salvietti, who as their guest would always come before them, followed by Jordan and in reverse birth order by Adam and his brothers.

The warmth of family love washed over him as he admired the pashmina scarf that Mrs. Salvietti had brought for his mom, the jars of peach preserves that his mom had gifted the older woman with, listened to the familiar tune playing in the music box and to the sounds of his brothers and Jordan teasing each other. He had thankfully only worked his regular single shift today but had been too late to sit down to dinner with the family. His dinner sat on a pretty filigree-edged dinner platter on a New York City souvenir tray.

Bennett and Jordan shared a brief but loving kiss when they exchanged gifts, and a wave of longing swept over him. When would it be his turn? And who was he going to make that journey with when the time came? Unbidden, the vision of a tall, dark flower shop owner popped into his mind. Isaac Hamilton ticked so many of his boxes. He found it easy to imagine the silver fox fitting into his family as easily as Jordan had done. He'd have a chance to test that theory on New Year's Day.

A sudden urge to hear Isaac's voice had him picking up the tray with his food and taking it out to the kitchen, covering it with a tea cloth on the table, and stepping into his father's study to make the call. He had, after all, promised that he'd call him back. Now was as good a time as any, he argued silently, as though he needed to reassure himself that it was okay to keep his word.

"Hello?" Isaac's voice was chocolate sin on chocolate ice cream.

"Hey, Isaac, it's Adam. Merry Christmas again!" How lame can you be, Adam?

"Thanks, Adam. I hope you had a good day, too."

"Well, I worked today, but at least it wasn't a double shift."

"That's good to know." There was a pause, as though Isaac were searching for something to say, before he added, "How's your family? Is Nova having a nice Christmas?"

Wow! He remembered her name. Too many people didn't even bother to try to remember it. They just called her 'your daughter' or 'your baby girl'. They both chuckled at the simultaneous questions.

"She's having a ball," Adam answered.

"Does she like the music box you bought her?"

Before he answered that question, he turned up the volume on his phone and walked out to the hallway close enough to the living room so he could hear but not be seen. Then he let Isaac listen as the tune that someone had once again wound up for Nova began to play.

"Did you hear it?" he asked as he walked back into the quiet study.

"Yes, I did. I'm glad she likes it."

Another pause, one that was becoming awkward to Adam, who was now worried that Isaac might think he was ridiculous for calling back when he had nothing to say. Should he tell him he'd bought him a little gift? Should he ask him how he'd spent his day? Should he ask when he was coming back home? Were any of those questions even legitimate?

"Are you working tomorrow as well?" Isaac asked, ending the silence between them.

Thank you! "No, I have the day off. How's Daytona Beach? What are your plans for tomorrow?"

"Daytona Beach is fine, thanks for asking. it's not too hot. We're going sailing tomorrow. I figured I should contribute something to the holiday. Today was pretty cool as well. Nothing much aside from pool time and dinner. The Mansfields have been really gracious hosts and the kids all loved their gifts."

"The Mansfields? Do you mean John Mansfield and his family?"

"Yes. Alex and David are best friends."

"Small world," Adam commented. "He's Aidan's captain. He's a cool guy."

"Yes, he is, and he has a great family."

Adam needed to know when Isaac was returning home because he wanted to see him again. He was coming to the conclusion that he was going to have to do something decisive with the older man like invite him out on a date...as soon as he figured out which way he swung. He knew he'd have to keep things very firmly in the friend zone if Isaac were straight, but he wasn't prepared to wait any longer to find out.

The urgency to move things along was beginning to eat away at him. And while he wasn't the player his younger brother had been, like Benny he did want to move on from meaningless hookups to something deeper and more long-lasting with someone worth his time and effort. And he sensed that Isaac could be that person and more and that he might reciprocate Adam's interest. He just needed to figure out how to find out without embarrassing either of them. Maybe he should wait until New Year's Day, when an opportunity might present itself.

"When are you coming back to town?" There really was no other way to find out than to ask.

"The day after tomorrow," Isaac replied. "David and I have an afternoon flight."

"What time are you getting back? Do you need a ride home from the airport?"

"We'll be landing at around six in the evening. And thanks, but you don't have to. We can take an Uber."

Adam took the plunge. "I know I don't have to, but I want to, Isaac."

Would Isaac intuit the things he was not saying from the things he was? Would he understand the inflection behind the word 'want'? And if he did, how would he respond? What if Isaac preferred to be the one doing the pursuing? He stiffened his spine, waiting for Isaac to answer. His shift ended at three, and if he tried to finish all his paperwork by the end of his shift, he could get to the airport in half an hour to pick them up. He found that he very much liked that scenario.

He waited patiently for Isaac to overcome his obvious reluctance to accept the favor. What was he thinking?

"I'd like that a lot, thanks, Adam."

Adam released the breath he'd been holding, taking another deep cleansing one before smiling so widely he was sure Isaac would hear it in his words.

"Good. I'll see you at around six thirty or so, then."

After he hung up, he remained in the armchair he'd been sitting in and thought back to their last encounter at Isaac's shop. Isaac had suggested that they might have dinner together again soon. Maybe he could buy them dinner so Isaac wouldn't have to cook when he got home. He'd have to figure out what to buy that they would all enjoy. He liked the idea, even if it meant sharing a meal with his son again. They would have time to be alone for dinner eventually. Pleased that he had a plan, he went back into the living room and sat down.

"Where'd you get off to?" Aidan asked.

"I had a phone call to make," Adam admitted, fighting to keep the telltale color off his cheeks.

Aidan eyed him speculatively but refrained from making any comments or asking any further questions. Adam was grateful. He might be getting ready to launch himself back into the dating world, but he didn't necessarily need a cheering section just yet. Maybe when — if — they got together, he would share more.

Half an hour later, after Adam packed their gifts in his car, the entire family went to see The Nutcracker at the theater as planned, emerging after almost two hours full of Christmas cheer and wreathed in smiles. Nova was thrilled that the song on her music box was part of the performance and Adam was hard pressed to stop her from squealing in delight. He and Nova exchanged hugs and kisses with the rest of the family and he drove them home to the condo. It had always felt a little lonesome to him, from the moment he had first bought it, but he had grown used to the heavy absence of sound. And then he'd met Isaac, and his imagination had been fired up. Now it was on a train about to run away with him aboard and stoked for the ride.

The next day, he spent a lazy morning lolling about in bed before rising to get Nova her breakfast, then playing and watching kiddie Christmas shows with her. Once she went down for her afternoon nap, after a lunch of peanut butter and jelly sandwiches, he tidied the kitchen and sprawled on the sofa in front of the widescreen television and fell asleep as well. He woke with a start when someone knocked on his door.

Nova was still asleep, and he'd need to wake her so she wouldn't have trouble falling asleep again at bedtime. But first he needed to deal with whoever was at his front door. Opening it, he found his brother and Jordan standing there, two large pizzas and a shopping bag in hand. He stepped aside to let them in and followed them to the kitchen where Benny put the pizzas on the table while Jordan unpacked the shopping bag. He put beer and juice in the refrigerator and dropped some snacks on the table next to the pizza.

"Is Pumpkin still napping?" Benny asked.

"Yes. I'm going to wake her now, or she'll be up all night, and I have the early shift tomorrow."

"I'll wake her," his brother said, walking away as he spoke. "Back in a tick."

When Benny returned with a rumpled, smiling Nova in his arms, Jordan and Adam were sitting in the living room. Adam's small Christmas tree was lit up and Nova went immediately to the music box that sat on the coffee table where she'd left it when she went for her nap.

"Uncle Benny, my music box is pretty."

"It sure is, Pumpkin. You like the music, don't you?"

Instead of answering, the little girl held up the box for Adam to wind it up and then she stood on her tippy toes and twirled around in place.

"Nova Madeleine is a ballerina!" she exclaimed, pausing in her pirouette to make sure all the men were watching her performance. Then she went back to her ballerina impression.

When she stopped again, the men all cheered and clapped, and Nova grinned happily. Adam wound up the box for her again and she danced some more before deciding she wanted Jordan to read to her from the pop-up book that he and Benny had given her for Christmas.

"Uncle Jordan, I know it's not the night before Christmas anymore, but can you please read this again for me?"

Jordan settled his back against the sofa and patted his lap. Nova climbed up and sat across his lap, her head resting on his shoulder and Jordan read to her. No one else was allowed to read to her when Jordan was in the house. it was the cutest thing, and Adam knew how deeply moved his almost-brother-in-law was by Nova's innocent affection for him. While Jordan read to his daughter, Benny sat on the coffee table facing him where he was in the wing-backed chair.

"Get your ass off my table!" Adam told him. "Pull up a chair, like a regular human being."

Benny chuckled but did as he ordered and pulled up a chair next to where he sat. Adam knew his little brother was about to be nosy and interfering, and he was equal parts irritated and grateful, which surprised the hell out of him. He never would have thought that he'd ever appreciate his siblings intruding into his life as they seemed to be doing with alarming regularity these days.

"What d'you want?" he asked ungraciously.

"Talk to me. Have you heard anything from your guy?"

Adam smiled reluctantly. It tickled him to hear Benny call Isaac his guy.

"Yes. He'll be coming on New Year's Day."

Benny high-fived him. "Way to go, bro. It's about damned time you found someone to take Cheryl's place. Who better than a silver fox?"

He waggled his eyebrows and Adam chuckled. He was ridiculous, but he was also right. And as the first one to bring a silver fox into the family, Benny must know what he was talking about. He was almost certain that Isaac was interested, but there was a niggling doubt, a fear that skittered up his spine at the thought of being rejected for having misinterpreted Isaac's friendliness for something more.

"Yeah, well, before you go getting all giddy, just remember, I'm still not sure he's into men. It could just be that he's friendly and doesn't kick puppies."

Benny rolled his eyes. "And I'm taking it you're the puppy in this analogy?"

Adam gave him the thumbs up sign in agreement. "I'm just going to take it slow, you know? Ease my way forward so I don't crash and burn."

"I know you. You're going to put it off, work doubles and forget, and talk yourself out of doing anything. So, I'm gonna be all up in your business until you get it right."

Adam didn't take Benny's threat lightly. Which was why he was glad he'd made the offer to pick Isaac up from the airport. Benny had offered to keep Nova with him for the night, and she was clearly thrilled that she was going to have another sleepover with Claus. He had grown closer to both Benny and Jordan since Jordan became a fixture in Benny's life, and he knew if he could find a guy — Isaac Hamilton — to treat him the way Jordan treated Benny, he'd be a very lucky guy.

The next day his brother took Nova off his hands before he went to work and he spent the whole day on pins and needles. Every time his phone rang his mind conjured things that could happen to Isaac and David, or reasons that Isaac might change his mind, until he was a wreck. Jill, one of the trauma nurses he worked with in the ER, pulled him aside during a lull in the action and asked,

"Are you okay?

"Yeah, sure. Why?"

He knew why she'd asked, but he wasn't about to let on to her that he did. He preferred to keep his private life out of the limelight, thank you very much. And he knew his colleagues…they were almost all incurable gossips.

"You look spaced out, man, very tense. You need to relax before you give yourself a headache."

Adam brushed her off with a smile. "Thanks, but I'm fine."

He managed to finish his reports only an hour after his shift ended and restrained himself from tearing out of the staff parking lot. He still had a couple of hours. He went home, showered and changed, remembering that he'd decided he'd take Isaac and David out to dinner. It'd be better than him having to reheat takeout when he got home. He made a reservation at La Cucina. Since Isaac and David loved mac and cheese, he assumed they wouldn't mind Italian.

He arrived at the airport when their plane was supposed to land and walked over to the arrivals terminal to wait for them. They were out in half an hour and easy to spot, since both man and boy were taller than most of the other passengers. He waited until they were close enough to see him before stepping out and waving a hand. Isaac's eyes caught his and he smiled. Adam's chest tightened with some feeling he didn't understand and his body warmed.

"Welcome back," he said, extending a hand when Isaac stepped close enough.

"Thanks."

"Right this way," he said, leading the way out to the car park. Once they were settled in, he added,

"I've taken the liberty of making a reservation for dinner. I hope you like Italian food."

Isaac's eyes widened in surprise. "That's very kind of you. And sure, we love Italian food."

"What's your favorite, David?" Adam asked, glancing at the boy sitting in the back seat.

"I love baked ziti," David answered.

"So does my daughter," Adam said. "Well, as much as she loves spaghetti with meat sauce."

Isaac laughed. "That used to be David's favorite when he was little."

Adam led the way into the restaurant, and once they were seated and had ordered their drinks, he turned to Isaac, who was sitting across from him in the booth.

"So, how was the sailing?"

David chimed in before his dad could answer. "It was so much fun! Even though the water was choppy because it got really windy when we were going back." His eyes were bright with remembered joy.

"I'm glad I chartered the boat, but I got to tell you, it's not something I could see myself doing often. It took me a while to get my sea legs under me."

Adam watched as David smirked at his dad. "Yeah. I have a video of Dad looking green."

Isaac didn't look bothered by his son's teasing. "It might have been better if I'd been in the water instead of on it," he commented with a laugh.

They devoured their food when it finally came. Adam and Isaac ordered lasagna and David had his baked ziti. The men each had a glass of wine with their meals while David had a soda. They didn't linger over the meal, because both men had to work the next day, and Adam didn't want to keep Isaac out longer than necessary.

He had never been to Isaac's home before, and when he got to the sprawling farm outside of town, he wished it were light enough for him to see. He could imagine the beauty of it, though.

"It must be great to wake up out here every morning," he commented as he parked in front of the refurbished farmhouse.

"It is," Isaac said quietly, and Adam could feel the other man's eyes on him.

They got out of the car and David turned to his father, who handed him the house keys. The boy turned back to Adam and said,

"Thanks for coming to get us, Dr. Kincaid. And thanks for dinner. Goodnight."

"You're welcome, David. Goodnight."

Adam felt rooted to the spot, unable to move as he waited to hear what Isaac would say. They had spent a good evening together, but they hadn't been alone, and he was certain, from the guarded glances that Isaac had cast his way over the course of dinner, that the man had questions. How could he not? And would he ask any of them now?

"Well, I'm guessing that you have work, like I do, in the morning, so I'd better get going myself. Like David said, thanks for everything." Isaac paused, looking into Adam's eyes. "I just need to know one thing, for now."

Adam tensed, though he kept his tone light. "Oh? What's that?"

"Why?"

Damn! Start with the hard question, why don't you? Adam didn't pretend to not understand what Isaac was asking him. How was he supposed to answer that? What could he say that wouldn't either earn him a fat lip or scare this man away? He inhaled slowly before replying,

"I like you." He didn't have any better words at the moment. Those would have to do.

Isaac quirked a brow and a small smile kicked up one corner of his mouth.

"Is that so, Dr. Kincaid? Intriguing!"

He didn't seem freaked out by it. Adam took that as a good sign. He liked the way Isaac's full lips curved when he smiled and he gave in to the sudden urge to feel the pillowy flesh beneath his own. Preparing himself for a painful rejection — better not to see the blow coming, though his gut told him he was safe with Isaac — he leaned in and closed his eyes.

Chapter Eight

Isaac watched Adam's SUV disappear down his long driveway. He was still standing on his front porch, his lips still tingling from where Adam had kissed him, where he'd kissed Adam. God help him, he'd kissed Adam Kincaid in front of his house where David could have seen him. What the hell had he been thinking? And more to the point, why wasn't he more freaked out about kissing a man than he was about possibly being caught doing so by his son?

He raised a trembling hand to his lips for the third time. By any standard, it had been a chaste kiss, but it had been no less powerful for being so. And it didn't matter now that he wondered at himself for having allowed the intimacy. Or had he initiated it? His muddled brain couldn't seem to get the sequence right. Had Adam leaned in before he did? Had they leaned in together? Because if they had, then the kiss was the result of a mutual desire, a shared need for it. Which didn't help him at all.

He couldn't go indoors just yet. He was still way too keyed up from a simple touch of warm, dry lips on his. The last time he had kissed someone other than his son had been…eleven years ago, on the day Rowena died. They'd shared the taste of each other as they kissed deeply before they'd finally managed to get dressed, he to go to work, she to go to the store for the last-minute items needed for their Christmas getaway. It was Christmas Eve, and David was still at his friend's house, where he'd slept over the night before, because he knew he'd be spending Christmas Day with his family.

Rowena had planned a three-day vacation that would begin that afternoon. They were to have gone up to the Finger Lakes region for some outdoor winter fun. He hadn't been especially keen on the outdoor activities, particularly the skiing that she had wanted them to try, but anything his love wanted he had always done his best to give her. The tender ache in his heart even now at the thought of that awful day reminded him of how much he had loved her.

He settled onto the porch swing, moving it slowly with a lazy push of his foot every now and again. They had loved sitting together on the swing, watching the night descend or gazing at the stars in the bejeweled sky. He looked up at them now, wondering when he had stopped pining for his lost love, and when his heart had begun to reawaken. And more to the point, when had it decided that it could handle being attracted to a man.

Isaac had never known himself to be interested in anyone but women in all his life. Sure, he could recognize and appreciate the beauty of the male face and form. He had had a couple of close friends in his youth and early adulthood who had been beyond gorgeous. He had noted it, had admired it, had even wished he had their flawless skin or perfect eyes or full lips. But he'd never gone beyond those thoughts. He'd never wanted to do anything with them that might have been even remotely considered questionable for a straight boy to do with another male.

But he had wanted that chaste press of lips earlier. He admitted it to himself now, sitting under the cold night sky, his coat keeping the freezing temperature at bay. Whatever move Adam may have made, Isaac acknowledged that he had also moved toward the younger man, and he'd leaned in deliberately to get a feel of those pink lips. He could still feel the faint pressure, the subtle warmth of them against his own, and his mind felt a sharp surprise at the thought that pushed into it.

He wanted to do that again. He wanted to feel those lips against his own again. He wanted them harder, for longer, and maybe with… What the fuck? He shut down his brain. He was definitely not ready for where that last thought had been headed. Hell, he wasn't even ready for the first one, where he wanted to kiss another guy a second time. This was too much to take in all at once, and after so little time together.

"Go to bed, Zac," he said aloud. "Work tomorrow."

He did that a lot…talked aloud to himself when he needed to bring himself back from some ledge or other. And this…whatever the hell this was with Adam Kincaid was most decidedly a ledge. A fucking high one, too. He went in, locking up behind him, picked up Sadie, and smiled as the other three cats followed him into his bedroom. He put the old female down and went into his bathroom. David had put his duffel on the chair by the window. He emptied the things into his hamper while the water heated and then took a slow shower.

His cock had been half hard since that kiss on his driveway and now, as he washed himself, it came to full attention under his hands. He hadn't even been aware on a conscious level that he was playing with himself until he noticed how hard he was. Damn! This was serious, if he was sporting wood for a guy. He couldn't recall the last time he'd gotten a hard-on for anyone. Even the few times in the past eleven years that he'd been propositioned he had felt nothing. There had been zero interest in anyone.

He remembered the couple of occasions when men had approached him wanting to get him off, and to get off on him. He had been shocked and then amused by the idea that he was sexually attractive to guys, but he had never thought of either of them in those terms. They had done nothing for him. They'd been short, slender boys, admittedly beautiful masculine specimens, and he had chalked up his lack of interest in them to the fact that they were male. Now, with the way his body seemed to light up at the very thought of a certain male, he had to wonder why he hadn't been interested in the past. Or if he'd been lying to himself all along.

Trying to ignore the now driving need that was stiffening his cock even more as he showered, he forced himself to think about work. Peaches would be going for her holiday on New Year's Eve. New Year's Day the store was closed, but the two days after he'd still be alone, except for David and Shannon. Both David and Shannon worked full days during the holiday break. Peaches had had Shannon with her while he was away. She was a hard worker, and very interested in horticulture and conservation.

He rinsed his body, recalling David's concern that he didn't know what he wanted to do when he finished high school. His son didn't mind working in the shop, but he seemed to be more interested in video games than anything else. In fact, he took every chance he got when he was at work to play the games he'd downloaded onto his phone. Maybe Isaac could have a look at those games to see if there was anything in them that might spark a career interest. He was a firm believer in the idea that there was no useless activity, that people did what they did, enjoyed what they enjoyed, because it met some basic need, and that within those needs lay the potential for growth in every area of their lives.

He shut off the shower, thankful that his cock had deflated somewhat. Maybe he'd be able to fall asleep tonight without a problem. If not, he'd just rub one out. It had been a while since he'd done that, anyway, and though it was mostly unsatisfying, it served a useful purpose. Empty balls, at least for the moment, meant a more relaxed mind and less tension. Which meant better sleep. A man did what he had to do.

He managed not to think about Adam again until lunch time the next day. David had gone to get their lunch and Shannon was heating hers in the microwave in the break room. Isaac was just ringing up the customer standing at the cash register when his cell phone rang. He smiled at the customer and wished her a good afternoon before answering, without looking to see who was calling.

"Good afternoon, Wine and Roses. How may I help you?"

He realized as soon as the words left his mouth that he was answering his personal phone not the store one. He stifled a chuckle.

"Good afternoon, Isaac. How are you?"

Adam's voice made his cock twitch. Damn! "I'm well, thank you, Adam. You?"

"Likewise, thanks." A small pause that felt oddly weighted followed before Adam spoke again. "Mom wants to know if you or David has any food allergies."

It took Isaac a moment to figure out why he was being asked that question.

"No, none, thanks. But since we're on the subject, is there anything I can bring? I don't mind whipping something up to contribute."

Another pause, this one filled with the sounds of a muted conversation before Adam returned.

"Sorry, I'm on my break but that doesn't mean too much if things get busy in the ER. Did you ask what you can bring?"

"Yes, I did." Isaac understood about work, so he wasn't offended.

"Well, if you tell me what you'd like to bring, I can tell her not to prepare it."

"Sounds good. I'll bring potato salad."

"Excellent! I'll let her know."

This time the pause was thoughtful. Isaac could almost hear the wheels turning in Adam's head, as if he were trying to figure out how to say what he wanted to say.

"Hey, Isaac, thanks for saying yes."

Isaac smiled. "Thanks for asking. I'll see you in a few days."

"Yes." The word was almost a whisper, but somehow it pierced Isaac 's calm like a dagger to the heart.

"Take care, Adam."

Long after the day was over, after dinner and dishes, when David was up in his room playing video games with his friends and the old tomcat Tom was snuggling next to his right thigh, the kittens to his left, and Sadie asleep on his lap, Isaac still couldn't get the sound of Adam's voice out of his head. It was sultry and a little husky. It made him think of Teddy

Pendergrass and Marvin Gaye songs, of dark, soulful nights and steamy sex. And it wasn't because the man's voice was all that deep. It was more about the texture...smooth, like melted chocolate and just as decadent.

Or maybe it was just his reawakened libido making him think things that weren't real. How was he to manage this unprecedented attraction to a man in whose company he was to spend a lot of time in four days? And worse, how was he going to hide his feelings among what sounded like it would be a crowd of people? He wasn't a man prone to subterfuge, but it seemed that at least on New Year's Day, he would need to hone those skills if he were to preserve his dignity.

Still, he couldn't deny the thrill that quickened his heart rate at the thought that he was back where he used to be when he first met Rowena, in those early days when all he could think about was her, when the sight and scent and sound of her set him on fire. Granted, he wasn't quite that far gone with Adam Kincaid, but this initial buzz, this simmering electricity made him feel young again. And if he let it happen, he knew he could get back to that place.

Isaac knew he wasn't an old man, but three years away from fifty didn't make him young, either. And after he married Rowena, he'd assumed she was it for him. He had given himself completely over to her and to the feelings she evoked in him. And her death had shut him down completely. But not forever, it now seemed. He was older now, though, so he'd need to be wiser about how he reacted, how he responded to the stimulus that was Adam Kincaid.

He had two big events to decorate for the New Year's celebrations, as well as the sanctuary for services, and although he hadn't told Adam about this, he planned to take along a plant for Mrs. Kincaid's home. He had spent a long time thinking about what he could give her that would reflect the respect and affection in which he held her and his rector. He had even asked Peaches, David, and Shannon for their input.

"What do you think would make a nice plant for the Kincaid's home?"

"Something that will bloom with yellow in it," Shannon had offered up, "because Mrs. Kincaid is such a sunny lady. She's always smiling."

"That's a good idea, Shannon," he'd told her. "You're right, too...I don't think I've ever seen Mrs. Kincaid without a smile on her face."

"A perennial would be nice. Maybe nasturtiums. Or marigolds."

"Or chrysanthemums?" David asked. "They're around a lot in winter."

"All good ideas," Isaac said, thanking them.

Eventually, he decided on a starter set of plants including daylilies, crocus bulbs, and clematis, so she could enjoy a variety of colors. He prepared the planters and on the morning of New Year's Day he packed them and the window boxes he was also giving her into the back of his truck. David had helped him with the potato salad, and they had gone up to get dressed after packing that in the car as well.

His son did him proud, wearing a pair of black jeans and a gray turtleneck. He had taken far longer to decide how he was to dress. He'd called Adam to ask about the dress code and the time of arrival.

"We start arriving before noon, but that's just us. Our guests usually start showing up around one or so in the afternoon. As to dress, wear what's comfortable. Since there's no snow so far, we're probably going to be out on the back porch, so make sure you're warm enough without getting overheated. There will be some space heaters out there for the ones who will need it."

So now he was looking down at his black boots, dark blue corduroy slacks and a gunmetal gray cable knit sweater over a collared dark blue shirt. He looked fine. Whether or not he felt fine was another matter, but he would never let anyone, beginning with his son, see how nervous he suddenly felt. He wished he could stop wanting to look good for a man who may not be where he was, even if he had showed Isaac that he was interested.

"Ready, son?" he asked, shutting down those thoughts and walking into the kitchen to find David standing by the table.

"Yeah, Dad. Did you remember your charger?"

Isaac grinned. David was never electronically unprepared. "Yes, son, I did. Let's get going."

When they got to the manse, there were already a number of cars in the driveway and on the patch of land left for parking extra vehicles. He pulled up behind an SUV with tinted windows.

"You take the potato salad inside, son. I'll come behind you with the plants and come back out for the rest."

They walked up to the front door and David rang the bell. The door swung open almost immediately and Reverend Kincaid smiled at them.

"Good afternoon, Isaac, David. Happy New Year and welcome! Come right in."

"Happy New Year, Rev," Isaac replied as they passed by him.

He directed David to follow him to the kitchen with the food, turning back to say, "Isaac, I'll just go get Anna. She will tell you where she wants these."

A moment later, Mrs. Kincaid appeared. Isaac straightened his spine as though he were meeting the principal of his son's school.

"Good afternoon, Mrs. Kincaid. Happy New Year to you."

"Happy New Year to you, too, Isaac. And thank you so much for these. I truly appreciate them."

"I have some other things in the car, so if you'll just tell me where you want these, I'll go get the rest."

He followed her out to the back porch where the others were gathered and showed him where to put the plants. He turned to her to say,

"The planter boxes I still have in the car should probably go someplace else until you're ready to use them."

She smiled at him and turned to speak to Adam, who was standing closest to her.

"Son, would you please go help Isaac with the rest of the things he's brought for me? The planter boxes can go into the garage for now."

Adam's eyes met his and something warm woke up in Isaac's chest. He returned Adam's smile and his quick hello before heading back out to his car. Adam kept pace with him and as they pulled the remaining plant and the boxes out, Adam said,

"Mom will love you forever. She's a real plant lover."

"I figured as much."

They didn't speak again until they were standing in the garage and Adam was pointing out where he could put the planter boxes. Isaac stacked them neatly before turning to back Adam, who said,

"Hi! Happy New Year!"

He smiled, a full, open, gut-twisting smile. At least, it twisted Isaac's gut; he couldn't speak for Adam. In fact, he was having a hard time speaking at all. He gathered himself, taking a calming breath so he could pretend to be grown up and unaffected by the sparks that always seemed to fly when they were together.

"Hi, yourself. Happy New Year! Thanks for your help."

"Any time, Isaac."

The smile shifted, just enough for Isaac to see that perhaps Adam was also feeling those sparks. And more, that he might be harboring the same kind of thoughts as Isaac. Well, damn! The day was definitely not going to be easy if he had to manage his emotions around this man at the same time as he was making nice with his family. He turned away to the door leading back into the house.

"Let's get back to the others, then," he said, brushing past Adam and refusing to give in to the senseless desire to lay one on his lips. The sound of his voice was already doing a number on his nerves.

He didn't need any further stimulation, thank you very much.

The porch was louder when they got back out there, with people Isaac didn't know milling about talking and laughing. He noted that Bennett and his fiancé were there, as was a handsome guy all in black who came over to hug Adam. Isaac was startled at the sharp pang of jealousy that ripped through him before he resolutely squashed it. Jealousy was an insecure man's emotion, not to mention being totally irrational since he and Adam weren't together. Shaking himself, he stepped away from them so he wouldn't be tempted to eavesdrop on their conversation and turned as Bennett called out,

"The McKenzies are here! The McKenzies are here!"

Laughter greeted his words, which he had uttered in the same way Chicken Little might have said "The sky is falling!" Adam watched as five people and a dog walked into the room. Mrs. Kincaid went over to greet them and they all hugged her. Isaac smiled when he noticed Ryland Tucker III standing with his arm around his husband. It was nice to see how completely the billionaire's blind heir had been accepted into his husband's family, and how the McKenzies loved their new in-law.

Thoughts of his own relationship with Rowena's family threatened to intrude but he stifled them. Since her death, he'd been pretty scarce around them, not wanting any reminders of what he'd lost. And he didn't want them today, either, especially not with the way he was reacting to Adam Kincaid. He turned as someone touched his elbow and barely managed to stop the moan that rose to his lips at the way Adam gently squeezed him there, almost as though he were flexing his fingers, before saying,

"I think your boy is smitten."

Isaac looked over at David, whose eyes were trained on the girl who had walked in with her family.

"Who is she?" he asked.

"She's Chan's baby sister, Chantal. She's a sophomore in college and a real sweetheart of a girl. He could do worse, once he's old enough for her."

Adam chuckled, clearly finding David's reaction amusing. Isaac smiled, though it felt a bit strained. David was too young for a sophomore in college.

"What does that make her? Nineteen?" He couldn't help the question.

"It does," Adam said, looking amused at him now. "Papa Bear doesn't want his son getting involved with an older woman, huh?"

Isaac felt hot and bothered suddenly, knowing how much he wanted to be involved with the younger man standing beside him teasing him. He knew that age didn't matter if two people clicked, but David was still a kid. He had a lot of time yet to decide who he wanted. Anyway, there was no indication that the girl — Chantal — had even noticed him, or that she'd even give him the time of day if she did. He needed to calm down.

He smiled at Adam, feigning nonchalance. "Well, he is only fifteen," he said. "He's got time, and I'm sure she's already got enough male attention that she won't even notice him."

"Come on, let me introduce you to your future daughter-in-law."

Between Adam's teasing words, the tone of those words, and the hand that now nestled at the base of his spine, Isaac was totally disarmed. He relaxed his shoulders as he walked, letting himself enjoy the warmth of Adam's hand on his back.

"Guys, meet Isaac Hamilton. Isaac, meet Chandler McKenzie-Tucker and his husband Ryland Tucker, III, and Chan's siblings, Chance, Channing, and Chantal." He paused as they shook hands and then added, "And Isaac's son David is over there with Nova and Thor."

All eyes turned to where David sat in a corner with the little girl, a book open on his lap, though they were both stroking the dog that had come in with the family when they arrived. Isaac relaxed. His son was engrossed in playing with the child and the dog, so he wasn't focused on Chantal anymore. That was all to the good, because he wasn't ready to explain why David couldn't be with an older woman. Any more than he was ready to explain why he shouldn't be with a younger man.

Life…what a pain, sometimes!

Chapter Nine

The party was in full swing. Everyone had arrived by one thirty, and all introductions had been made. The back porch was wide enough for the sixteen people now gathered around the coffee table that Mrs. Kincaid had placed in the center of the space. They were playing charades because the Kincaid family loved the shenanigans that ensued every time. They had divided themselves into three groups, two of four and one of five people. That had been the beginning of the fun times.

Adam laughed at the look on Isaac's face when he got stuck with Rob on his team, which happily included Adam and David. Was that a spark of jealousy in Isaac's eyes? Surely not! He and Rob were friends, but Isaac wouldn't know that would he? Still, Adam smiled at the thought. Aidan and his partner and her husband got stuck in with Benny and Jordan while the McKenzies were together.

The guesses when the younger members of the group took their turn with the cards were hilarious beyond belief. Most people were really bad at it, but Adam found, to his immense delight, that Isaac and David were excellent at it. His team won handily, while the McKenzies were unanimously declared the best losers and given the prize.

Oh, yeah, that was part of the fun of these New Year's Day parties. His parents had prizes for Best Loser, Worse Liar, and other such unusual categories. And the prizes were as hilarious as the games they played. After charades, Mrs. Kincaid stood up and said, as she turned to go in to begin the final prep for dinner,

"Dinner will be ready in about half an hour. That gives you all enough time to shoot some hoops or play catch or talk amongst yourselves. And I'll need some help in the kitchen, if anyone wants to volunteer."

Adam stood up. He didn't need his mother's eyes slanting over to him to know it was his turn among the siblings to help, and he got to pick his own helper. Obviously, he chose Isaac and made sure he didn't look at Aidan or Benny, both of whom he knew were watching him with expressions he didn't wish to see on their faces. That did not stop the piercing wolf whistles that echoed around the space.

In the kitchen, Mrs. Kincaid set them to work. Isaac took over making the salad, which left Adam free to set the table. Isaac helped his mother carve the ham and the chickens and he set them expertly on the two large platters that she had ready to receive them. Together they took everything out to the side table which had been stripped of its usual occupants so that some of the hot food could be placed there. The potato salad and chef's salad sat on the dining table, as did the green beans and corn on the cob. Adam saw Isaac's smile when he brought out the mac and cheese and he grinned.

"I told mom that David loved it, and since you brought potato salad, she decided to substitute this for her special mashed potatoes."

Isaac's eyes widened and a warm smile curved his lips upward. "You didn't have to do that," he said slowly.

Adam shrugged. "I know. But I thought it would be nice to do something special for him, since he's the youngest guest here today."

Isaac stared at him for a long moment before shaking his head. "You're something else, aren't you?" he said, walking away before Adam could respond.

Once everything was laid out, Adam went to call everyone to dinner. He went to get Nova but found she was already in David's arms, and something uncoiled in his belly at the sight. It was good to see his baby interacting with someone other than her family and her babysitter. She'd be in afternoon pre-K after the holidays and he needed to know that she'd be okay with new people. And that she seemed to enjoy David's company boded well for any future he and Isaac might share.

He blinked. What the hell! Future? What future? They didn't even have a present, for crying out loud! They weren't an item. Neither of them had made any move that said they wanted more than this sizzling foreplay-like pseudo-friendship. Hell, he didn't even know what to call what they had going on. He didn't notice when Isaac took hold of his left hand and Benny took hold of his right as they stood in a circle.

"Amen!"

Shit! He'd missed his dad saying grace. What else had he missed? Moving to the back of the line forming by the buffet, he didn't have long to wait to find out.

"Where'd you go there, big bro?" Aidan asked, stepping in behind him where he stood behind Isaac.

Adam turned his head to look at his twin. "What?" He wasn't sure what Aidan was asking.

"Your eyes glazed over back there. What's on your mind?"

"Nothing!" His answer was sharper than he had meant to make it, but he couldn't stop it. Any more than he could stop his next words. "How about you stop watching me, Detective, and get your dinner?"

Aidan laughed unrepentantly. "Something's got you majorly rattled, hasn't it?" He looked beyond Adam to where Isaac stood, speaking quietly to his son. "Is it the hunky florist, I wonder?"

Adam lowered his eyes from his brother's face and stepped out of the line. He ignored Aidan's amused chuckle and went to stand at the very back of it. He didn't want anyone watching him. And he sure as hell didn't like feeling so flustered. He needed to manage the emotion before he snapped at anyone else. Maybe if he could avoid Isaac for a little bit, he could get himself back under control.

They say when men make plans, God laughs. Adam could hear the Almighty chuckling heartily now as he found himself sitting next to Isaac in the only available seat left at the table. Thankfully, aside from Aidan, who smirked at him and then went back to minding his own business, no one else appeared to be watching him. He speared some of the salad that had been served into the bowl for him, chewed and swallowed, not sparing a thought for who had served his plate. Rinse and repeat.

That's it. One forkful at a time, Adam.

Fortunately for him, his mouth was empty when Isaac asked, "Have I done something to offend you?"

"What?" He knew his eyes were wide with shock. "No! Of course not?" He sipped some of the water that had also been poured into his glass for him. "Why?"

You know why, fucker! Stop pretending!

"One minute we were standing in line together, the next you were at the back of the line," Isaac said. Adam took another sip of water as Isaac continued. "Was it that crack your brother made about me?"

Adam choked on the water and Isaac tapped him gently on his back until his hacking cough subsided.

"You all right there?" he asked, his lips quirked up in a small smile.

"Yeah." Adam's voice was hoarse from the coughing.

He sipped some more water, giving himself time to figure out how he wanted to respond to Isaac's question. He'd never been one for subterfuge, because he knew how things could end — witness the near miss with Rob — and he wasn't going to start now. So, although he wished he could deny his principles just this once if it would help him save face, he finally looked back at the man sitting next to him and said,

"My going to the end of the line had nothing to do with you, Isaac. At least, not because of anything you said or did."

Maybe he could leave it there and Isaac would let the subject drop. He really didn't want to go into specifics, and definitely not at his parents' extended dining table. Seemed like God was having a field day at his expense this evening, because once again, divine laughter echoed in his mind when Isaac asked,

"But it was about me, still, wasn't it?"

Adam looked away. "Persistent much, Isaac?" He didn't realize he'd said it aloud until Isaac replied,

"When I think it's important, yes." Then, at what was no doubt a look of absolute horror on Adam's face, he chuckled and added, "You didn't mean to ask me that out loud, did you? Sorry."

He didn't look sorry, Adam decided. In fact, he looked like he knew all Adam's secrets and was smugly amused. That didn't sit well with Adam, but he was at a loss for how to fix it. He decided to ignore the comment and applied himself to his dinner. They didn't speak to each other again until dinner was over and Mrs. Kincaid invited them all to return to the patio for dessert and more party games.

It was fully dark outside by the time Adam and his brothers finished clearing the table and loading the dishwasher with the first load of the evening. His dad and Jordan had been pressed into service setting up the dessert table and adding more drinks to the cooler. Adam had been more than happy to escape from Isaac's bewitching presence for a while. Time he spent getting himself back under complete control, so he wouldn't blurt out the first thing that came to his mind again in mixed company. He even managed not to snap at his brothers, who were teasing him about being so alternately distracted and taciturn all evening.

"I mean, I get it, you know?" Aidan had said with a smirk as he scraped food remains into the trash. "The dude's hot as fuck. A regular silver fox, emphasis on 'fox'. And that bald thing he has going on? Mm, mm, mm, mm, mm!"

Aidan licked his lips after the last sound, making Benny laugh uproariously. Adam had managed to keep his voice even when he retorted,

"Just in case he didn't hear that, like he did the last time you opened your gob about him in the line,

I'll be sure to report your assessment of his charms the next time I speak to him."

He hoped his tone was laced with enough sarcasm to disguise any emotion that Aidan's words might have let slip.

"Oh, don't make any sacrifices on my account, big brother," Aidan said, his teasing tone unmistakable.

Adam gave him the middle finger, making Benny laugh again. Aidan chuckled and reached over to pull him in for a hard bro hug.

"If you really like this guy, you need to do something about it, Adam," he said, suddenly serious. "It's been way too long. What if this is the man who can finally make you happy?"

Adam looked up at him. "Who says I'm unhappy?" he asked quietly.

"We do," both Benny and Aidan said together, as though they'd rehearsed the response for the occasion.

"Come on, Adam, you know that if it wasn't for Nova and game night you would be a completely pathetic single guy."

Benny's words were also teasing, but they stung just a little because they were also true. Adam hadn't answered...what was he going to say? A denial would have been blatantly false but he wasn't ready to agree just yet. Thankfully, they'd both let the subject drop after that. And now they were back out on the patio waiting to get at the array of dessert choices. Adam was grateful that other people had taken over looking after Nova for him, because he realized he'd been a poor father all evening.

At her request, she'd been seated between Benny and Jordan who had both made sure she was not only well fed but entertained. Now she was sitting with Chan and Ry, playing with Thor while David, who was sitting with the McKenzies, fed her pie and ice cream. It made him smile to see how well she handled being around Isaac and David. He cast his eyes around the space, searching for Rob and found his friend sitting next to one of the McKenzie twins…Chance. Their heads were close together and they seemed to be looking at something on Rob's phone.

Adam was glad that Rob was relaxing enough to pay attention to another guy, even if the interest wasn't sexual. It didn't have to be and anyway, Rob needed a few new friends, as well. He was glad he'd made the decision to invite him. This would be a better year for the two of them. He could feel it in the air. Now if only he could be as certain about what would happen between him and a man he wasn't sure was as into Adam as Adam was into him.

"I'm glad I accepted your invitation."

Think of the devil. Adam turned his head and managed a calm smile — well, he hoped it was calm — at Isaac.

"So am I," he replied. "I take it you're enjoying yourself?"

"I am. David and I don't get out much. I'm always glad for occasions to remind him that he's part of a larger community than just the two of us."

Adam frowned. "He seems like a well-balanced, fully socialized teenager to me."

He turned back to watch David and Nova. She was now sitting right up against his thigh while he held a book between the two of them and read to her. As he watched, she giggled and covered her mouth. It made him smile.

"My son has fallen under your daughter's spell," Isaac commented with a slow grin when Adam looked back to him. "I'm not at all surprised. She's a doll!"

"Thank you," he replied, preening just a little. Nova was a beautiful child, and he knew someday he'd have to watch out for her so the sharks wouldn't snatch her up. "David seems like a caring guy. He'd make a great teacher or pediatrician. He's got the right something that those people need to work with little kids."

Isaac nodded. "You know, you're right. Maybe you can tell him that some time. He's been agonizing about what he wants to do when he grows up. College visits to his school set him off and I haven't really known what to tell him, since I didn't decide on a path for myself, aside from not going into the military like my dad, until after I had a bachelor's degree in landscape architecture with a minor in horticultural science."

Adam was impressed and said as much. "Where did you get your degree?" he asked as they finally made it to the dessert table and were helping themselves to its offerings. "And what made you decide to open a flower and gift shop?"

He hoped those weren't intrusive or inquisitive questions, but despite himself, he wanted to know everything he could about Isaac Hamilton. He was relieved when Isaac answered without hesitation.

"I went to college because my dad said either that or the Army. I wasn't going anywhere near the military, so I enrolled in a college as far from home as

I could get. That's where I met Rowena, my wife," he explained, obviously seeing the question in Adam's eyes. "She always knew she wanted to open a gift shop, so she was there for a business admin degree already. She was specializing in entrepreneurship."

Adam didn't want to break the spell, but he had to ask, "'So, you fell in love and decided you wanted to be her partner?"

Isaac laughed softly. "Not at all. We were on a date at the botanical gardens and I was fascinated by the story of the flowers. Between that and loving the way the gardens were laid out, I got to thinking that maybe I could do the same thing, too, if I knew what the hell I was talking about. Maybe I could teach people the story of plants, their meaning and function. And maybe I could sell them my expertise as a designer of outdoor spaces. That's when I decided on my major and minor."

They found seats together on a loveseat that had been recently vacated by Benny and Jordan. Adam was intrigued by this interesting, fresh new look into Isaac's life. He wanted the rest of the story, so when it looked like Isaac was done talking, he urged him on.

"Well, don't leave me hanging. I'm sure there's more to the story than that. How long were you in business together before she passed away? Did you have any other jobs before the shop opened?"

"I helped her in her family's store until her mom passed. She hadn't meant to stay there that long, but once her mom got sick, she didn't have a choice. Her older brother had four years left in the Army so she was also doing it for him, since the business would go to him once her mom died."

Adam wished he dared ask the next question that came to his mind. But inquiring about how long they had been married might be beyond presumptuous. He hoped they'd eventually become good enough friends that he could ask. Isaac kept talking.

"I found out I liked the idea of teaching other people, but not enough to go back for another degree in education. And that meant I'd have to find a way to use my degree for my career…one I still had no idea about. And then Rowena's mom died and suddenly we were free to do what we wanted. She was set on opening a gift shop where she would sell unique gifts. She suggested I start a flower shop and I could give lessons on flower arranging. gardening, and landscaping on the side. And here we are today."

That sounded like a true partnership to Adam. But how long had they been together then, if he had first met her in college? The question he had avoided asking earlier seemed more acceptable now.

"How long were you married?"

"Five years." Isaac's eyes grew shadowed. "David was four when she died."

They would have been married for twenty years if she had lived. Adam's heart ached for him. But it also seemed that they had been together a long time before getting married, which was about right for the kind of man Isaac appeared to be…deliberate, thoughtful, in no hurry for anything. To know someone so well was a dream Adam could only see escaping him more with every passing day.

"I'm sorry for your loss, Isaac," he said, feeling inadequate suddenly.

There was nothing that he could offer to a man like Isaac, with his years of experience both as a businessman and as a husband and father. Any hopes he might even wish to harbor for anything more than friendship between them had to be squashed ruthlessly if he were to retain his sanity. He would try his damndest to keep his thoughts in the friend zone. He had to stop himself from going any further along the path his brain kept taking him.

"You disappeared there for a minute."

Isaac's observation made Adam's cheeks heat. He really had to stop acting like a lovesick schoolboy and keep it together around this man. Just until he had his emotions back under control. He was allowed to feel deep admiration and respect. Anything else was completely off limits. He stopped asking questions then, deliberately turning his attention away from the man sitting next to him, watching the others interact and wishing he could be as carefree.

"Well, it's the beginning of a New Year, and as is our family tradition, we have to speak our goals into the air and into the ears of at least one other person who will keep us accountable."

His mom's voice broke into the general hum of chatter and everyone turned to look at her. She continued with a smile.

"Just like we do on Thanksgiving, when we each say something we've been thankful for all year, on New Year's Day we each say one thing we think is important for us to remember or to work on in the new year to help us grow as human beings. Oh, and none of these things must be physical, unless that's especially important to our personal growth. It's too easy to say we want to lose weight and feel better."

Everyone groaned, but she only smiled and said, "We'll begin with the oldest. That will give Adam time to help Nova figure out what she wants to say."

His mother looked meaningfully at him and he turned to find Nova already approaching him. He smiled and pulled her onto his lap.

"Thanks, Mom," he said. "I mean, I was getting free babysitting before you messed with my mojo."

Everyone laughed and then his dad began to speak. Adam hugged his daughter to his chest and listened as his dad said he wanted a second grandchild. No one was surprised, though his mom did protest.

"That's my line, mister!" she said sassily. "It's a good thing I have a backup plan." She turned her eyes all around the room and continued, "I want to take the vacation we've kept putting off because we we've been waiting for the boys to be settled."

Adam looked at Aidan and they both shrugged at the same time. That meant they had no idea what their mother meant but they'd find out soon enough. Because they both knew that the only one who was "settled" was Benny. Once she stopped speaking, she said,

"So as not to out any other old folks around here" — loud laughter accompanied that remark — "how about we leave my sons and granddaughter for last and the rest of you get to go in any order you choose?"

A general murmur of agreement was followed in quick succession by Jordan, Chandler, Ryland, the other McKenzies, Rob, Aidan's partner and her husband. Their goals included everything from starting a garden — "Isaac, sounds like you're gonna have a new customer!" Mrs. Kincaid said in response to that one — to making a budget. That last one was Chance, who was working with a high-end law firm while he studied for the bar.

Then it was David's turn. Adam watched as the boy looked first at his father and then at the rest of the group.

"I like the feeling I have right now," he said. "I want to keep it."

Simple words, spoken quietly, with faint embarrassment and lowered eyes, but Adam felt every one of them echoing in his heart. What must it be like to grow up as an only child needing outsiders to keep you from falling off the deep end into depression or fear or any other negative emotion? And to be a motherless only child must be even worse. Thank God he had a man like Isaac for his father.

Adam watched as his mother rose and went over to where David sat, pulling him up and into her arms. The boy's eyes lit up and he returned her hug, neither letting go of the other for a long moment. Then it was Isaac's turn. Adam wondered if he was worried about what he'd say, especially after his son's own poignant wish.

"Sometimes, it takes a son to show a father what's possible. Thank you, son."

He held his arms open to David, who walked unashamedly into them. Father and son embraced for an even longer moment, and Isaac didn't completely release David when he added, "I look forward to all the future lessons. Letting go was hard. Moving on is harder, but I'm trying."

Damn! This man was deep, and the love he shared with his son was heartwarming and affirming.

Cryptic words, unless you knew the man and enough of his story to know what he meant. Was Isaac saying he was ready to move on from his wife? Had he found someone to do that with? The questions made Adam unaccountably anxious and a little bit scared. He knew who he would like the other man to be moving on with, even if he didn't think he was worthy of the honor. He might not have anything new to offer Isaac, and it might not be smart to keep hope alive, but that didn't stop the wanting.

Logic and common sense didn't matter when his attraction to Isaac was an ever-rising tide. He closed his eyes for a moment, thinking about the little girl on his lap. He hoped he was as good a father to her as Isaac was to his son. At least he was certain that he was ready to move on, as well. And he knew exactly who he wanted to do that with, logic and common sense be damned.

"Adam, you're up!"

His mother's voice startled him out of his thoughts. It brooked no argument, so even though he didn't really know what he wanted to say, he opened his mouth anyway and hoped that what came out wouldn't embarrass him or anyone else.

"I'm with Isaac...about the moving on," he hastened to add.

He didn't need anyone thinking he meant...fuck it! He secretly did mean that that was his wish, but no one else needed to know that. At least not until Isaac did. His response would determine the direction that Adam moved in. He finished his thought.

"I'm ready for a change."

"Well, it's about damned time!" Aidan said, making everyone laugh.

Adam looked down at Nova before kissing the top of her head. He had more or less withdrawn after Cheryl's death and let his job take the place of a person in his life. But now that he'd met someone who made him want to come alive again, made him want to be that vibrant, engaged, passionate man he once was, he didn't think he could push that side of himself back down any longer. He didn't want to.

He didn't hear what his brothers said until his mother asked,

"Nova, if you could have anything in the world this year, what would you like?"

The little girl looked up into Adam's face, her eyes bright with love, before she looked at her grandmother and said,

"I want my daddy to be happy like you and Papa, Nana."

"Aww!" issued from the lips of every person sitting there in a poignant harmony.

Tears pricked Adam's eyes but he closed the lids to contain them. It wasn't as though he was surprised by his daughter's response. She asked him at least once a week why he wasn't happy like Nana and Papa. And he knew exactly what it was that she saw in his parents and didn't see in him. Well, maybe the time was now to change all that.

"As always, out of the mouth of babes..."

His father looked at Adam with love and concern in his gaze before he said,

"Well, this has been a wonderful day. The 'official' parts are all done. Feel free to stay as long as you like, but from now on, the entertainment is on you. Just make sure you finish the rest of the food and drink before you leave."

Laughter echoed around him, but Adam didn't join in. His gaze was riveted on Isaac, who had looked at him for one long, penetrating moment after he had said his piece. The look was weighted with so much emotion that Adam needed to know what it meant. What was Isaac thinking? Would he share if Adam asked him? You can't know if you don't try, bucko! Setting Nova on her feet, he whispered in her ear,

"Go ask Nana for more pie, sweetie! I'll come get you when it's time to go home, okay?" The permission was possibly going to come back to bite him in the ass, but he couldn't summon the will to care just then.

Nova studied him for a minute before she said, "Okay, Daddy. But can I get ice cream, too?"

Adam laughed, feeling suddenly light. "Only if Nana says you can, baby girl."

"Okay, Daddy."

Adam watched her skip away to her grandmother's side before he turned to Isaac and wasn't surprised to find the other man watching him. He approached him with a smile.

"Can we talk?"

Chapter Ten

Isaac considered him for a moment before nodding. "Sure. Where's good?"

"Follow me."

Adam turned away, knowing Isaac was right behind him, and they walked together into the living room. It was a semi-private space, far enough away from the patio that they wouldn't need to speak loudly to hear each other.

"Have a seat," he said, gesturing around him.

Isaac sat in the overstuffed chair and crossed one ankle over the other knee. He waited, eyes on Adam, hoping he was exuding calm. He wondered if Adam was buying it, if he looked zen, or if he was also silently buzzing with the knowledge of the possibilities in the chemistry between them. He hoped he hadn't misread Adam's words from earlier because he knew there was no denying the connection they shared. Not after the unintended insights of the last half hour.

"What's on your mind?" Isaac sensed that Adam needed a push to get going. Maybe it would be best if he helped him out with a question.

"What did you mean about letting go and moving on?" Adam began.

Isaac leveled him with another considering gaze before he answered. "I've been alone for eleven years. I haven't once tried to fill the gap that Rowena left. I haven't wanted to. There was always work and there was always David and they were enough. Or so I thought. I wasn't even attracted to any of the people who made a pass, came on to me, stalked me. I wasn't interested."

He paused, looking down at his hands. Could Adam hear the wheels turning in his head as he decided how to go on with his answer? What else should he say? Would it be anything that Adam wanted to hear? He went on doggedly, determined to be honest from the start...if this was really to be the start and not the end of anything between them. He didn't know how to do this anymore...he was too old for this level of sexual anxiety, or whatever the hell it was that was making his limbs tremble despite his best efforts to remain calm.

"Then you walked into this house last November, and suddenly, I'm aware of another man in a way I've never ever been before with any man. Or at least, not consciously. But every time I see you, I wonder if the other times when I thought I was looking at an attractive man dispassionately, the way I'd look at a painting or one of those sweet music boxes, I was lying to myself. Was I admiring those men because they were beautiful creatures or because I wanted them?"

Isaac's heart beat hard in his chest. He really wanted to know the answers to his questions. But did it matter, if Adam wasn't interested in finding out, as well? His anxiety rose, but he tamped it down. He'd be done baring his soul in a minute and then whatever was going to happen would happen. This too shall pass, Zac. He felt like a condemned man facing the gas chamber.

"And? What have you decided?" Adam clearly needed to hear the rest sooner rather than later.

Isaac sighed. "I'm still not sure. You confuse me. Or rather, my reaction, my responses to you...they confuse me." Another soft huff of air and then he added, "You've probably been told this a lot, but I need to say it. You're a very attractive man. My teenage helper Shannon would describe you as 'sexy as hell,' and she wouldn't be wrong."

Adam's endearing blush warred with the amused chuckle that escaped him at that. Isaac found the expression amusing, as well, so he smiled. But what he really found himself wanting to do was to test how warm Adam's cheeks were by feathering soft kisses all over them. He swallowed and focused on what he still had to say.

"But I think the way I'm reacting to you is more than how I'd admire a museum piece. What I'm feeling is more than what I think about when I look at a beautiful work of art."

Suddenly, he stood up, needing to put some distance between himself and the doctor before he gave away how tense he really was. He paced away from Adam, moving to stand by the window that looked out over the garden and the street beyond it. Adam didn't speak. Maybe he wanted to hear it all before he spoke his own truths. That was only fair, Isaac supposed. He hadn't wanted to pussyfoot around but had gone straight to the heart of the matter. He had to stop stalling and finish what he started.

"At any rate, to answer your question completely, I'm letting go of Rowena. I realize I hadn't really done that, even though the hurt has faded. I've been keeping her enshrined so I wouldn't have to engage with anyone new. Everything in its time, huh?"

He had spoken those words with his eyes on the darkness outside the window. He turned back to the room to face Adam before ending,

"As to the moving on, I'll admit I don't know how to do that with..." he paused, looking Adam dead in the eye and swallowing before continuing, "...with you, because this is all new to me. But I know what I'm feeling. I've only ever felt it once before, but I've never forgotten it."

Adam stood up then, too. The tension between them was almost palpable. Had he also needed to move, to stop himself from giving away how keyed up he was? Despite the revelations that he was laying bare to Adam, Isaac did his best to appear cool, almost detached. Maybe Adam was pretending just as hard that he was cool and calm.

"So, you're saying you want to move ahead with me?"

Smart man! It was best to get things crystal clear. Isaac was certain that Adam didn't want to make a fool of himself. He couldn't blame him...he wouldn't want to take that chance, either.

Isaac moved back across the room to where he stood and faced him without touching him.

"Yes."

He waited silently, everything he had wanted to say finally laid bare between them. He had lobbed the ball firmly back into Adam's court. How would he respond? Had Isaac been a fool to open himself up like that to a man he was only just getting to know? Was he going to get let down gently but with clinical precision? And if he wasn't, how was he going to react to a positive answer? How should he react? He didn't know how it went between men. It hadn't been this hard with Rowena...had it?

A hand on his brought him back into the moment. He looked down at their joined hands, then up into Adam's face. He could see the younger man trying to find the words to say what he was feeling. He would help him again. He was older, more experienced. He should help when and where he could. This time, an even more direct question seemed called for.

"So, you said that you're with me on the moving forward, that you're ready for a change. Was I reading you wrong, or did you mean that you wanted that change...that moving forward, to be with me?"

"Yes."

Isaac smiled. They were a pair, weren't they, unable at the last to do more than agree. But since that was what he wanted to hear, he didn't care if Adam's answer was lacking in eloquence. There would be time for that, if things developed well.

"So, where do we go from here?" One more question was necessary.

Adam looked toward the door that led out to the rest of the house. Then he looked back at Isaac.

"How would you like to come over for game night next Saturday?"

Isaac smiled. "I'm usually open later on weekends. What time does game night begin?"

"Eight. That's the best time since I don't usually get home much before then most evenings. Will that be too late for you?"

Isaac hesitated. He didn't care so much about the time as about what he'd do with David. Unless his son had plans with Alex, he'd be alone at the farm. Isaac knew the boy could look after himself, but he didn't like leaving him alone for too long all the way out there. Maybe...

"Can David tag along, or will it be too grown for him?"

"Sure he can. He can always play with Nova, and Benny has a cat named Claus that she loves, so they'll both be entertained."

"I'm sure being anywhere near his hero will make his night."

Adam smiled. "And when we have it at the McKenzie house, he'll have people closer to his age to hang with."

Isaac was intrigued, despite the momentary twitch he felt at the idea of David being in closer contact with Chantal. How great that must be, having a support system.

"So, game night moves around?"

"Yep. A different home every time, unless something happens — usually with me — and it has to go back to the venue from the time before. It's the easiest way for us to stay connected."

"Is that your only escape from work?" Isaac needed to know exactly how much he and Adam were alike.

The other man lowered his eyes at the question for a moment before he looked back up and nodded.

"Between my job and Nova, I don't have a lot of time for socializing."

Isaac couldn't judge him for that because that was his truth as well.

"I hear that," he said. "No judgment here. I don't even have a game night to look forward to."

"Well, now you do, if you want to. Of the six of us, Jordan is the only one with a social life that doesn't include just us. He hangs with his buddies on Friday nights. Sometimes, if they can, they join game nights with us. It's even more fun, then."

The possibility of meeting new people and perhaps even making new friends warmed Isaac. This was an opportunity to do what he'd said he would do, and he would grasp it with both hands. Being with Adam, learning about him and seeing where this attraction went might have been the basis for this decision, but it was no longer the only reason to do it. And that made him feel better, somehow.

"Is game night a weekly thing, then?" he wanted to know next.

He didn't think he could do that because he really did enjoy being on his own. Solitude was restorative for him, but it was still good to know. He didn't have to say yes to every invitation but he was sure that Adam wouldn't mind. At least, he hoped he wouldn't.

"Usually it's every two weeks, since that's when Aidan is most likely to be free. But he's often absent because he's working a case, and sometimes I'm absent if I have to pick up a shift. Benny's away only when he's out of town on a gig, which isn't often anymore."

Voices approaching interrupted their conversation. Both looked toward the open doorway in time to see Rob heading toward them, walking next to Chance, whose face was wreathed in smiles. Adam chuckled and Isaac looked at him curiously.

"What's funny?" he wondered.

Adam turned away from the men who had now passed by on their way to the front door.

"Nothing, really. I'm just glad Rob has noticed someone else."

Someone else? What was that about? Isaac wanted to ask, but he was again interrupted by the approach of the rest of the McKenzie clan, including Ryland, who was being led by his husband, the big dog taking up point on his other side.

"I guess it's time I got going," he said, looking back at Adam. "I'll just go get David. Text me the details...venue address and what I'm to bring with me."

He went in search of his son, whom he found heading in his direction with Nova in his arms. She was whispering something in his ear that made him grin, and he whispered back, making her giggle. He waited for them to get to him before he said,

"Hey, son. You've got a new fan, I see."

David looked up with a smile. "Nova's cool, aren't you?"

He raised his hand and she high-fived him with a tinkling little laugh. Isaac felt Adam move in beside him and he had to forcibly ignore the awareness that made his nerves zing all along his left side. Nova reached for her father, and Adam took her with a smile.

"Did you have a good time, baby girl?" he asked, planting a soft kiss on her temple.

"Yes, Daddy. Nana gave me more ice cream and David played Operation and matching with me and Chantal and Nana."

"Sounds like you had fun," Adam said with a chuckle, turning to eye Isaac with amusement.

"Wait till she's old enough," Isaac groused, but without heat.

He knew Adam was laughing at him over his concern that David seemed to like Chantal, who was four years his senior. He could admit that he was probably being absurd, since the young woman didn't even seem to notice his son. He hoped her disinterest wouldn't depress David. He didn't need a moody teenager right now when he had his own love life to figure out.

Everyone was busy putting on hats, coats, and gloves, and goodbyes were ringing out through the front door. Isaac found himself next to Adam and it seemed natural to help him with his coat before he put his own on. Pulling on his gloves, he watched as Adam kissed his mother and hugged his dad.

"I'll call you," he promised his mother in answer to whatever she had spoken into his ear.

Isaac noted the faint flush on his cheeks but couldn't be sure what had caused it, since the air in the hallway was distinctly chilly now from the front door being opened to discharge the Kincaid guests into the frigid night air. Then he was up next and found himself being hugged by Mrs. Kincaid.

"I hope you enjoyed your day with us, Isaac," she said as she released him.

"I did indeed, thank you," he replied, watching as she took David into her arms for the same treatment.

She said something quietly to his son as well that had David looking bashful even as he said,

"Yes, ma'am. I will. And thanks."

Hmm…what was that about? He figured it was something good that she'd said to him, and Isaac supposed if David wanted him to know, he'd tell him. He was trying to give the teenager more space as he grew older, because the last thing he wanted was to be the overbearing parent his own father had been to him. And then his eyes opened wide when David was approached by Chantal, who said, loud enough for everyone around them to hear,

"It was nice to meet you, David. I hope you can figure out what you really like soon. Talk to Mr. DeLongo. He helped me a lot when I was trying to figure out what I wanted."

She smiled at him and Isaac saw his son's eyes widen in shock. He could understand the reaction. Chantal was pretty, but her smile transformed her into a rare beauty. She was going to be a heartbreaker, if she wasn't already, and Isaac felt his gut tighten at the thought of his son's heart breaking. Something in his demeanor must have shown on his face because Adam said, next to him,

"Easy does it, Papa Bear. It'll be okay, I promise."

Isaac turned to look him in the eye. "Stop watching me," he commanded him.

Adam chuckled. "Too late."

They followed the McKenzies to the door and David turned to him.

"Dad, I'll go start the car."

Isaac handed him his keys and then smiled when David offered to start Adam's as well. Adam quickly handed over his also, pointing out where his car was with a quiet word of thanks. They stayed inside a few more minutes while the rest of the Kincaid clan came to get their winter gear. Eventually, he and Adam walked out to their cars and he waited until Adam had buckled Nova into her car seat and stood up again, closing her inside.

"Well, I'll see you next Saturday. I'll text you details when I get home."

"Looking forward to it," Isaac said, no longer surprised to know he meant it.

"Me too."

Something in Adam's eyes told Isaac there was some other message in his words than the one he understood. But it was cold out, and they were standing on his parents' driveway with the rest of his family out and about to see their interactions. He didn't need to broadcast to anyone that he had more than a friendly interest in Adam, so he smiled and stepped away to the driver side of his car. He opened the door and just before he slid into the seat, he said,

"Drive safe."

Then he ducked into the seat, closed the door and put it in reverse. David was bopping his head to something he was listening to on his phone, his cordless earpods glowing in the dark car. With nothing else to distract him, Isaac let himself go over the conversation with Adam. Now that they had openly acknowledged the connection they felt with each other, they'd be spending more time together. What would that time look like? Was he ready to start dating again? And what would his son think about him with another man?

Isaac knew only too well that when it came to family, people's views were often fickle. What was fine for other people was anathema if it involved a family member. He knew David wasn't homophobic, but that truth had only been tested in the public sphere, in his knowledge and acceptance of his favorite teacher as a gay man. David might sing a different tune when it came to him. Isaac knew he had to be prepared to deal with the fallout of this decision to explore the chemistry between him and Adam.

He also knew that pushback would definitely come from his father. The Major didn't consider himself a homophobe, but Isaac knew his father was never comfortable even discussing the subject of gay rights in general, so there was no way he'd be happy that Adam was who Isaac was choosing to rediscover his need for companionship with. Not only was Adam gay, but he was also white, and the Major would see that as another big mark in the 'No' column.

He sighed, wishing his life could be simpler. It would have been so much easier to stay away from Adam, to refuse to explore the feelings he was stirring up, to avoid any more contact than he had already. Easier…and deadly dull, he knew. Despite the faint trepidation that was making his blood fizz, he felt more alive than he had in the last eleven years, and it was a good feeling. He remembered how it used to be when his heart was whole and his life was filled with love and laughter. He wanted that again and he'd take it, however it was given.

Sleep came slowly when he got home later. He'd be at the store by eight the next morning, but it would be a slow day unless something unexpected happened, so it wouldn't matter if he were a little bit sleepy. Nobody would notice. He tossed and turned on his bed, got up to go get water, plumped his pillows and cursed the day of his birth. Nothing seemed to help him relax enough to drift off to sleep.

Then his cellphone dinged. He had forgotten that Adam said he'd send him a text message with the rest of the details about game night. He picked up the phone and opened the message.

Adam: Hi! Game night is on for my place at eight. The address is 2549 Juniper Drive, Apartment 2C.

Even as he dashed off a quick "Got it. What do I bring with me?" Isaac was seeing the area where Adam lived in his mind's eye. It was one of the newer communities growing on the outskirts of town, where the younger married set lived because the communities had been built to include swimming pools, tennis and basketball courts, and playgrounds to meet their varied single and married needs.

Adam: We usually have pizza and wings with snack foods. And of course, beer.

Isaac: Okay, I'll let you know what I'm bringing before the day of.

When a couple of minutes went by without a response, Isaac assumed Adam had gone to bed. He slid the phone under his pillow, then removed it with a shake of his head. Whatever that had been about, he needed to nip it in the bud. The phone vibrated in his hand before he could set it back on the nightstand. Another message from Adam.

Adam: You don't have to go out of your way to make anything. Just bring some chips and dip. That'll be good enough.

He sent him a thumbs up in return, then put the phone away and turned on his side. Chips and dip were fine if he were a kid, but he was a grown man a breath away from fifty. He'd make some real food for them to eat. He had six days to figure something out.

He could do this…he had raised a child all on his own for eleven years, and built and run his own business as well. He could handle a bunch of guys, no problem.

He refused to dwell on the fact that he was joining the group as someone with a personal interest in one of its members. He wouldn't let himself worry about how that might be received. Maybe it wouldn't even come up. After all, he and Adam wouldn't be the only male couple there. It was no biggie.

When he told David they'd be spending Saturday evening with the Kincaids and their friends, his son's eyes lit up like fairy lights on a Christmas tree. Isaac was amused by the teenager's excitement at the thought of seeing Adam's daughter again, though he suspected that David might also be harboring the hope that he would see Chantal McKenzie as well. He didn't bother to disabuse him of that notion. He was all about letting sleeping dogs lie and all that.

Peaches reminded him that he was to start a new set of flower arranging classes the following week, and she and he sat and planned the first session. The post-holiday surplus of flowers would be perfect for the work he'd be doing with the motley crew of beginners he'd have. They had decided the first time he'd offered them that he'd run the classes from his workshop, which was why he had enlarged the space by taking some from the break room.

He asked Peaches what she thought would be good to take with him to game night. Aside from wings done any way but raw, he couldn't think of anything that wouldn't make it seem like he was trying too hard. And he didn't want to give anyone, least of all Adam, the impression that he was desperate for acceptance. He wasn't desperate, exactly, but he knew that now that his heart was cracked open again, he wanted to feel like a part of something bigger than himself.

He decided to go with barbecued bacon-wrapped chicken bites. It wasn't hard to make, especially if he bought the wings already deboned. He made them every year on his and David's birthdays, and paired them with a chef's salad and mac and cheese for David. He figured the guys would like the meat-on-meat, and since they were only bites, they wouldn't worry too much about the extra fat and calories.

He texted Adam, though by Thursday he found himself desperate to hear his voice, and told him what he planned to take with him. His phone buzzed a second later. He looked down to see who was calling and then checked the time...it was almost five thirty in the afternoon.

"Hey, Adam." Isaac did his best to keep the sharp pleasure he felt at hearing the younger man's voice from leaching into his own.

"Hi! That sounds delicious, but I don't want you to go out of your way to make anything. This is supposed to be a fun, easy night, not more work for you."

Isaac smiled. "It's no trouble. I make it for David's and my birthday every year and really all I have to do is wrap the chicken on bacon and pop it in the oven coated in barbecue sauce."

He didn't bother to tell him that the sauce was homemade. better not to get into that now. If it came up on Saturday night, he'd tell the story. If not, it wasn't important.

"Well, if you're sure. There'll be other food, so you don't have to make a whole lot," he added.

Isaac chuckled. "Somehow I don't think your buddies would agree with that. I'm probably going to be the oldest guy there, and I eat a lot of them. It's not a problem, really. David will be beside himself when he finds out I'm making them for something other than a birthday."

Now it was Adam's turn to chuckle. "Have you told him yet?"

"I have, and he's chuffed to be hanging with the guys, as he put it. Plus, he thinks this will give him major babysitting cred."

The slight pause that greeted his last words puzzled Isaac until Adam said, "I hope neither you nor he thinks I'm having him over to babysit Nova, because that's not it at all."

Another wall crumbled bit more in Isaac's chest. The thought hadn't crossed his mind, but it made something inside him warm to know Adam was worried that he might take offense. When was the last time anyone cared not just about his feelings but about his son's? This was certainly another of the things they'd need to discuss, because children brought complications with them into any relationship.

He didn't want his son to be taken advantage of, for sure, but he didn't want Adam to feel like Nova would be a burden because she was a toddler, either. She needed more hands-on parenting than his teenager did, but it wouldn't be a hardship for Isaac to share his wisdom with Adam or to spend time with her. She was a sweetheart, by the looks of things, and David was already bowled over by her. She was probably going to be like the little sister he would never have now, no matter what happened between Isaac and Adam.

"I know. Don't worry about it. David likes her. He stopped asking about this when he was still a little boy, but I know he's always wanted a little sister. So, I'm sure things will work out fine, as long as we don't make it weird."

The conversation played over in his mind as he checked the oven on Saturday afternoon. Peaches was minding the store with Shannon, having informed him in no uncertain terms that he was not going to show up at his first social event in years looking like something the cat dragged in. She was the older sister he had never had, and he was grateful for her friendship and support. Isaac chuckled even now as he recalled her sassy grin and teasing words.

"You need to rest a bit, especially since you're making food to take with you. I'll see you on Monday, and I'll want a full update on your date."

The second batch of bacon-wrapped chicken poppers, which was what he called them, was almost done. David had helped him prepare them, and had asked if he could make something as well, for Nova. Isaac hadn't seen a problem with it, and watched as his son made a dozen fried Oreos and placed them carefully in a glass dish in the refrigerator. He would take them out at the last minute and transfer them to an insulated bag which he had put in the freezer.

They ate dinner early, so there'd be room for the food at the party later. It was nothing too difficult... David would never say no to pasta of any kind, so he volunteered to make spaghetti and meatballs. Isaac left him to it, knowing he'd add the already fully-cooked frozen meatballs to the rest of the pasta sauce that Isaac had made the week before. He chose his outfit while his son made dinner, and after they ate and tidied the kitchen, they went up to shower and dress.

Isaac took in his son's casual jeans and t-shirt look before he pulled a hoodie over his head and put on his jacket. Isaac wondered if he was overdressed. Sure, he was wearing jeans, but they were almost new, and he'd paired them with a button-down shirt and a round-necked sweater. He'd pulled the collar of the shirt over the neck of the sweater, so he looked like a professor rocking it in class on casual Friday.

It was too late to change now. He packed the poppers while David went out to start the car, put food out for the animals, replenished their water supply and then followed his son out to the car, which David had backed onto the driveway. As the garage door slid down, he turned the car and drove off. His hands shook slightly, and it wasn't from the cold. Tonight was going to be another game changer.

Chapter Eleven

"Relax, Adam." Aidan walked by his twin as Adam stood in front of the refrigerator peering in. "Game nights are supposed to be a fun, relaxing time, but you're so wound up, you'll crash and burn before the night is over."

He squeezed Adam's shoulders once and it felt so good he moaned.

"Come on," he said, "sit here. Let me work these knots out before your man gets here, so you can meet him with a cheerful smile instead of a constipated imitation of one."

Adam turned to glare at his sibling. "Shut up! And he's not my man. He's just a friend."

"Mhm…and I am the King of Siam."

Before Adam could protest further, Aidan manhandled him over to the kitchen table and shoved him down onto a chair. He relented, letting himself relax and feeling his shoulders loosen as his brother massaged them. The front door opened and Adam knew who it was before they walked into the kitchen.

"I smell brownies," Aidan said, still kneading Adam's shoulders.

He was right. Benny had made his signature brownies and the glorious scent of sugar, butter and chocolate was permeating the room even now.

"Nervous, big bro?" Benny asked, passing by him to place the two pans of brownies on the table.

"Tired," Adam replied before Aidan could say anything. Of course, that didn't stop his twin from responding. He should have known it wouldn't.

"Yeah, that's what he's calling it tonight."

The sharp retort ready on his tongue was halted by the doorbell. Instantly, Adam was back to feeling as anxious as before, his shoulders hiked up again.

"Hey! Calm the fuck down, bro. He's just a guy. And if he's as into you as you're into him, he'll not be happy to find you so tense you can only grimace at him. Take a chill pill, for Pete's sake!"

Aidan squeezed his shoulders again, and Adam forcibly relaxed them. Benny had gone to answer the door, but it was just Ry and Chan, bringing with them Chan's newest favorite game night treat, jalapeño poppers. Jordan carried a case of beer to help relieve the hot lips and tongues they were going to have from the poppers.

"You know where to put stuff," Aidan said when they came in to say hi. "We're just waiting for the guest of honor to arrive, and trying not to lose our shit. Well, Adam here is. I'm just the moral support."

He sounded far too amused for Adam's liking, but since there was nothing he could do about it, he made do with another glare at his twin, who just laughed at him.

"You said he was bringing something with bacon, right?" Chan asked when he walked in. "That'll go nicely with the poppers. We're gonna have a feast tonight, it seems. Good thing I didn't make anything heavy for dinner."

"He's bringing his son," Adam said, twisting to look at his guests. "I'm sure he'll clean up whatever we don't. He's a growing boy. I mean, have you seen the kid? He's barely shorter than me."

"Is it any wonder? Have you seen his dad?" Aidan chimed in before anyone else could answer.

"Yeah, he's a big dude for sure," Chan agreed.

"How big?" Ry asked.

Chan hummed. "I'd say maybe six inches or so taller than you. You'd have to look up at him, if you could see him."

"Where's Nova?" Jordan asked, coming back into the room from the kitchen.

"She's napping. Mom tried to get her to go down earlier but she wasn't having any of it. Then she fell out in the car."

Adam stood, giving his twin a thank-you hug for the massage, and moved away to go check on her, adding as he went, "It's fine, though. She likes Isaac's son. I figure she'll be tired again by the time they leave, so she can spend some time with her crush."

The men all chuckled at that and he walked away to wake his daughter. The doorbell chimed before he had quite made it to the hallway. Jordan appeared at his side as if by magic and said,

"Why don't you go answer the door, hm? I'll get Nova." He winked as he said it, then smiled easily and added, "Us older guys like it when our crushes show an interest, too, you know?"

Adam blushed, a full-on coloring up off his cheeks. He felt the color travel down his neck to his chest. He shook his head and sighed.

"Thanks, old man," he quipped. "Take her to the bathroom before you bring her out, please."

"No problem. I'll be back in a few!"

Adam hurried to the door, opening it after taking a deep breath. Isaac and David both smiled at him as he stepped aside, saying,

"Come on in and welcome."

Closing the door after they passed him, he said again, "Follow me. I'll show you where to put the food."

"Um, I made some fried Oreos for me and Nova, sir," David said. "May I put it in the fridge till it's time to eat them?" He indicated the insulated bag that he held in his hand.

"Sure thing, David," Adam replied with a smile. "Just don't tell her about them till I say so or she'll pester you to get it before she's had anything else."

"Hasn't she eaten already?" Isaac asked, looking concerned.

"Mom gave her some dinner, but she barely ate any because she was too excited about seeing her Uncle Jordan again."

Isaac's eyes warmed with understanding. "Kids, right?"

Adam smiled, grateful that he wasn't being deemed a bad parent. Nova had very few friends. That was one of the reasons that he was putting her in afternoon pre-K. But in the meantime, he had done what he could, between her babysitter and his mom, making sure she was taught age-appropriate things, that she was read to and taken on excursions once in a while. And when he had her, he did everything he could to occupy her mind without wearing her out.

"I figure one night of kiddie debauchery won't kill her," he said, making an apologetic shrug, just in case.

Isaac laughed and the sound heated Adam's insides. He turned away abruptly, not willing to let Isaac see how he was affecting him. Besides, there was a teenager in the room. He didn't need to broadcast anything Isaac's son might pick up on.

"Let's get you settled," he said to David. "I hope you won't mind playing out here with us. She's not likely to want to stay in her room because Jordan is here. And she loves her blood uncles just as much, so she's gonna be pretty stoked to be out here with us."

"It's okay," David told him. "I brought my Beats and some extra earphones, in case she wants to play games on my tablet."

"That's pretty sweet of you, son," Adam said, and then stopped speaking when he realized what had slipped out of his mouth.

He hadn't meant to call David 'son', and he truthfully hadn't even thought of him in that way before. But the gesture was so kind and Adam was so appreciative of it that he said the first thing that came to his mind. Now he wondered if either the boy or his father would take offense at the familiarity. He didn't really want to know, so he stepped away from the two of them and walked into the living room, hoping they'd follow.

The others were already gathered around the coffee table, and Nova was sitting on Aidan's lap, cupping his ear in her little hand and whispering to him. Aidan's eyes were trained on Jordan and he was laughing silently at whatever she was telling him. Adam watched them for a moment more, but when Aidan could no longer contain his laughter and it escaped in a burst of sound, everyone turned to look at him.

"Nova Madeleine Kincaid, what mischief are you getting into over there?" Aidan asked. "Are you trying to get your Uncle Aidan into trouble?"

"That wouldn't be too hard to do, little brother," Adam answered for his daughter. The men all laughed at that, and then Adam continued, "Everyone, say hi to Isaac and David. Isaac's here to play, David's here to hang with Nova. And we're all here to eat. Let's get the ball rolling with some food."

David left his father's side and went to Nova who smiled at him and said hi shyly, as though she hadn't been leaning against him a week earlier. She tried to cling to her uncle but Aidan handed her over, saying something to her that had her smiling. David went with her to sit in the big comfy couch that Adam had bought so he could sit with her while he read to her. it was a pretty little reading nook with books and games on the table next to the couch.

Adam went into the kitchen and got a plate for Nova, turning to ask Isaac, who was just behind him, if he would make a plate for his son.

"Once we get going, we don't stop for a bit," he explained.

Once everyone was settled with plates and the chips and dip were set in the center of the coffee table, the men all settled in to eat and shoot the breeze. Because Isaac was the newbie, the conversation was mostly directed at him. They asked him all sorts of questions, but Adam was happy that they kept the really personal ones off the table. He didn't want Isaac to be offended. He wanted him to have a good time so he'd be willing to come back again and again.

"So, is it true that every flower has a story?" Aidan asked, licking his fingers after popping one of Isaac's bites into his mouth.

"It is," Isaac said, grinning at them. "Everything from apologies to friendship to declarations of love."

"Oh yeah? So, what kind of flowers say, "I'm sorry I fu…messed up?" Aidan quickly corrected himself, knowing Adam didn't want cursing around Nova.

Isaac chuckled. "That depends on who you're apologizing to. I'm sure if you searched online you would find answers that may be better than mine, but since you asked, here goes. If it's for a lover or spouse, then red roses are great. But lilies and tulips are also good for that. If you're apologizing to a friend, yellow roses are a good choice. Just remember that most roses aren't the hardiest or most long-lasting of blooms, even with plant food. Orchids are great, too, if you're apologizing to a guy. And if it's a female relative, light-colored tulips are a great choice."

"Should we be taking notes?" Benny asked with a smirk.

Isaac laughed. "I don't know. Have you pissed someone off lately?" He glanced at Jordan as he spoke, a brow raised curiously.

General laugher greeted his question before he added, "Of course, not everyone is into flowers. You should find a way that will have the most impact on the person you need to make things up with. So, if a hamper full of goodies would be better, go with that. Or if a unique gift will do the trick, then get it. And then, for some people, it's not what they receive that will work, it's what you say. You all know that, though. I'm sure I'm preaching to the choir."

Adam smiled, doing his best to ignore the unaccountable pride he felt at how well Isaac was handling himself. He was fitting in fine in the part of the evening that could have been the most fraught with traps for the unwary. He hadn't refused to answer any questions so far, and he had asked one or two himself, like the one he'd just asked Benny. They ate companionably as they talked, and Adam finally relaxed enough to enjoy the chicken snack that Isaac had prepared.

Afterwards, they started with gin rummy, which it appeared Isaac was great at. He didn't lose a single game, and finally they gave up in disgust.

"So, you're a card shark, are you?" Aidan asked, turning a stern eye on Isaac.

Adam turned to watch how he would react. He knew his brother was teasing, but nothing in Aidan's expression or posture gave it away. He seemed genuinely serious and a little miffed.

"If by that you mean I know when to hold and when to knock, then yes, I am."

Isaac looked his twin dead in the eye, face equally expressionless, neither of them twitching until Aidan lost the battle with his amusement and burst into tear-jerking laughter. Isaac just shook his head and grinned while the others, who had seemed a bit nervous at the question joined in relieved laughter.

"So, what's a game you don't play well?" Aidan asked, gathering the cards together.

"I'll bet it's not poker," Chan said, causing more laughter.

He was probably right. Isaac could clearly adopt an inscrutable poker face when the situation warranted it. That probably meant he could probably also throw the best surprise parties and keep secrets like Fort Knox kept gold.

"I lose at poker sometimes," he said. "I mean, a guy can't be good at everything all the time. Imagine the pressure."

The smirk that accompanied that comment amused the guys as well, but they decided to go for poker next. They liked to play Texas Hold 'Em, and Isaac was game. And he hadn't lied. He did lose one or two, but just barely. Aidan prevailed this time, and he broke into song, his rich baritone making love to the chorus of Kenny Rogers' "The Gambler". That also met with laughter.

"I'm ready for the sweet snacks now," Ry said, having finally shut down the story he was listening to on his tablet. "What have we got?"

"You mean aside from Benny's brownies?" Chan asked with a smile at his husband.

"Well, there's always at least ice cream to go with that," Ry said.

Adam looked over at David. "Hey David, how many of those treats did you make?"

He was careful not to name it. He wanted David to surprise Nova, who had been remarkably silent this whole time, with the gift he had made for her.

"A dozen, sir. Are we ready for those now?"

The boy's eyes lit up, making Adam chuckle. Some things never changed. Kids' love affair with sweets was one of them.

"Yes, we are. It's okay, you can stay," he added when the teenager made as if to stand. "I'll deal with it. You stay with Nova. I'll bring them out so you can surprise her with it."

Benny and Aidan helped clear up from the first round of eating, and then Benny served the slices of brownie onto plates and added plastic forks that were laid out already on the table, in case anyone wanted clean fingers. Adam took the fried Oreos and placed them on a platter. He placed two on one of Nova's little plastic heart-shaped plates and took that and the platter back out to the living room. Beckoning David over as Benny came in with more beer and juice for the kids, he said,

"This is her favorite plate. She'll love that you gave her the treat on it. Help yourself to what you want, but I think you need to do it now before these disappear."

David smiled at him and moved three of the treats onto a napkin before heading back to the corner with Nova. Adam watched as he carefully placed his own serving on the chair and knelt next to her to present her with his gift. Her eyes widened in surprise and pleasure and she hugged him fiercely before taking the plate and immediately beginning to nibble on one. David's face was a study in pleasure, and Adam had a sneaking suspicion that he had taken one extra so he could sneak it to her when he thought no one would notice. He decided he wouldn't notice, even if he did.

"These are good," Ry said, chewing on one. "Who made them?"

"Isaac's boy," Adam said with pride in his voice. "And they are good, aren't they? Sinful!"

Jordan turned an enquiring glance Isaac's way. "So, what's it like handling a thriving business and raising a teenage son?"

Adam knew the word he had left out was 'alone'. They had briefly discussed what they felt comfortable talking about with him there, and had decided that any conversation about his being single would have to be one he started. Not that he thought Isaac would shy away from the question if it came up, but he just didn't want them to be the ones who raised it.

"Well, I started when he was four, so it's been eleven years of trial and error. It was really stressful in the beginning, after his mother passed, but I gradually learned how to balance my time, and how to make sure he knew he was my priority. I wanted to make sure he grew up well-adjusted."

There was a hint of something in his voice as he answered the question that made Adam study his face closely. His expression gave nothing away, but his eyes met Adam's and something flashed in them for a brief moment before it disappeared.

"Based on the way he's been behaving so far, I'd say you've done a pretty bang-up job," Aidan commented, all seriousness this time. "I've seen too many cases of kids his age having no rudder or anchor and their lives have been so much harder because of it."

"And sometimes they end up in my ER," Adam added. "I'm sure David won't ever end up there for any of the reasons that the others do. So good job, Dad."

It was clear by this point that Isaac was becoming uncomfortable with the praise. He avoided eye contact, for one thing, and didn't respond to either his or Aidan's remarks. Thankfully, Benny broke what could have become an awkward silence by reminding them that they each had a piece of brownie to polish off, as well.

By the time the food had all disappeared again, it was late enough that Isaac began to look at his watch.

"Well, fellas, this has been great, but if I'm going to manage to keep David awake and not fall asleep myself in church tomorrow, I need to get home."

He turned to Adam. "Thanks for inviting me."

"My pleasure," Adam said, wishing suddenly that they were alone.

He wanted to try for another kiss goodnight, but he wouldn't do that in front of a bunch of witnesses who would only tease him mercilessly about it afterwards. Besides, he didn't think Isaac was ready for any PDAs in front of his son and he certainly wasn't ready to play the twenty-questions game with Nova if she saw it.

"Next time we'll be at home with my siblings," Chan said. "David will have more company closer to his age. I hope you can make it again. And feel free to bring more of the same. My brothers and sister will demolish anything you bring."

"I'll bear that in mind," Isaac said with a smile. "And I'll let you know if I can make it."

Nova's voice interrupted the conversation. "Daddy, can I show Davey Claus, please?"

She was holding David by the hand in a totally proprietary manner as she spoke, much to Adam's amusement. He also understood that this was her way of extending her time with the boy, whom she had taken a serious liking to. He didn't see the harm in it, if Benny didn't mind. She was already up way later than her normal bedtime. Another five minutes wouldn't hurt.

"Why don't you ask Uncle Benny, babygirl?" he replied.

The little girl turned her wide eyes to her uncle, who grinned at the puppy dog look in them and nodded.

"Sure thing, Pumpkin." He looked over at Adam and added, "Why don't you take them while Aidan and I clear up here?"

Adam narrowed his eyes. Benny was up to something and it became clear he was right when his little brother winked at him when Isaac's back was turned. He'd find out what soon enough, but for now, he fetched the keys to his brother's apartment from the hook by the door and led the way next door to Benny's place. This was a good opportunity to find a moment alone with Isaac, and he had never been one to look a gift horse in the mouth.

"I'll go in first, because that cat likes to play escape artist, and I'd rather not have to go chasing after him," he told Isaac.

"Claws because he's got sharp ones?" Isaac asked as they stepped inside.

"Claus, as in Santa," Adam corrected him just as Benny's white Persian came strutting in from the back bedroom.

"David, come on! That's Claus!"

Nova's squeal of delight made Isaac's eyes light up with amusement and Adam stood back and

185

watched as the older man's face softened with affection as he studied his son and Nova on the floor with the fat white cat, who was soaking up all the love they were bestowing on him with their belly rubs.

He could watch Isaac Hamilton forever. He was a beautiful man, and the more Adam looked, the more he wanted another taste of him. A real taste, to get him through till the next time they could see each other. They'd need to talk about that…maybe after the kiss goodnight? He needed a plan but couldn't think of anything. And then his daughter struck.

"Wanna see where he sleeps?" she asked David. "Uncle Benny bought him a new bed. It's so big, Davey!"

She pulled him along behind her toward the back and left her father and Isaac alone by the front door.

Maybe the Universe liked him after all.

Chapter Twelve

For a moment, the silence was deafening. Isaac watched as the little girl pulled his son along behind her to where the cat slept, aware all the while of the man standing next to him, eyes firmly planted on him. He turned slightly so he could look back and said,

"She's a little dynamo, isn't she? You're gonna have your work cut out for you when she gets to David's age."

He was trying, he really was, to keep them both on an even keel, because if Adam wanted to kiss him as much as he had been doing all evening, any touch between them might ignite a fire they would be hard pressed to put out. It had been the best evening out he had spent in…eleven years, even better than Christmas with the Mansfields. The camaraderie between the men was heartwarming. The teasing made him feel like part of the family, something he hadn't realized he had been missing until the last few hours had made it clear to him.

And to see his son take to Nova the way he had melted his already softening heart. Which didn't do anything to slow the attraction for Adam that was even now pushing against the restraint he had been keeping on himself all evening. He turned fully and looked Adam in the eyes even though he knew he shouldn't.

"She's way too smart for her age," Adam agreed. "But I wouldn't have her any other way."

He held Isaac's gaze, telegraphing through them a need as strong as Isaac's for something more than words between them. The moment seemed to demand action. How long did they have before their children returned and took this chance away from them? When

Adam stepped closer to him, he leaned in and whispered,

"I'll have to figure out what it is about you that I'm finding so incredibly irresistible, but in the meantime, how about another kiss?"

Adam smiled. "You mean a real one, like this?"

And before Isaac could reply, the younger man's mouth was on his. This time, there was nothing even remotely chaste about it. Beyond the first momentary press of lips, the kiss drove deeper, tasted more, sought and found the tongues it needed to share flavors and textures. Isaac pulled away from the first frenzied meeting of their tongues to taste his way around Adam's plump lips before licking back into his open mouth, giving him the chance to suckle on him gently before even that became a battle to satisfy their hunger and desire for each other.

He pulled away again, panting lightly and pleased to see that Adam was just as breathless. At least they could acknowledge that they were both equally turned on.

"You're dangerous," he murmured, reaching up to stroke Adam's bottom lip, pulling it away from his teeth. "You should come with a warning label."

"I try," Adam retorted with a sexy smirk. "Next time you won't even see me coming."

"Next time?"

Isaac lowered his lashes so Adam couldn't see his eyes completely. Would there be a next time that was about more than playing poker and winning card games? He sure as hell hoped so, but he knew better than to presume.

"Thanks for the warning." He winked. "When that time comes," — he wanted to make sure Adam understood he wanted more, too — "you can be sure I'll ready."

Adam leaned in and kissed him again, making Isaac's balls tighten in his slacks. He chose not to stifle the moan that rose in his throat, because he wanted Adam to know just how potent he found him.

"You taste really good," Adam informed him, leaning in to inhale against his neck. "And you smell amazing and sexy as fuck."

Isaac pulled him into his arms then, needing to bridge that last gap, if only for a moment. He needed to feel the press of Adam's body against his. He was aware that it might set him off like firecrackers, but he also sensed that it would quiet his jangling nerves and settle him. Typical reactions to the man gazing at him with startled eyes.

"Fuck! And you feel like..."

Isaac smiled when Adam slid his arms around his waist for a moment, squeezing him tightly before loosening his hold and stepping back.

"Feel like what?" he asked, allowing the stepping away. They both needed to cool off before the kids returned.

Adam shrugged. "Like...I don't know. It doesn't matter. Just know I like how you feel, too."

"Likewise.

"When's your next day off? Can we meet again before the next game night?" Isaac asked, clearing his throat and shoving his hands into his pockets to stop himself from reaching for Adam again.

It was past time that he took the reins and moved things forward. The last time it had been left to Adam, but there was no excuse for letting things stay that way. He may not know how he was going to adjust his life to make room for a love interest, but he sure as hell was going to do his best to figure it out.

"I'm off again tomorrow." Adam hesitated, then added, "Too soon?"

"I don't know, really. I'm hoping you remember more about dating than I do."

He chuckled wryly as he ended, knowing his confession wouldn't surprise Adam but still needing to prepare him for the truth.

"I remember enough to know it's always good when each guy is into the other. And if those hot-as-fuck kisses are any evidence at all, they prove we're into each other."

David's voice interrupted their conversation and Isaac said, "I'll text you."

He turned away to watch his son and the little girl walk back toward them, Nova holding Claus, who rested his front paws against her shoulder.

"Daddy, Davey has four cats!" she exclaimed, putting Claus down.

"Does he now?" Adam asked, and Isaac could feel his eyes on him.

"Yes. Their names are Sadie, Tom, Charlie, and Lola."

"Cool cat names! Who named them?" Adam asked.

"I named the old cats, and David named the kittens," Isaac explained. "He loved the Charlie and

Lola books that I used to read to him. His mom had bought them for him for Christmas the year she passed away."

Isaac had grown used to the fact of Rowena's absence by now, and mentioning her or the things she had done for them didn't hurt him anymore. But one look at Adam's face and he saw how pained and sad his eyes were. He moved closer to him, ignoring the children for the moment, pitching his voice low enough so only Adam would hear him and said,

"Hey! It's okay. We're not hurting anymore."

Adam inhaled and Isaac stepped away again, moving toward the front door.

"Come on, Nova," he said, reaching out a hand to the child. "Time for bed again." He picked her up and kissed her temple. "Otherwise, you're gonna be a grouchy sleepyhead in the morning."

They all stepped out and Adam locked the door and pocketed the key.

"Wait just a moment, please," Adam implored him, taking Nova back to his own place first and getting her in the door with a whispered word in her ear before shutting it on her and turning back to Isaac.

"Walk you out?"

Isaac nodded and again handed David the keys to the car, watching him hurry out to start it. The night was cold but his coat kept him warm. Adam was only wearing the thick sweater he'd had on indoors.

"You should go in," he told him. "It's cold out here."

"I'm good for another minute," Adam said. "I just need another moment with you."

"Seductive talk, Dr. Kincaid." Isaac smiled at him affectionately.

"Is it working?" Adam asked, smirking impishly.

The look of almost boyish delight on his face at Isaac's comment was endearing, and another spurt of affection warmed his chest. He was really coming to like the young man standing next to him as much as he found himself desiring him. He could certainly see himself falling for him if he allowed it to happen. And the more he thought on it, the more he found he wanted it to happen, challenges be damned. He had faced off a whole host of problems when Rowena had died. He could do it again.

But for now, wisdom cautioned him to be patient. He supposed he could invite Adam over for Sunday dinner, but he didn't remember what he and David had planned. He'd talk to his son first and then decide. There was no rush. He wasn't going anywhere, and neither was Adam. They had time to get to the more that those steamy kisses indicated they both wanted.

"It's working," he admitted with a wink. "Now, I'm really gonna go. I'll text you by the time I get home to let you know whether or not we're on for tomorrow. And then we can talk about some other time."

Adam nodded, trying to hide his disappointment, much to Isaac's secret amusement. In that moment, he didn't look like a successful doctor and single parent of a smart toddler, but more like David pouting at not getting what he wanted when he wanted it. Somehow, though, he didn't think that characterization would go over well with Adam, so he bit his lips and walked away, stopping to wave a hand before getting into the car.

The drive home was fairly quiet. David was bopping his head to whatever was playing on his phone, and Isaac was basking in the warm glow that still enveloped him at the memory of Adam's kisses. He had always loved kissing, whether giving or receiving, and Adam had now joined his very short list — heck, it wasn't even a list since there had only been one name on it before tonight — of people he really enjoyed kissing. Rowena had had the ability to make him leak precum like a faucet when she kissed him, and it would appear that Adam had also been blessed with that talent.

"Dad, can we have Nova over to play with the cats?"

David's voice interrupted his heated thoughts and he was glad for the darkness in the car so David didn't see the way he started guiltily at his question.

"You like her, don't you?" he asked, glancing at his son instead of answering the question.

David nodded. "She's a cool little girl," he said.

He opened his mouth as if to add to his comment, then changed his mind and went silent. Isaac decided to answer his question. Whatever else he had on his mind, he'd spit it out when he was ready.

"I'll ask her dad and see what he says."

"If he's too busy, I can babysit her and we'd kill two birds with one stone," David suggested eagerly, his tone making it clear he thought that was an admirable solution to the problem.

"You're aware she has grandparents and uncles, as well as a babysitter, right?" he replied, chuckling. "She doesn't need another child minder."

"Yeah, but..." he paused. "Well, I'm just saying." He didn't sound at all happy.

"Don't go getting your hopes up, but we'll see what her dad says."

He could give his son that, if nothing else. He didn't anticipate Adam refusing, but he would rather David not ignore the possibility that he mightn't get his way. Still, at least it gave him a reason to ask Adam over that had nothing to do with their feelings for each other. Assuming Adam had feelings for him and wasn't just looking to scratch an itch. An itch that Isaac still didn't know if he could scratch, if he were to be honest about it. Because what he knew about men loving men was a big fat zero.

Once back at home, he lavished the cats with affection and grinned as David scooped up the kittens and took them upstairs with him to his room.

"Goodnight, son," he called after him as he walked away. "Don't stay up too much later. We have service in the morning."

David turned back to say goodnight and then disappeared up the stairs. Isaac went to the kitchen and poured himself a glass of water. He swallowed it quickly before heading up to bed himself. Before he changed — because he felt oddly reluctant to be in just his skivvies while talking to the man he wanted — he dialed Adam's number. Pleasure pierced his chest when the doctor answered on the first ring.

"Hey! Home safe, I guess?"

"Yes. I'm about to go to bed, but David asked if he could have Nova over to meet our cats. I said I'd ask you."

"Seems like our kids want us to spend more time together," Adam said with a chuckle. "Nova loves cats, so she'll be in seventh heaven if I tell her we're going to see her crush's cats."

Isaac laughed. "Her crush, huh?"

"You have no idea," he replied. Isaac could hear the grin in his tone. "Aside from Jordan, whom she fell in love with almost immediately, she's usually pretty shy for the first meeting or two. So yeah, major crush, apparently."

"So, we eat dinner a little earlier on Sundays. And I'll be in second service in the morning. What time can you be here?"

"I'll come to that service, as well, so we can leave together," Adam said. "Where do you sit?"

This guy's gonna kill me! "Three rows from the back."

"I'll find you." Adam's voice went low as he added, "I like kissing you."

The unexpected comment sent heat shooting through Isaac's veins as he recalled how passionately they'd kissed each other less than an hour before. The need that had awakened inside him after their first kiss had bloomed more, and being reminded of it now was not helping to control it.

"Adam, you shouldn't tease me. I'm older than you. Show some respect."

He tried to lighten the mood, to give himself a moment to control his heart rate. He was gratified when Adam laughed softly in his ear.

"You can hope," he informed Isaac, "or you can enjoy it. Teasing is…stimulating."

Fuck! Isaac rarely cursed, but Adam was opening him up and spreading him wide, leaving him with no defenses. The next words out of his mouth felt almost destined; he couldn't keep them in if he tried.

"You like teasing, but can you handle it yourself?"

"Mmm! I can handle whatever you choose to throw at me. Tease away, Isaac!"

Adam was unrepentant and sexy as hell with it. Isaac gritted his teeth, trying to control the desire rising inside him at just the sound of Adam's seductive tone. More unfiltered words burst from his lips.

"Call me Zac." What the hell? Have you lost your mind?

"Okay, Zac." Adam's sultry tone made Isaac's name sound like the dirtiest, sexiest word on the planet.

Jesus, Lord, help me! "I'd better get to bed," he said, instead of voicing the prayer in his mind.

He had to get off the phone so he could do something he hadn't done in a long time. If he didn't get hands on his dick in the next minute he was going to explode. He had no idea what was happening to him, or why suddenly he needed a release more than he needed his next breath. Or why the thought of having that release with Adam was making his already hardening cock pulse in his pants.

"Running away again, Zac?"

"I never run away," he defended himself immediately. "But you seem intent on seducing me, and I'm not ready for that just yet."

"So, when will you be ready? Hmm?"

The blatant flirtatiousness and the raw sensuality of his tone were not lost on Isaac. He might not be ready in his mind, but his body was beyond ready by this point. This was what happened when he chose celibacy. The first sexy thing to smile at him and he was on the verge of orgasm. Well, maybe not quite as bad as all that, but this was pretty close.

"Goodnight, Adam," he said firmly, refusing to answer his question. "I'll see you tomorrow."

Adam's chuckle before he whispered goodnight and hung up stayed with Isaac long after the call ended. It was still ringing in his ear as he brushed his teeth, emptied his bladder and washed his hands. He could still hear his name on Adam's tongue like fingertips across his skin. His cock had not deflated completely, and it took him another half an hour to will it down enough so he could finally doze off.

But when morning came, his morning wood demanded that he do something about it, or he'd be sporting a tent all through service. Taking himself in hand in the shower, he rubbed one out quickly, feeling embarrassed that he needed to do this in order to face his son and the man that the erection belonged to. Thankfully, he managed to relieve enough of his tension to make it to service without any noticeable shift in his clothing. And equally thankfully, he didn't see Adam as he took his seat. He chose to sit at the end of the pew, which made David the one who sat next to him. He wasn't sure that he would make it through service if Adam was directly next to him.

"Morning!"

Isaac caught a whiff of Adam's cologne a moment before he turned to find the younger man standing next to him holding Nova's hand. He shifted so they could pass him into the pew and offered him a smile but didn't touch him. Better safe than sorry and all that.

"Daddy, can I sit beside Davey, please?'

Nova's voice piped the question into the growing silence in the sanctuary, and Adam shushed her even as he motioned David to scoot over so they were sitting together, and the very thing Isaac had tried to avoid happened. Adam's leg brushed against his.

Jesus, Lord, help me! he prayed silently again. He was definitely going to explode. Deep breaths, Zac. Deep breaths. That was all he could do. He knew logically that Adam was not deliberately inflaming him, yet every accidental touch burned him, and only by a supreme act of concentration was he able to follow the service. And that's what saved his body from reacting any more visibly. Thank God for prayers and hymns...he had never needed them more than he did now.

Reverend Kincaid's homily seemed especially pointed, as well, given Isaac's turmoil. He spoke about temptation and about how human beings' responses to it were a demonstration of not only their deepest desires but also of their greatest weaknesses. He spoke about the line in the Lord's Prayer that specifically addressed mankind's need to manage temptation, which was an everyday expectation.

"How are you managing your temptations?" he asked.

Isaac glanced at Adam then, and found the younger man's eyes on him. They were heated with meaning. He looked away instantly. Now was neither the time nor the place to answer the question not only in the sermon but also in Adam's eyes. He doggedly returned his attention to the priest and was immensely relieved when at last the final prayers were said and the congregants encouraged to keep the faith in the week to come.

Isaac looked at his son who was waiting for him to step out of the pew. He had told him at breakfast that Adam had agreed to bring Nova over to play with the cats and that they were having them as guests for dinner.

"Ready?"

"Yeah, Dad."

"Mind if I take Nova to say hi to her grandma before we leave?" Adam interjected.

"No problem."

Adam reached for Nova, who was holding David's hand. "Come on, babygirl. Let's go say hi to Nana and Papa."

She raised her arms and Adam chuckled as he picked her up. Isaac watched them walk away and turned to his son.

"Go start the car. I'll be right out."

David took the keys and they both made their way to the front of the church. Reverend Kincaid was greeting the worshippers leaving the building, his face wreathed in smiles. Isaac waited his turn, and when he finally made it to the rector, he smiled as well.

"Great sermon today, Rev," he said. "Very thought-provoking."

"It was certainly that for me, Isaac," he said. "I hope you have a triumphant week."

His eyes twinkled as he spoke the wish, as though he knew how much harder this week would be for Isaac than the one just gone. Sometimes ignorance was bliss indeed. Before acknowledging that his interest in Adam was less than innocent, his days and nights had been far more peaceful. One kiss, and suddenly he was in Temptation Central and unable to control a libido he had long thought dormant.

Dormant isn't dead, Zac. And wasn't that the truth!

"Thank you, Rev. I hope I'll be as successful at resisting as I'm sure you are."

Reverend Kincaid's booming laugh warmed Isaac and somehow it made him relax, lose the tension that had taken up residence in his spine from the moment Adam had sat next to him.

"I'm glad you think I'm some paragon of virtue, Isaac," the rector said. "Just don't talk to my wife and kids, okay?"

Now it was Isaac's turn to laugh, but his was less hearty. He raised a hand in farewell as he stepped away from the door and walked toward his car. David was leaning against the side of the hood on his phone as usual. Isaac looked around until he saw Adam coming toward him carrying Nova, whose pink-clad arms were wrapped around his neck. He was bouncing her on his hip as he walked and she was giggling. The sound rang out in the midday air, sweet and pure.

"Davey, Daddy says I can play with your cats today!" Her voice rang with excitement. "Are we gonna go see them now?" She turned to look at her dad. "Are we, Daddy?" She looked from Adam to David, then turned her eyes to Isaac's face. "Are we?"

Adam chuckled. "We are, but you have to promise to be a good girl when we get there. Do you promise? No running around or going where you're not invited."

Nova put her forehead against her dad's and stared into his eyes. "I promise, Daddy. I promise so much."

"Let's go, then," Isaac said, stifling a laugh at her cuteness.

Adam began to walk away, then turned back to say, "David, how'd you like to ride with us?"

He looked at Isaac then, as if realizing he should have asked him first. Isaac winked and nodded. It didn't bother him that Adam hadn't asked him first, but it was nice to be given the respect. He liked that about Adam. He was careful not to tread on any toes. He supposed that was part of what it meant to grow up in a preacher's house. The motto in such a house was probably different and put others' welfare above your own.

David slanted him a look as well. Isaac nodded again and watched his son walking behind Adam so he could play with Nova. Whatever he was doing was keeping her in stitches. He must be making faces at her. Isaac shook his head indulgently as he got into the car. He backed out of the spot and waited until he saw Adam's SUV pulling in behind him before moving off. He let himself feel the thrill that knowing Adam was coming home for dinner.

He very rarely had guests over, preferring to have David visit his friends. And as he himself had had no one he wanted to spend his off hours with, their home had been a kind of desert. Until now. Now, someone he liked, someone who fired him up, someone whom he could honestly call his temptation, was coming home to brighten up the dark places, and lighten the mood. He was as excited as he was sure David was. It had been too long!

He pulled his car into the garage, making room for Adam's vehicle beside his own. Then he waited until David unbuckled Nova from her car seat and they all headed into the house through the kitchen door.

"Come in," he said, standing aside to let Adam enter. Once David and Nova were in, he closed the door.

Sadie immediately appeared, winding her way between his legs and mewling her demand to be picked up. He obliged with a laugh, while Nova squealed at the sight of her.

"Daddy, a kitty!"

Adam chuckled. "Yes, babygirl."

"David, please show the Kincaids into the sitting room. Oh, and you might see if Nova needs a potty break while you're at it."

"I'll do that," Adam said. "Just point me in the right direction, please."

"But Daddy, I want to see the kitty," Nova complained.

"And you will. But let's get settled first, okay? The kitties aren't going anywhere."

Isaac let Adam handle the bathroom duty while he got out the chicken breasts he had left in the refrigerator to thaw. He also pulled out the vegetables he'd need for the vegetable stir fry he planned, and when David walked back into the kitchen he asked,

"Did you remember to take the mac and cheese out of the freezer before we left this morning?"

"Yeah, Dad. I'll put that in after I make the salad."

"Okay. I won't need you to do that for a bit, so you can take Nova to meet the cats now."

David scurried away and a moment later Adam strolled into the kitchen, his hands in his pockets, a smile on his face.

"This seems like a great house," he began. "It's got character."

"Old houses usually do," Isaac replied, keeping his hands busy prepping the chicken.

"I'm hoping you'll have a chance to show me around before I have to go," his guest continued, something in his tone making Isaac look up at him.

"Soon as I'm done with the chicken," he promised. "I like my meat to marinate a bit before cooking, so it will absorb all the flavor it can. I hope you like oven-baked chicken breasts and stir-fried vegetables."

"What, no mac and cheese? How will David survive?"

Isaac laughed. "He's reheating that. We always make two sets when we make it, since it's kind of labor intensive on the prep end."

"What can I do to help?" Adam sidled closer, hands still in his pockets.

"Nothing. Would you like something to drink before dinner?"

"Sure. What's on offer?"

"Coffee, tea, hot chocolate. What will it be?"

"Whatever you're having will be fine with me." Adam sat at the kitchen table, clasping his hands on it.

"Should I make something for Nova as well?" he asked next, reaching for milk from the refrigerator.

"Yes, thanks."

"I'll make us all a little snack to go with it," he announced.

He could feel Adam's eyes on him and heard the little gasp when he pulled the cocoa powder and chocolate chips out.

"Decadent, aren't you?" he said, his eyes gleaming.

"If you're gonna do something, best to do it right, no?" Isaac turned to look at him, hoping Adam could read his eyes telegraphing the deeper meaning behind his words.

"Absolutely!" He paused, his expression serious. "You seem like the kind of guy who always does it right."

They definitely weren't talking about food anymore, Isaac was sure of it. Adam's voice had grown a little bit husky and as usual, it tested the limits of Isaac's patience to remain where he was stirring the milk before adding the other ingredients. He was definitely not going to mess up whatever was beginning between them.

Chapter Thirteen

"This is delicious."

Adam licked his lips as he drained the mug. The hot chocolate was just the right degree of rich chocolatey sweetness, and it warmed his insides nicely. He helped Nova clean up and when she asked for a bit more, he watched as David poured her another half cup. He loved to see her so attached to someone who wasn't a relative.

"Thank you, Davey. Do you want some, too?"

David nodded and poured himself another half cup as well, while his dad busied himself pouring what was left in the pot into a car mug.

"This is for you," Isaac said, handing the car mug to Adam. "So, you can have some more before bedtime."

He winked as he said it and Adam couldn't stop the grin that split his face in two. It would be so damn easy to fall for this man. He was like the antidote to Adam's frenetic work life, the calm in the middle of a storm. And yet, with only a few kisses between them, he could tell Isaac Hamilton would blow his mind if they ever got to where his imagination sometimes took him. Skin on skin contact could never be disappointing with him. Adam was sure that that was a safe bet.

"Thanks," he said, pulling his thoughts away from a naked Isaac.

He wasn't doing himself any favors letting his mind wander like that, especially not with minors in the room. Taking a deep, fortifying breath, he tried to find something to say that would be PG. He was still casting about for safe topics when his daughter once again saved the day. He heard her ask David, in a comical stage whisper, as though she was certain Isaac couldn't hear her,

"What's your dad's name?"

David looked surprised. "Isaac Hamilton. Why do you want to know?"

"I want to ask him a question, but I don't know what to call him."

David smiled, even as Adam stifled a grin. He looked over at Isaac and saw his back turned and his shoulders shaking. The grin became a chuckle he disguised as a cough. He waited to hear where else the conversation would go.

"You can call him Mr. Hamilton," David said.

She nodded. "Okay." Turning her head, she said more loudly, "Mr. Hamilton, can I ask you a question?"

Isaac turned back to face her with a twinkle in his eyes. "You certainly can, little lady."

She giggled. "How old is Sadie? Davey doesn't know."

Isaac's eyes darkened with an emotion that Adam couldn't read. "She's sixteen years old, Nova. That's why David doesn't know. She was already a year old when he was born."

Adam's heart squeezed in his chest. That emotion was sadness. Isaac's wife had been alive when they got the old cat, and she was still with them.

"Wow, she's vintage, Dad!" David exclaimed, and the moment dissolved into laughter all round.

"Why don't you take Nova back into the study with the vintage cat and maybe find her a book she'd like to listen to?" Isaac suggested with a chuckle.

David nodded. "We already know what I'm going to read to her," he said. "She chose them right away. But she wants to play a game as well, so I'm looking to see which of mine she'll like."

"Thank you for taking such good care of her for me, David," Adam said. "I really appreciate it."

"It's no problem, Dr. Kincaid. I like Nova. She's a cool kid!"

When they were out of earshot, Adam said, "Your son is the real cool kid here. You do know that don't you?"

Isaac smiled. "Yeah. The good Lord blessed me with a really uncomplicated teenager."

"There aren't enough of those around," Adam agreed.

"Anyway, ready for the tour?"

"Yes, please."

Isaac led the way through the first floor, including the study where Nova was helping David to hold the book he was reading to her from and giggling at the voices he was making as he read the different parts. Their heads were close together and they were clearly engrossed in what they were sharing. Adam paused to listen, watching unseen and pleased that his gut didn't set off any alarms about the boy. One could never be too careful these days, but David Hamilton's vibe with Nova was one of innocent affection. And given what he knew of his dad, nothing would have surprised Adam more than if he had triggered any concern.

"He's as much under her spell as she is under his," Isaac murmured quietly next to him. "And it's good for him. She's the little sister he'll never have. Or the little cousin, at any rate."

Something in the way he hurried to add the last sentence made Adam look up at him. There was a question in his eyes, a question that Adam understood only too well. How was it that he was so in sync with a man he had only known a couple of months? It was uncanny.

"He'd make a really good babysitter for her, if you agreed and I was ever in a bind. I trust him. He's got a good head on his shoulders, and an awesome dad."

Isaac looked away, and Adam was sure he was blushing. Which was adorable in such a big, brawny man.

"Come on, show me the rest of the house. I love the way you kept the layout down here authentic even with the updates," he commented.

"Rowena wanted it that way, and I agreed with her." Isaac paused at the foot of the stairs, which led from the kitchen up to the bedroom floors. "We cut into the parlor to make a powder room, but mostly it's the same as it was. And we finished the attic."

He led the way up the stairs, the rich dark wood adorned by a dark red runner that muffled their footsteps as they walked up to the second floor. The house smelled faintly of pine up here. Adam loved the dark wood paneling that extended only halfway up the walls of the hallway. The rest was covered in butter-yellow paint. It gave the room brightness without being either bland or blinding.

"There are three bedrooms up here, and two bathrooms," Isaac informed him. "The master bedroom is at that end," he pointed to their left, "and this is the rest."

He showed Adam David's room and the bathroom that was next to it. Across the hall was a large guest room, the hall closet, and a small laundry room. Back beyond the stairs on the other side, Isaac opened up double doors and revealed a suite that floored Adam with its gorgeous masculinity. His eye caught the ceiling at the window and he gasped.

"Is that wallpaper on the ceiling?" he asked, looking up to get the full effect.

"It is. Rowena was a free spirit and decided that she could put wallpaper wherever the hell she pleased. It's fabulous, I agree. She did the same thing in the hallway."

Adam took a step back into the hallway and looked up. The antique gold color of the wallpaper there caught the light from the wall color and deepened it, adding somehow to the sunny effect. It was indeed fabulous. Back in the master bedroom, the navy-blue antique pattern of the wallpaper was a sharp yet soothing contrast to the much lighter blue of the bedroom walls. He could imagine looking up at night, with only the moon for light, and thinking he was looking at the stars in the night sky overhead. He realized that what gave the ceiling its starry effect was the silver flecks in the antique pattern. He loved it.

"It's definitely not something I've ever seen before, but what a great idea!" he enthused.

Isaac turned to look at him. "Glad you like it," he said with a smirk. "Bathroom's through here."

He led Adam into a spacious room, elegantly modern and the least period-authentic space in the house.

"Seems like your wife loved her mod cons as well, though," Adam said with a chuckle.

Isaac laughed. "She did. We took the small sitting room that was up here and included it in the new suite. Hence the sitting area by the bay window, which we also added. And she wanted a large space so we could shower together, as well as a soaking tub that had claw feet. Very particular, was Rowena."

He spoke fondly, no pain sounding in his voice, only loving affection. Adam didn't respond. He didn't know what to say, especially because despite his best efforts to control his rambling thoughts, they had once again taken him to a naked Isaac standing beneath the high shower, water sluicing down his dark skin, droplets like diamonds sparkling everywhere on his body. He blinked and stepped back, unable to admire the sea foam blue of the walls or the other modern appointments that made the room stunning.

"You okay there?" Isaac asked, coming back through the door to watch him.

Adam swallowed and nodded. He'd speak again in a minute. Just as soon as he got his tongue under control and could make it say only the most appropriate things. If he spoke too soon, he'd say what he was thinking, and he was still a grown man who could marshal his thoughts and censor his words. Besides, there were still children in the house.

He waited until they were once again in the hallway before he spoke.

"You have a lovely home, Isaac. I can almost feel the love."

Isaac looked down into his eyes and Adam could feel the intensity of their searching gaze. What was he looking for? What was he hoping he'd see? He held his stare for a moment, then turned to head back down the stairs. He didn't hear Isaac move, but the hand on his shoulder stopped him. He turned back.

"What?" he asked. "Tell me."

Isaac shook his head. "I've never had any interest in a man before you," he began. "What is it about you?"

He looked sincerely puzzled and it made Adam smile. He might be the younger of the two, but he understood the power of attraction. And he hadn't been in an emotional desert for eleven years.

"I'm good looking? I'm young? I'm irresistible?" he asked with a smirk, wanting to keep the intimacy intact but knowing that he should probably burst the bubble before it got too intimate and they did things they shouldn't do.

"You sure are all of those," Isaac agreed with a chuckle. "And let's not forget that you're sexy, too." His eyes twinkled with mirth.

Adam blushed. He couldn't help it. It pushed all his buttons to know that Isaac found him attractive. He looked into Isaac's golden eyes and said,

"Ditto, Zac." Then he leaned up and kissed the corner of his mouth.

When Isaac cupped his chin and opened his mouth over Adam's, he moaned a little bit but kissed him back, disappointed when Isaac slid his lips away after way too short a moment.

"Not here. Let's go down. I'll make dinner and after we eat, we can sit on the porch for a bit. I'm assuming Nova will need a nap by that time."

"Most likely," Adam said. "It's a good time to nap, after Sunday dinner, though it's usually a bit later at my house, so she naps before dinner."

They had just reached the bottom of the stairs when they heard Nova's happy laughter.

"Who knows?" Adam added. "She may just forego napping altogether so she can hang with her new bestie."

"You've got a point there," Isaac conceded. "When she's ready to nap, you can settle her down here in the big couch, or you can take her up to my room."

"Thanks." Adam's smile was wide and warm.

Eventually, Isaac let Adam help him with dinner, and once they got everything to the dining table, he called the children.

"Take Nova to wash her hands please, son," Isaac said.

Then they sat down to a meal that was as happy and full of laughter as any Adam had shared with his own family. Isaac regaled them with stories of what he called his "misspent youth", though he noticed there was never a mention of his dad alone. It was always about him and both his parents. Did that mean he and his father didn't get along? He remembered that Isaac didn't call him 'Dad', he called him 'Major'. What was that all about? He couldn't imagine not having a good relationship with his own father. What could have caused such a rift that even now he couldn't speak of the man whose DNA he shared?

None of those questions would be appropriate to ask unless they talked about what was happening between them. That kiss at the top of the stairs had seemed almost like a capitulation, like Isaac was giving in completely to the pull between them for more than just that moment. Could he do this? Could he be the one to show Isaac that love between men could be as fulfilling as between a man and a woman?

He'd never had anything long term with a man, but he knew instinctively that what was beginning to bloom between them would be even better than what he had had with Cheryl. Would Isaac think the same about him? Would he be at least as good as Rowena had been? Could he be? Should he even want to be? It didn't sound right to be in competition with Isaac's dead wife.

"Daddy, can I go look at the flowers with Davey?"

Nova's voice drew him out of his musing. He looked at Isaac.

"Flowers? Where?"

"I have a heated greenhouse," Isaac told him. "It's how I manage to have some flowers in the winter months without having to get them all from suppliers." He turned to Nova and said, "If you promise your dad you'll take a nap afterwards, I'll persuade him to say yes."

Nova turned pleading eyes to Adam's face. "I'll take a nap, Daddy," she promised. "Can I see the flowers now, please?"

She stretched out the 'please' and stuck out her bottom lip. Everyone else at the table laughed at that blatant 'poor me' look. She kept it up until Adam nodded and then she squealed and did a happy chair dance. Isaac was right...he was going to have his hands full when she got older if she was already this savvy.

They finished the meal quickly after that, and while David took Nova to see the flowers — which Adam admitted he also wanted to see, but not with anyone else along — they washed the dishes and tidied the kitchen. Then, once Adam had settled his daughter in bed, he followed Isaac out to his greenhouse. The old barn he had noticed at the south side of the house as he had driven into the garage had been transformed into a flourishing, vibrant space.

He could smell several familiar scents in amongst ones he didn't recognize. The colors were surprising and lush as Isaac took him on a brief tour, explaining why he had planted the vegetables he had, why the herbs were where they were and which flowers were easiest to cultivate in a greenhouse.

"This is amazing!" he exclaimed. "I had no idea cultivating flowers could be such a delicate process. I knew it was time-consuming, because I used to watch my mom weeding and mulching and pruning. She seemed to find comfort in doing it, too."

He turned to look at Isaac and caught him watching him with an intense concentration that would have been unnerving if he hadn't also seen the desire flaming out at him. He breathed deeply and continued speaking.

"Do you find gardening to be peaceful as well, Zac?"

Isaac strolled toward him from where he stood by the wintergreen's planter boxes over to where Adam stood next to a row of brightly colored pansies.

"I do," he said. "And seeing you here in my peaceful place also does it for me, it seems." He held out his hands "You fit right in."

"That must be some kind of miracle, since I know next to nothing about gardening."

"You don't need to know anything about it." He reached across the small space he had left between them and stroked a finger down Adam's cheek.

"You fit right in yourself, big guy," he said, answering Isaac's comment as he leaned into the touch.

"Are you enjoying your afternoon?"

Was Isaac's hand trembling just a little bit? Adam smiled and nodded, inordinately pleased. Could this big, strong, confident guy be feeling a little anxious right now? That would definitely be a surprise.

"I have such great admiration for your talent with beautiful things. It's not just the flowers. It's the gifts in the shop. It's the way you handle your staff. It's…"

Isaac ran his thumb over Adam's lips, effectively stopping his outburst.

"Are you as nervous I am?" he asked, cutting right to the chase.

"Why are you nervous?" Adam asked, instead of answering him.

"The things I'm feeling right now are all new to me. New, exciting…strange, and yet so familiar. What am I gonna do about them?"

"What kind of feelings?" Adam whispered against his thumb.

Isaac sighed heavily. "Rowena and I were like a gas fire that no one could put out. She was the one who had the idea for the greenhouse, and we had even begun to outfit the barn for it when she died. But before she did, when we were cleaning it out in here, we had one of our hottest lovemaking sessions over there."

He pointed to the far corner, closest to the house. "There were some hay bales and some old horse blankets there then and we made good use of them more than once before we fell asleep."

Why was Isaac sharing such an intimate memory with him? Unless he wanted a repeat with a different partner? But why would he when he wasn't in love...? Surely not! In lust, maybe, but love happened slowly, in measured beats. Adam was certain of it. Not that he minded being in lust with Isaac. He could definitely do with a little lust relief, but he wasn't going to call it anything else. And he sincerely hoped that that wasn't where Isaac was headed, as he would have to politely refuse, and it would break his heart to break Isaac's heart. He was a good man who deserved all the happiness he could get.

As though he could read the conflict raging in Adam's mind, Isaac said, "I don't know why that memory came back to me just now. Maybe it's because I am feeling some of what I was feeling that day right now, standing here in front of you just talking."

He reached out again, this time to cup Adam's cheek. Once again, Adam dared to lean into the touch, to draw comfort and strength from it, to let himself open up to the possibilities of being with this man. He stepped in, closing the gap between their bodies, and looked up into Isaac's face.

"Care to demonstrate what you're feeling there, big guy? I'm a fast learner. Maybe I can help you understand them. You know what they say!"

Isaac's eyes mirrored the amusement that was making him grin. "What they say about what?" he asked obligingly when Adam paused to wait for the question.

"About two heads," Adam supplied.

He waited again. He wanted Isaac to actually say the words so he could kiss them right off his lips. Isaac didn't disappoint him.

"You mean the one that says two heads are better than...?"

His voice had gone all growly and in his eyes Adam could see the increasing lust darkening those golden irises. He closed the final inch-wide gap and pressed an open-mouthed kiss on Isaac's lips. Immediately, Isaac responded to him, pulling him fully into his embrace. Adam pressed his body tightly against him from chest to knees, letting him feel his burgeoning hardness. His second head definitely wanted freedom to play, and even though he knew it wasn't likely to happen this time, he could dream.

They strained together, two grown men afraid to let go of the last of the restraints that kept them apart. Had this been any other man, Adam would already have had him in his bed. But he knew that just as soon as he was done shagging the man's brains out, he would have sent him on his way or have left his house and not looked back.

He didn't want to leave Isaac's house. He didn't want to leave his side. He wanted to do exactly what he was doing right now. And he wanted to do more. Oh, God help him, he wanted to do so much more! He pressed in against Isaac's equally evident erection and smiled against his lips when the other man groaned and pressed back. He wrapped his arms around Isaac's waist and rolled his hips experimentally. When Isaac answered with his own hips, thrusting against Adam, he whimpered feverishly and kept pushing into him.

They kissed and humped each other for another long, excruciatingly arousing minute until they had to drag their mouths away to breathe. Adam's limbs trembled and he would swear he had begun to leak precum inside his boxers.

"Fuck!"

The swear word escaped his control, but it did nothing to convey the power of the moment between them.

"The preacher's kid with the potty mouth," Isaac murmured, tenderly pushing a stray lock of his blond hair back behind his ears.

Adam chuckled. "Wait till you hang out with Aidan," he warned him. "I'll be the saintly brother after that."

Isaac's gaze was smoldering. "I don't need a saint," he said. "Apparently I need a man. And apparently that man is you."

Isaac leaned down and took Adam's mouth again, and with this kiss every functioning brain cell shut down as Adam gave himself over to the raw feelings. How the hell had he lived without the touch of passion for so long? He had been so intent on work that he had let his need for companionship, for a human touch, fall by the wayside. And now, as Isaac devoured him and drove his lust higher with every thrust of his hips, Adam understood why he had given up on hookups.

This was why. This moment, so filled with the possibility for more, this connection with a man he might never have met except for serendipity, this man with his maturity and his drive and his strength. He was why. Adam hadn't realized that all these years he had been saving himself for that special someone. But now, as he pulled his mouth away to breathe, dropping his head against Isaac's shoulder, feeling the older man's chest heaving with his own breathless desire beneath the hand he put there to steady himself…now, he knew with an absolute certainty that this man was the right man to end the drought in his love life. Maybe this wasn't love, but maybe it could grow to be, if he let it.

Chapter Fourteen

Isaac's body burned; his heart raced; his breath came in small gasps. The last time he had been this out of control, he'd been a married man, and the love of his life had been a woman. He knew he had never had any feelings like the ones he was now fighting to control for any man. Until this man, this beautiful, kind, strong man with the bright hair and the stormy eyes.

Adam Kincaid was undoing him completely. Could he really be with a man? Before Adam, the answer would have been an emphatic, resounding, and perhaps even scandalized "No!" Before Adam, he had been in the wilderness, an automaton, controlled only by the need to provide and care for his son and the need to keep his business successful so that he could fulfill that first mandate. Before Adam, he had given up on sex, on passion, on lovemaking. Before Adam, he had given up on love.

Now, there was Adam, confusing and turning him on, driving his body wild with need, making him wish for things he had never even considered doing with anyone other than Rowena. Now, there was Adam, holding him and humping him and making him crazy with longing. Now, there was Adam, and God help him, his heart didn't want to give him up even though his mind told him this was just lust and it would pass.

His heart knew better. No matter how his hips thrust against the younger man, needing to feel his hardness, he knew that what he wanted was more than just the satisfaction of a mind-blowing orgasm. What he wanted from Adam was a soul connection that would make anything they did together more than just sex. What he wanted was something he had only ever had with one other person in his life, and she had been a woman.

He pulled away from Adam's arms, steadying himself before looking into the younger man's eyes. He had to say something, but he didn't know what to say. He wanted to apologize for…what? Losing control and humping him like a dog? Could he be honest with Adam? Should he risk rejection if all the doctor wanted was a roll in the hay? Should he deny himself the chance to have what could be great sex because he wanted more?

Get out of your head, Zac! Now isn't the time for this. Say something to him before he gets the wrong impression.

"It's been a long time," he began, still searching for words but holding Adam's gaze for a moment more before looking down at his hands.

"For me, too," Adam said, his voice gruff. "But I'm glad I waited."

Isaac looked back at him then. "Waited?" He didn't understand. What had Adam been waiting for?

"I haven't been with anyone for a very long time, and I kept telling myself it was because I didn't have the time." He huffed out a wry laugh. "But after…well, after this, I realize that I was lying to myself. I didn't hook up with anyone because I was waiting for someone special to make out with. In a greenhouse, no less. On a Sunday afternoon after church."

His smile drew Isaac in. He felt like a fish on a line probably felt as the fisherman reeled it in. Resistance was futile…wasn't that the saying? His capitulation was inevitable, inexorable. It felt almost fated. But he was older, and should be wiser. They couldn't let themselves go hog wild as though there wouldn't be consequences for their actions. Life wasn't like that, as he well knew.

"Adam..."

He didn't get a chance to finish, which was probably a good thing, since he really didn't know what to say or even what he should say. He felt overwhelmed, flushed, needy, uncertain. He didn't like the feeling, but he had no ammunition for combatting it.

"Look, I know I'm a shock to your system," Adam interrupted him. "I wasn't really prepared for you, either." He shrugged and spread his hands in a 'who knew'?' gesture. "But I'm not confused about how you make me feel, or about what I want to do with you."

"That's just lust, Adam. You have to know that."

"It's more. And I think you know that, too, Zac."

Way to call him on his bullshit! Adam had balls, he'd give him that. And it made him even more attractive to Isaac. How did he admit to the truth of Adam's words without admitting to all the other feelings that should not be spoken of between two people who had barely begun to know each other?

Adam stepped back into his personal space and laid his hands on his chest, over his still too rapidly beating heart.

"Can we please give this a try? Can we date? Get to know each other? Decide what we want to happen between us, and take our time getting there?"

His eyes pleaded with Isaac to agree. Isaac put his hands over Adam's and squeezed them gently. Then he removed both pairs of hands from his chest and stepped back again. He wanted to…no, he would take a chance. He closed his eyes briefly and prayed he wasn't making the biggest mistake of his life.

"Okay." Once again he was lost for words. He turned awkwardly instead. "Let's go back to the house," he said. Then he walked away, hoping Adam would follow him.

The house was quiet when they got back inside, except for the drone of David's voice as he talked, presumably on his phone.

"How much longer will Nova nap?" he asked, making his way to the refrigerator.

"Maybe another half hour to forty-five minutes," Adam replied, consulting his watch. "We have time…unless you want us gone and need me to wake her now? I don't want to mess with your routine."

Hell, no! That hadn't been why he'd asked the question, and Isaac hated that Adam immediately went there. If they were going to find more than their lust for each other in common, they'd have to communicate clearly and build trust.

"That's not what I meant," he said, turning around to look at Adam. "I was just curious. David never managed to nap for long before Rowena died, and afterwards, he had a hard time sleeping for a while. So, I don't really know what's normal for little ones anymore."

Adam studied his face, and Isaac tried to keep his expression open. But he wasn't prepared for the words that came out of his mouth.

"It must have been hard for you to sleep, too."

It had been. It had taken him a lot longer than it had taken his son for him to be able to sleep for more than a couple of hours at a time. And his sleep had been disturbed, so when he woke he was always exhausted. He nodded.

"It was. But we managed. Life goes on, you know."

Adam sighed. "It seems like you did more than just manage," he said. "Seems to me like you aced it and now you're both so much stronger than you ever were."

Isaac smiled. "How'd you get to be so smart?" he asked, needing to lighten the mood.

He really enjoyed how insightful Adam was. It must come from having to spend so much of his time working with a range of human beings, all presenting with their differing physical and emotional needs.

"I went to smart school," he quipped with a laugh. "Passed with flying colors, too."

"Guess that makes you a smartass, then, huh?"

Adam laughed, the sound warming Isaac's heart. "Nobody can ever say you're slow either," he replied at once. "Silver fox got brains and beauty." He winked at Isaac, making him laugh, too.

"Flirt!" Isaac could think of nothing else to say in response to that. 'Thank you' just seemed too precious.

"And you like that about me," Adam returned confidently. "Don't even try to lie about it."

Only if it's me you're flirting with. That wasn't something Isaac would ever permit himself to admit to aloud, though he admitted to himself that it was startlingly true. Instead of responding, he started working on dessert, to give himself something to do, something to help him handle the jitters he was still feeling from their kisses. He made a simple syrup, added freshly squeezed lemon juice, and asked Adam to hand him the cherry-flavored seltzer that he kept in the pantry.

"I'm sure Nova will love this with her dessert. I have two choices…apple or coconut cream pie. Which would y'all rather have?"

"Did you make both?" Adam asked, his eyes wide.

Isaac chuckled. "Not this time, no. But my son loves the coconut cream pie from Granny's Place, and since we sometimes eat in on the weekends, I bought one of each to keep. He takes lunch to school, and that's what the apple pie is for…dessert after his sandwich."

"You're just one organized beast, aren't you?"

Adam's admiration made Isaac's chest puff with pride. Which was ridiculous because he didn't need anyone's approval to know he was a good father to his son. Telling himself that now, though, did nothing to stem the feeling. It was hearing the words from Adam's lips that was doing a number on his ego. Who knew he'd needed to hear those words about himself spoken with such pride? He sure as hell hadn't realized just how much he had missed being appreciated and admired.

He never would have thought he needed it, if he were to be honest. His father's image flitted across his mind and he understood why at once. The Major would not be flattered by anyone's praises of him doing his job. He would not have wanted it and would have seen taking any pride in such praise as a sign of weakness of character. Damn! Maybe he'd picked up more of his father's thinking than he realized.

"You've got to be when a kid needs help tying his shoelaces and zipping up his jacket." Ignoring his unsettling thoughts, he answered Adam's comment, turning a sharp eye on him. "But you already know this. You've got a little one yourself."

"True," Adam said. "When I'm off work and solely responsible for her care, it surprises me how much I have to do just to stay on top of things."

Isaac put the seltzer in the refrigerator when Adam handed the two-liter bottle to him and then checked on the apple pie that he had taken out of the freezer to thaw earlier. By the time Nova woke up, it'd be fine to be reheated. He had bought a coconut cream pie on Friday, and the half of it that was left sat in the refrigerator.

Eventually, Nova woke up and they had dessert, with Isaac finally feeling more relaxed. Neither he nor Adam had spoken further about what they would do going forward, but he knew the conversation wasn't over. Nor did he want it to be. He added the by-now cold seltzer to the lemon-flavored syrup and added crushed ice. It went over well with the kids, much to his delight. They talked about nothing, laughed at Nova' antics, and he answered more questions about the cats.

Once they were done, Adam looked over at him with a smile.

"We need to get going now," he said. "Nova, it's time to go, honey. Let's go clean up."

He led her to the powder room while David fetched her winter gear. When they walked back into the kitchen, Isaac watched as David helped the little girl into her pink jacket, as solicitous as any self-respecting older brother would be, watching her as she put on her mittens. Then, while Adam went out to start the car, David sat with her while she pulled on her booties.

"Ready, baby girl?" Adam asked when he walked back into the kitchen.

"Yes, Daddy."

"And what do you say to David and Mr. Hamilton?" Adam prompted her.

She pursed her lips before replying, as though she were sifting through the best way to say what was on her mind.

"Thanks for letting me play with the kitties, Mr. Hamilton." She paused, then added, "And thanks for letting me play with Davey. He's fun!"

Isaac stifled a laugh at how serious she was, even as she placed David and the cats in the same category.

"You're very welcome, little one."

Then she did the most surprising thing, startling Isaac as well as her dad. She walked over to where he stood and raised her arms. Knowing that was the universal toddler sign language for "Pick me up", he obliged and found himself face to face with the little girl. She proceeded to cup his ear and whisper into it, her sweet baby breath fanning over his neck as she spoke.

"Maybe if you think I was a good girl I can come over and play again? Because Davey is my bestie."

This time Isaac couldn't restrain the laughter. Adam eyed him curiously, but he didn't respond to the question in his eyes. Instead, he whispered in her ear,

"You were a very good girl, honey, but you'll have to get your daddy's permission before you can come back to visit. You ask him, and he'll let me know what he says, okay?"

"Okay."

Just as he went to put her down, she wrapped her arms around his neck and planted a solid kiss on his jaw.

"You're a nice daddy, too, Mr. Hamilton, just like my daddy."

She made the announcement aloud so her father and David heard. Isaac was struck dumb. He had no words for her as he set her gently on her feet again. She walked over to Adam and took his hand while Isaac tried to find his tongue. Adam headed for the door while David went to the kitchen to clear up the dessert mess and make himself lunch for school. Isaac followed Adam to the door. It had just gone dark, and the night sky was clear enough for a million stars to shine through.

"I enjoyed my afternoon, Isaac. Especially the tours."

Adam's voice held no inflection, but his eyes danced merrily as he teased Isaac. An overwhelming desire to kiss the innocent look off his face, to leave him feeling electrified and energized, swept over him. He had to get a grip.

"I'm glad you did," he said instead. "Drive safely."

"I'll text you when I get home, Dad," Adam teased again.

Isaac rolled his eyes but he was chuckling as Adam went out to his car and strapped the little girl into her seat. He waited until he couldn't see the car any longer before going back into the house, heading straight for his study and the bottle of Scotch he had stowed in there for when he needed a drink.

Something told him that his life was never going to be the same from now on. Adam Kincaid had slipped through the chinks in his armor and opened him up in ways he had stopped thinking about. He was as unexpected as snow in the Sahara, but nowhere near as fleeting as that would be. Maybe a better way of seeing him was like sand dunes in the Arctic. Even when the snow melted, the sand would still be there. Just like Adam would be.

There was no way to escape the knowledge that what they had done in the greenhouse was as far from innocent as it could get. The kisses they had shared, the way their bodies had sought pleasure from each other, had been a sure sign that even if Isaac had been straight before, he was definitely more than that now.

What would he tell David? How would he explain himself? What if his son had found him kissing Adam and pushing his aching cock against him? Sex education was never supposed to be hands on or, in this case, eyes on. It was supposed to be, at the very least, a conversation without demonstrations. He had lost himself for those moments when he and Adam were wrapped in each other's arms, seeking something more than pleasure from the press of lips and tongues and hips.

How had he lived for eleven years with just his hand for release? How had he managed to give up the pleasure of another person to hold, to share pleasure with...to treasure? He couldn't account for his restraint, except to assume that his heart just hadn't been ready. And without his heart involved, his body had not been interested. That was how it had always been with him, even back in his youthful days.

Hookups had been rare back then, something he had done once in a while, he realized now, because he'd thought he was supposed to, to show that he was a man and not a boy. But once he'd met Rowena, even before he acknowledged that he was falling in love with her, his desire had shifted from the need for a quick fuck to prove himself to the need to make love, to cherish, to have someone as his own forever. He hadn't slept with anyone but her, and they had explored their passion together, once she had let him in and trusted him with her heart.

Lord help him, his heart was flooded with feelings now, and though he knew how he should respond — caution had always been his watchword — he couldn't get his mind to focus on reason and common sense. He wanted Adam. He wanted to explore what they seemed to have unleashed between them. He wanted to understand how it happened that he was now enamored of a man. But above all, he wanted to feel the connection between them grow, strengthen, deepen, become everything Adam's responses had promised it could become, everything his gut said it would become.

He must have dozed off because when he woke two hours later it was to the scent of bacon cooking. He got up, went to relieve himself, and headed to the kitchen. David was making breakfast for supper.

"Hey, Dad," he said when he saw Isaac. "I was hungry."

Isaac chuckled. "I'll bet," he said. "Is there enough for me there, son?"

"Yeah, Dad. And I made pancakes. They're in the oven keeping warm." He paused to look at his dad and then added, "I'll make eggs if you make more hot chocolate."

His tone wasn't quite wheedling, but it was definitely hopeful. Isaac chuckled again and went to do as his son requested. They ate slowly, each lost in his own thoughts. He wondered if Adam had texted him like he'd said he would but managed to stop himself from checking his phone. The rule was no cellphones at the table. He'd check after they cleaned up the supper things and tidied the kitchen.

Back in his study, he poured another two fingers of smooth liquor and settled back into the leather recliner he'd been in before, stretching his legs out and crossing them at the ankles. He checked his cellphone and found a message from two hours ago.

Adam: We're home. Nova can't stop babbling about David. Everything is David this and David that.

Isaac cringed. What was Adam thinking? He could be forgiven for thinking Isaac was rude and had blown him off. Shit! He needed to fix it.

Isaac: Sorry, Adam. I dozed off and just saw this.

There was no answer. He drowned his disappointment in the rest of his drink, and went to pour himself some more. Might as well chalk up the shitty end of his day to bad luck and missed text messages. He would not dwell on it or let the curious ache of what felt like sadness bloom inside him.

He closed his eyes instead, reliving the fervid kisses that had been his wakeup call. If they ever managed to get beyond making out like teenagers, what would Adam be like as a lover? His cock twitched at the thought of getting naked with the doctor. He'd have to find out what making love with a man involved. He had a general idea, of course, but he wanted to be prepared before anything happened. He had no intention of looking like a fool.

A soft chuckle escaped his lips at the direction his thoughts had taken. What the hell was he even thinking? Who said they'd ever get there? All Adam had asked was that they date each other. In his experience, limited though it had been before Rowena, dates did not always end in sex. In fact, they rarely had, for him. Maybe times had changed in twenty-odd years. He had never been one to follow the crowd, so even back then he would have been out of the loop on what the correct etiquette for dating should be.

"Dad, I'm going up to bed now. Do you need me to do anything else?"

David's voice broke into his daze. He opened his eyes and looked at his son, standing in the doorway. He was big for being only fifteen. Adam only had six inches on him. Would he keep growing physically? They said boys kept growing till they were twenty-one, but he'd stopped growing when he was nineteen. Maybe David would, too. He'd just had a growth spurt...

"Dad?"

Isaac jerked. Jeez, he'd been so busy distracting himself that he hadn't answered his son's question.

"Sorry, son. No, I don't need you to do anything. But…"

He paused, then decided to plunge on. Better to get the question over with now. If they needed to, they could revisit the conversation another day, but he had to ask the question that would get the ball rolling.

"How would you feel if I…?"

How the hell did he even word the question? He hadn't had a relationship with anyone else since Rowena's death, so David had no way of knowing what to expect, or of knowing how to respond if Isaac did pick someone else. Did he even remember his mom? It wasn't as though he was asking permission. He was asking to give a heads up, as well as to try to find out how David would react.

"If you what, Dad?"

David stepped further into the room, looking at his father with a look that was a cross between curious and impatient. Isaac cleared his throat, took another sip of his drink, and resumed his question.

"How would you feel if I started dating?" There, that wasn't too bad, was it?

David's expression went blank for a moment before something like comprehension dawned, and with it a smile that Isaac didn't understand.

"Dating who, Dad?"

His smile became almost a smirk, and Isaac feared he already knew the answer. Dammit! He hadn't expected it to get there that fast! Still, he had never lied to his son, so he wouldn't start now.

"Dr. Kincaid and I are considering it."

Well, that wasn't exactly the whole truth, but it wasn't a lie, either. They had already agreed to date, but hadn't set a time. They hadn't done much more than say they would. He braced himself for the next question, knowing his son was just like him, methodical in his thinking. He wasn't sure what he would ask next, but there was bound to be a question about the fact that they were men.

David was silent for so long that Isaac began to worry that he was angry. He didn't need to deal with any drama in his own home, but he was prepared to weather any storm that blew up because of it. He'd been blessed with a pretty even-tempered, laid-back teenager. If he threw a tantrum this one time, Isaac would have to forgive it. Still, he hoped he didn't have to deal with any negative feelings.

"Will I get to babysit Nova more, then?"

A surprised laugh burst from Isaac's lips. Talk about unpredictable! That had definitely not been the question he had been expecting.

"I guess you'll have to ask him the next time you see him, son," Isaac said, still chuckling. "So, does that mean you're okay with me dating him?"

"Sure, Dad. He's cool. That's probably why Nova's such a cute kid."

"She is that son," Isaac agreed. "Anyway, that was what I wanted to ask."

David smiled at him. "If you guys get together, she and I would become family."

Something hard twisted in Isaac's chest. Behind his son's words was a feeling he understood only too well. At the end of the day, they both wanted to feel like they belonged to other people, like they were part of something bigger than just the two of them. He had deprived his son of the chance for a family for eleven years. If, as David said, he and Adam got together — however that would look — David would have four other men to look up to in addition to Isaac and the Major, and a little girl to dote on.

"That's right." Isaac smiled at the way his son's eyes lit up at the thought. "It's a nice thought to go to sleep with. Goodnight, son." He would have time to think about found family later. "Sweet dreams."

"Night, Dad."

His phone vibrated as he was going up to his bedroom. His heart leapt when he saw it was a text message from Adam.

Adam: Sorry about the delay. I was putting Nova to bed.

Isaac paused on the middle rung of the stairs to send a quick answer.

Isaac: I'm going up to bed now. Have a great week.

He added a smile emoji and went the rest of the way up to his room. He was brushing his teeth when the response came back. He rinsed, spat, and wiped his mouth before taking his phone back with him into his bed.

Adam: Thanks. You too.

Isaac watched the three little typing bubbles spin for what seemed like forever before Adam's next words came through.

Adam: I had a really good time today, but next time, I want us to be alone. Do you want that as much as I do?

Isaac's hands trembled on the cellphone.

Isaac: You have no idea.

He dropped the phone onto the mattress and inhaled deeply, calming himself. Text messaging had never been his favorite thing to do. He preferred the immediacy and intimacy of a phone call. But for some reason texting with Adam was making his dick twitch. What the hell was that about?

Adam: I'm on the next four days, then off two, then on the next three. Will you be at the next game night? It'll be at the McKenzie home this time.

Isaac had rather enjoyed his first game night, so he wouldn't mind doing it again. This time, he'd make sure David had plans. Maybe they could do something together before or after? They had said they wanted to date, after all. He knew Adam needed to use his time wisely since he worked such long hours.

Isaac: Which night? I can make sure David can spend the night at his friend's.

Adam: No! Bring him. He can hang out with Chantal and the boys. Aside from Chance, who sometimes joins our games, they usually prefer other games like Codenames or Cards Against Humanity.

Isaac paused. David had shown an unusual interest in the McKenzie girl, but she had not returned it. He was probably being stupid to worry about his kid falling for an older woman, but he was suddenly feeling protective of him. Still, the boy was almost sixteen and Isaac knew he couldn't protect him from the inevitable. Maybe if his first crush was on a girl whom Adam knew, he could ask for advice on how to help David when his heart got broken.

Adam: Hey! Did you doze off again?

Adam's question brought him out of his haze. He chuckled and sent him a quirked lip emoji, to which Adam immediately replied,

Adam: Don't worry, Papa Bear. Chantal is a sweet young woman. She won't lead him on.

This texting back and forth was getting to him. How the hell did young folk do this? He had already lost all patience with it, and it hadn't even been five minutes. He dialed Adam's number and breathed a sigh of relief when he answered at once.

"Does she have a boyfriend?" he asked, without preamble. He couldn't help asking the question.

"I don't know. Do you want me to ask?" Amusement laced Adam's reply.

Isaac sighed. He was being a fool and he knew it. "No. Don't mind me. I'm being ridiculous. And yes, I'll come for game night again."

"Can't wait."

Adam sounded like he meant it, which caused a thrill that Isaac hadn't expected to feel.

"But that's not a date."

Adam's reminder of their agreement had Isaac grinning into the phone.

"I know. When will you be available for that?"

"It'll have to be a midweek night, unless you're willing to wait a couple of weeks if you can't do that."

Isaac didn't want to mess with the routine he and David had going. Midweek nights were spent at home, since David had tutoring and whichever sport he trained for each semester. He'd be going out for track soon, and Isaac knew the training would begin shortly. Weekends would be better and he said so.

"No problem. Let's finalize those plans at game night."

"Okay. Good night, Adam."

"Night, Zac."

Long after they'd hung up, Isaac lay in his bed, hard and aching, reliving the sound of his name on Adam's lips. How could a man's voice be so powerful? He'd never had anything like it happen to him before Adam Kincaid walked into his life two months earlier. He shifted on the bed, trying to find a comfortable spot to fall asleep in. After another ten minutes of thrashing about, he settled enough to doze off.

The week flew by. David had trouble with his first math assessment of the new year and asked if he could see his math tutor for an extra session so he could retake the test to get a passing grade. Isaac was pleased that his son took his studies so seriously, especially since his dyscalculia would be a challenge he faced for the rest of his life. He stayed after school on Thursday and Friday, and asked if he could hang out with his best friend overnight.

"Don't forget you have work on Saturday morning, and we're visiting the Major in the afternoon. Am I coming to pick you up on the way in?"

"Yeah, Dad, thanks."

David called him on Friday after his tutoring session to say he was on the way to the Mansfields.

"Have fun, son. And say hi to everyone for me."

"I will. Thanks, Dad."

He was clearing away the detritus of two bouquets someone had ordered for a party when the bell over the front door of the shop dinged. He heard

Peaches telling the person that the store would be closing in half an hour. The voice that responded sent shivers up his spine. Why was Adam here? He stood up, ready to go out to meet him, when the swinging doors opened and Adam walked in.

"Hi! Peaches said I could come back. I hope that's okay?"

His smile was at once beautiful and uncertain. Isaac returned it and walked around the worktable to stand before him.

"It's fine," he said, wishing he knew what to do with his hands.

Should he shake Adam's hand? He discarded that idea. They were well beyond the handshake stage of greeting. Those kisses on Sunday had pushed them into intimate new territory, So, maybe he should kiss his cheek? His lips? Maybe he shouldn't do anything at all and get back to work so he could close the shop on time for once.

Adam took the decision out of his hands a moment before he moved to get back to cleaning up. He stepped into Isaac's personal space and cupped his cheek with one hand, while resting the other lightly at his waist.

"Did you miss me?" he asked, his voice husky. "Because I sure as hell missed you. And I know we're going to see each other again, but I was off today and I tried to stay away."

Isaac chuckled, despite the way his limbs trembled with tension. "So, what straw broke the camel's back?" he asked with a smirk.

"This." He leaned in then and kissed Isaac's lips gently. "I wanted to do this."

He opened his mouth over Isaac's again, and though Isaac desperately wanted to relax into the kiss, he stiffened instead and pulled away. Adam dropped his hands and stepped back as well, confusion and hurt warring in his gaze. Isaac fisted his hands at his sides to stop himself from reaching for the man whose kisses he wanted to drink like good Scotch.

"I can't do this here, Adam. This is my place of business. Peaches could walk back here at any moment, and I'm not giving her or anyone else anything to speculate about. My private life is private."

He'd put on his dad voice, trying to remain calm and reasonable, hoping that his explanation would placate the man whose face had shuttered as he spoke. Realistically, he knew that if they were dating, showing affection to each other in a semi-private space was okay. In fact, it was probably normal. But they weren't there yet, despite the intimacies they had shared days earlier.

"Sorry," Adam said, putting up his hands, palms out in a gesture of conciliation.

He paused as though he were trying to figure out what to say next. Isaac didn't know how to help him, and he didn't want to say anything else to widen the gap he could feel forming between them. So, he went back to cleaning up the cut stems and leaves from the flowers and dumping them in a garbage bag. He'd use them as composting for his greenhouse.

"I'll go then, since you're busy. I'll see you next week."

Damn! This was not how he wanted their unexpected encounter to end. He hadn't meant to shut down Adam's advances, just to slow his roll. He still wouldn't be comfortable with displays of affection at his job, but maybe they could go somewhere private. He hastened to speak as he saw Adam turn to walk back out.

"Adam, wait. Please."

The doctor stopped and looked over his shoulder, but he didn't say anything. His face remained closed off, his eyes half hidden by lashes held at half-mast.

"You said you were off today?" He had an idea.

"Yes."

"Where's Nova?"

Isaac wouldn't disturb Adam's routine with his daughter. Family always came first as far as he was concerned, and the little girl deserved to have her dad with her as often as she could.

"She's with her grandparents." He was clearly confused by the question.

"Would you like to come by my place? David's at his friend's tonight."

Adam turned back around. "Are we going to hide this?"

"No!" Isaac answered immediately

Hell, this was not going the way he wanted it to. It hadn't even occurred to him that it could seem like that was what he was doing. But he was also a little annoyed that Adam couldn't see his side. Why was he acting like a toddler throwing a tantrum because he couldn't get his way?

"How would it look if I showed up at the hospital and laid one on you where anyone could walk in and see us?"

He knew that his voice sounded fiercer than he had intended it to be, and by the way Adam's eyes widened, he probably sounded more pissed off than he really was. That impression was validated when Adam held up his hands again.

"Whoa! I said I was sorry. I get it. No PDAs."

He sounded huffy, which meant he was upset, but Isaac wouldn't back down from this. He didn't say anything though, sensing instinctively that the younger man wasn't done speaking.

"I asked because I clearly don't know you well enough and just wanted to be clear about why we'd be going to your place tonight."

Isaac bit back the retort that sprang to his lips. He wasn't going to argue with Adam, whom he felt was being childish, because that would serve no useful purpose. He could withdraw the invitation, but somehow he knew that would go over even worse than the invitation had done. And really, even if it did feel like Adam was pitching a bit of a hissy fit, he was right. He didn't know Isaac well enough to know how he felt about how they should conduct their fledgling relationship.

"We can get to know each other better, if that's what you want," he said slowly, "but for now, I'd rather we do it in private. And for the record, I don't think PDAs at work are okay. I'm old school like that. I suppose I could change my mind, but for now, I'm not comfortable with it."

Might as well get it all out now and give him his first lesson in Understanding Isaac 101. He waited with bated breath, wishing there were more stalks and leaves to clean up. He'd need to sweep, but that would have to wait until this conflict was resolved. Either Adam would wait for him in the shop, or he'd leave. He tried to ignore the hope that Adam would wait in the shop. He hadn't even thought about hope in so long that it hurt to feel it tug his heartstrings now.

"Okay." Adam didn't look at him as he added after agreeing, "I'll be in the shop."

Then he was gone, leaving Isaac alone with his thoughts. As he plied the broom, sweeping up the mess on the floor, he wondered how he was going to break the ice when they finally made it to the farm. They could have leftovers…he had meatloaf and mashed potatoes. He could make a salad to add to that for dinner.

That's what he'd do…he'd ask Adam to help him make the salad to go with dinner. He had learned that involving David in shared activities for their mutual enjoyment and benefit invariably smoothed things over when they had disagreements. Something about doing stuff together and working with your hands was like therapy for the spirit. He didn't want to be Adam's dad, but he knew they had to get past this first hiccup.

Hope, that irrepressible thing, sprang anew, despite his best efforts to squash it.

Chapter Fifteen

Shame washed over Adam as he followed Isaac's truck back to the older man's farmhouse. He knew he had overreacted back at the shop when Isaac had called a halt to the kissing. He was thirty-five, not four. He should know better than to act like Nova when she didn't get her way. He was only a step above her, since he hadn't cried and thrown an actual tantrum.

Still, he wondered how he was going to face the man he was becoming more and more attracted to every day when they finally got to his home. He'd have to apologize...a real one this time. He didn't want to muck this up with juvenile behavior. And Isaac was right. They weren't kids, they were grownups. They had to behave in a manner consistent with their age and experience.

Besides, he was the preacher's kid. He was expected to live up to a certain standard of behavior. And he was expected to be respectful of other people's boundaries. He had run roughshod over Isaac's boundaries back there in the shop, and had gotten his feelings all hurt when Isaac had called him on it. Not especially mature and adult of him, and not at all the way his parents had raised him.

Sighing heavily, he pulled in behind Isaac's truck, which he'd parked next to another smaller vehicle. Isaac left the garage door open and Adam followed him into the house through the door that led to the kitchen.

"Go through," Isaac said, gesturing toward the living room. "Would you like something hot or cold to drink?"

"Whatever's easiest," he answered. "I just need to make a pit stop."

He headed off to the powder room without waiting for an answer. All the way through relieving himself and washing and drying his hands, he tried to think of a way to begin the awkward conversation he knew was inevitable. Maybe this was another reason that he had shied away from getting serious with anyone. Fights were bound to happen and he wasn't very good at dealing with them. He wasn't a confrontational man by nature, and arguments or fights just made him tense and stressed out.

He opened the door to find Isaac coming toward him, his eyes full of a purpose Adam didn't understand. He had changed into a t-shirt and jeans, both of which hugged his body like a glove. He looked edible. Adam stopped just outside the door, waiting uncertainly. Isaac came to a halt as well and leaned casually against the wall, hands in his pockets.

"Talk to me," he said. "We're never going to figure out what we want if we hide from each other or don't speak our minds. I don't want to waste time pussyfooting around, do you?"

Adam exhaled loudly. Time to put up shut up. Or no...not shut up, speak up.

"I'm sorry, Isaac," he said. "I overreacted at the shop. You were right to call me on it."

He held Isaac's gaze for a second, then lowered his eyes to the top of his shirt. Why was he suddenly so insecure? He may not be combative, but he had always been confident. What the hell was happening to him?

"Apology accepted."

Adam welcomed the rush of relief that spread through him, and then uttered a surprised oomph when he felt Isaac's lips on his.

"You can kiss me now."

Adam could hear the amusement in Isaac's voice, and feel the smile against his lips. Didn't need to ask him twice. He didn't know when Isaac had moved, but they were close enough now that he could reach up and cup the back of his neck, pulling him closer so he could feed him his tongue. He loved the feel of Isaac's hands at his waist, holding him in place as they kissed.

"Better?" Isaac asked when they pulled away to breathe.

"Yes." Adam pecked his lips again before adding, "Thank you."

"Come on, let's go reheat dinner."

They walked back into the kitchen. Isaac handed him the beer he'd taken from the beverage cooler and he took a sip before setting it down. He had also pulled two covered containers from the freezer as well as the fixings for a salad.

"Help me make the salad?" he asked.

"Sure."

Adam was glad for something to do with his hands, because now that he knew he'd been forgiven, he wanted nothing more than to maul Isaac right here in his kitchen. But he knew that he had to be more careful and less impulsive, so he began to chop the onions and radishes, while Isaac shredded the lettuce and rinsed it. While he used the salad spinner to get rid of the excess water, Adam sliced tomatoes. Then they put it together with carrot sticks, tossed it all and added some of Isaac's homemade salad dressing.

The food was delicious. He had never been a lover of meatloaf, but this was juicy and smoky and perfect, and the mashed potatoes were smooth but not soupy. Isaac had added a sprinkling of parsley, paprika, and cheese on top, all of which added an extra touch of flavor. He ate everything on his plate and took seconds when they were offered. He finished his beer and took another, sipping it while Isaac packed the dishwasher.

"No, you're my guest. Maybe next time," he'd said when Adam had offered to help with cleanup.

Next time…Adam liked the sound of that. A lot.

"Would you like dessert now, or would you rather wait for it?"

"I'll wait."

Adam wasn't sure he'd care if he didn't have a sweet treat as long as he could have more kisses. But again, he held his tongue. If it was going to happen, it would, and him hurrying it along wouldn't help his cause.

Isaac nodded. "Okay, then let's go sit in the living room." They carried their beers with them.

"Thanks for dinner. That was great," he said as he sat back on the sofa and rested one ankle over the other knee.

Isaac settled his big body on the deep brown leather recliner by the fireplace. Adam loved the way his looked, his legs crossed at the ankles, his hands cupping the beer bottle. He watched as Isaac took a sip, helpless against the need to stare at his Adam's apple as it moved when he swallowed. He blinked when Isaac spoke.

"You're welcome. I don't cook every day because who has time? And some days when I get home all I want to do is lie on a flat surface somewhere and sleep."

Adam chuckled, hoping he hadn't been caught staring like a pervert. "I feel you, man. Do you pass out and have to figure out where you are when you wake up?"

Isaac laughed at that. "Haven't done that in a long while," he said. "I almost always know where I am and I always know who I am with."

Adam eyed him for a second, wondering if he could venture back into territory he had been in danger of losing access to a couple of hours earlier. Deciding he'd try again — because hadn't Isaac said they should speak their minds? — he made a confession.

"I've had to make the walk of shame a time or two in my younger years, and each time, not only did I not know where I was when I woke up, but I also had a hard time remembering my hookup's name."

Isaac's eyes flew to his face, a question in them that Adam didn't understand.

"What?" he asked, suddenly apprehensive again.

Another long moment went by before Isaac said, "Walk of shame, huh? Is that what you envision happening here?"

Damn, but this man was intense! "No! No, Zac, no!"

He was at a loss for words. He didn't want Isaac to ever think he was just a booty call, or that Adam was ashamed of what they wanted to do with each other. And he for sure didn't want him to think he was forgettable in any way, shape, or form.

"No, Zac." He sat forward, repeating the denial. "I'm proud to be with you, however you want that to happen. I'm proud to know you, to be your friend. You're a truly amazing man."

He stopped talking because in his ears, he sounded like he was overcompensating. The gentleman doth protest too much and all that. All he could do now was wait to hear how Isaac would respond,

"Thank you. That's good to know." He tipped the beer to his lips and swallowed, then continued, "So what does a typical day off look like for you?"

Adam relaxed his shoulders and sighed quietly in relief. He appreciated the change of subject. He could handle nice, mundane topics like how he spent his days off. There was no way he could mess that up.

"As you know, toddlers are hard work. So, I'm up as early as if I were going to work. Nova always wants to help me make her meals, so we do an easy breakfast, so she can choose the fruit and the flavor of yogurt."

He chuckled at the memory. His daughter was a firecracker, despite how young she was, and he dreaded the time when she would be grown enough to argue with him.

"I usually do some lessons with her and we watch some kiddie TV. I read to her, we play whatever game she's currently wild about, and I take her to the church preschool in the afternoon. After that it's chores and errands and a nap."

Isaac's soft laugh curled inside him like Scotch whisky, going down to his most secret places smooth and heated. He adjusted his body on the sofa and crossed his legs at the knees, hoping to ward off an inconvenient chubby. It might be barely excusable to fantasize about what he and Isaac could get up to together if they decided to take it there, but it was definitely not okay to let his interest show without being certain it would be welcome.

He knew that Isaac was attracted to him. Their kisses had made that abundantly clear. And he knew that the older man wanted to explore their connection further. But wanting to date someone was not the same as wanting to do the nasty with him, especially after so few meetings and still no real date. Today was not a date…he had shown up uninvited to Isaac's workplace and the man had been kind enough to help him save face by having him over for dinner. Not the same as a date.

So, until they had their first real date, maybe he should hold off on the daydreaming and keep control of himself. For the first time in his life, he knew it would be hard — pun intended — to keep his body under control around someone he was interested in having sex with. And the reason was clear…Isaac Hamilton was more than a booty call. He mattered to Adam and he wasn't about to screw up his chances with him by doing anything else stupid. One impulsive act might be understandable and forgivable; a second was pushing it.

"What games does Nova like to play?"

Isaac's question snapped him out of his head. "Right now, she's very much into Don't Break The Ice, but she also loves Boggle, Jr. and Concentration."

Isaac smiled. "I barely remember any of the games I played with David when I had the time," he said. "I do remember that he loved Concentration, though. These days, we play card games and dominoes mostly, when we're not watching TV together. Usually, when we choose to hang out together in the same space, I'm listening to my music and he's playing whatever on his phone."

Adam considered that for a moment. "He seems like a really chill kid."

"He really is," Isaac agreed. "I'm grateful that he still talks to me and doesn't mind being seen in my company."

They both laughed at that. Adam looked over at Isaac again and this time the older man's eyes were also on him. They held each other's gaze for a long moment before Isaac said,

"I'm glad you like my son, because he's fine with us dating, since he thinks it means he'll be allowed to babysit Nova." He grinned at that. "I've told him he needs to ask you about that. But what I really want to tell you is that he thinks if we get together — his words — then he and Nova would be family."

Adam's heart swelled. He remembered Isaac telling him that David had wanted a baby sister, and it seemed like the boy was now hoping to make it happen. It was a sweet wish and he couldn't say he disagreed. Because he could see Isaac being his family, too.

"Family is good," he said, aware that his voice was hoarse from an excess of emotion. "I wouldn't mind having him in my family. Nova could do with a big brother like him."

"Just Nova?" Isaac's voice was in no better shape than his own. "What about you? Could you handle having a teenaged son? Being a dad to two kids?"

Adam held his gaze. "I could if you could."

Tension stretched between them, taut and electric. When Isaac stood up from the recliner, placing his beer bottle on the coffee table before he walked over to where Adam still sat, his movements were filled with intention. Adam braced himself, releasing the bottle he had been holding tightly when Isaac reached for it and put it next to his.

"All this talk of blending families and we haven't even been on a date as yet," he murmured, pulling Adam up to stand before him. "I'm an old school kind of guy, so I think we can't even consider all that before we manage to figure out if we belong together."

"That's really smart thinking." Adam tried not to sound as breathless as he felt.

"Well, you're not the only smart one in this relationship, you know."

Isaac's lips were tantalizingly close. All Adam would have to do was raise his head and lean up just a little. He was sure Isaac would take the hint and meet him halfway. The kiss would be one for the books, just like the others they'd already shared had been. He was beginning to think that every kiss he shared with Isaac would be memorable. He blinked. This wasn't his play...he would need to cool his jets and leave Isaac in charge. For now. He smiled instead, and replied with a chuckle,

"As one smartass to another…"

Isaac swooped and shut him up with a fierce kiss. It shot heat straight to the erection he'd been fighting off since they'd sat down in the living room.

"You only get to talk if you've got something helpful to say. Wise cracks are not permitted."

Isaac's voice had gone growly now, arousing Adam even more. Apparently Isaac's voice, however it sounded, would always be a turn-on for him. Who knew his eardrums were an erogenous zone? What would it be like if Isaac nibbled on his ear while he was talking to him? The thought made his knees weak. He gripped Isaac's waist with both hands to steady himself and could only manage a tame,

"That sounds like a good plan."

Isaac smirked at him, then leaned down to kiss him lightly again. "I'm glad we're in agreement on the important things. So," he eased back to look into Adam's eyes, "what happens next?"

"You mean I can speak now?" Adam dared to sass him, because he desperately needed to hold on to his control, and being this close to Isaac was wreaking havoc with his system. It didn't help that the older man was rocking the alpha vibe while still managing to be playful. Sexy didn't begin to describe what Adam felt about that.

Isaac bent to his lips again, but this time he nipped the bottom one hard in punishment. Adam gasped and opened his mouth, and Isaac accepted the invitation to explore him. Kisses were supposed to be foreplay, right? That's what he'd always thought, but this one was taking that to a whole new level, adjusting the lyrics, upping the beat, changing the essence into something more akin to lovemaking.

That's what it was…Isaac was making love to his mouth. It inspired Adam's next words, shocking even him as he spoke them.

"Next depends on how fast you can strip, because I'm suddenly ravenous for a taste of you."

That was no less than the truth, but he hadn't planned on speaking the desire aloud so soon. Still, he meant every word of it. He wanted Isaac naked, so he could kiss his way down that strong, dark, sexy body before he took him into his mouth and gave the proper attention to his cock. Although if he were honest, he'd be just as happy sucking him off without the rest of the body treatment this first time.

"You want me naked?"

Isaac sounded as shocked as Adam felt, but he nodded. He had walked right through the door Isaac had opened and he wasn't leaving till he got what he craved. He was taking Isaac's question as permission to get down and dirty, or at least to begin the journey.

"Will that be a problem?"

Might as well be sure. After all, Isaac had never been with anyone but a woman as far as he knew…

"Have you ever…?" He paused, not sure how to ask the question without making it sound intrusive.

"I've never been with a man, no."

Adam registered uncertainty in Isaac's eyes. He needed to reassure the man he wanted as his lover that he would take care of him, that he'd be patient, that he'd make their lovemaking as memorable as Adam wanted it to be for himself, as well.

"Hey, we don't have to do anything you don't want to do," he said, reaching up to cup Isaac's cheeks in his hands. "We can go at any pace you set."

Isaac's laugh was strangled. "I might just shock you if I set the pace," he commented. "Because the way my body feels right now, anything we do would end up being a sprint not a jog."

Fuuuuck! Adam's hands trembled as he reached for the hem of Isaac's t-shirt and pulled it up. Isaac finished the job, tossing the garment aside carelessly. Adam could feel his eyes on him as he unsnapped the waistband of his jeans and pulled the zipper down. His delight in the way Isaac held his body tightly, tension radiating off him in waves, made him grin and lean in to buss his lips lightly.

"Relax. I won't hurt you, big guy! Promise."

Isaac rewarded him with an unexpectedly shy smile and raised a slightly trembling hand to cup Adam's cheek as he lowered himself to his knees in front of him.

"Are you sure?" he asked Adam, his eyes filled with both doubt and desire.

Adam pulled the jeans down his legs and mouthed Isaac's cock though his boxers. Isaac groaned and Adam could feel him tightening his thigh muscles. He got it, he really did. It had been eleven years for Isaac, but if he felt like Adam did, he was worried he'd blow too soon and it'd be over before they'd started.

"Easy there, Zac. I've got you. I'll take care of you, okay?"

Isaac didn't respond and when Adam looked up to gauge his reaction, his eyes were closed and his jaw was clenched. Damn if that look wasn't hot as fuck! Inhaling deeply to calm his own rising lust, he peeled the plain cotton boxers down to reveal a big, beautiful cock leaking precum. Fancifully, he could almost imagine it calling his name. He chuckled as he leaned in and licked the head, collecting the bitter, salty precum on his tongue, then rising to share his taste with Isaac.

"Oh, fuck!" Isaac swore harshly when Adam released his lips.

He was openly trembling now, as though the taste of his essence had broken down the last barrier to his control. He pulled Adam back in for another kiss, then rested his hands on his shoulders, urging him silently to return to his cock. Adam smiled at him, kissing his lips quickly before doing what he wanted.

Adam hadn't known what to expect when he saw Isaac's cock for the first time, but he was not surprised to find it was proportionate for a man of his size. Which was code for fucking huge. He knew the myth about a man's foot or hand size and his cock was unfounded, but he had apparently had a secret belief that it could be true. He felt inordinately pleased that Isaac was big all over. Thank fuck!

"Please, Adam."

Adam looked up at him as he grasped his cock in both hands. Isaac's eyes had darkened almost to copper, and the sight stoked Adam's masculine pride. He had done that to Isaac. He had made him lose control.

"Impatient much?" he teased.

"You started it," Isaac groused. "Now stop looking and suck me."

Adam smirked. He didn't have a problem with that.

Chapter Sixteen

His heart was beating so hard in his chest that Isaac was afraid he was going to have a heart attack. The last time he'd been this turned on had been…too damn long ago, in another lifetime, with a woman. Wonder and trepidation and lust warred in his veins as Adam knelt in front of him on the rug and sucked his hard-as-steel cock. He had always loved being blown, and Rowena had been pretty good at it. Now though, as he watched Adam twirl his tongue around the dark crown of his uncut dick, he knew he was in for something above and beyond anything he'd ever experienced before.

Trying to hold himself still, he spread his legs apart, bracing his feet hard against the floor. The sight of Adam's pink lips against his brown flesh was pretty beyond words and when he stuck his tongue out to lick a stripe down the length of him, Isaac barely managed to stifle the groan that rose hard and sharp in his throat. He inhaled through his mouth as Adam licked and suckled him, taking shallow breaths to help him regulate his oxygen intake but still feeling lightheaded.

And then Adam swallowed him down to the root. Isaac could feel the tip of his cock at Adam's throat, and the scream that was ripped from him was as inevitable as high tide. He could no more have held it back than he could stop the sun from rising. Panting, he rested his hands on Adam's shoulders, slamming his eyes shut as though that would help him contain the ecstasy coursing through him or the need to bust a nut down Adam's throat. Unaccustomed swear words rose against his tongue, more welcome this time than ever, because they said what he was feeling in his bones more than anything else could.

"Motherf…!"

He bit off the expletive as Adam deep-throated him again. He needed air for more important things than words, like breathing. Panting didn't seem to be getting enough oxygen to his brain, and he fought to remain conscious while his lover twisted him into tighter and tighter knots of need and want and ravenous hunger.

"Adam!" he growled when his human brain blinked out and the animal in him rose to take control. "Fuck, Adam!"

"Let go, Zac! I've got you, babe! Let go for me!"

Isaac obeyed. He had no will or power to do anything other than cum so hard he blacked out for a second, regaining his senses to find himself sitting on the coffee table bare-assed, fighting for breath. He couldn't speak, couldn't think, couldn't do anything but work to get air into his lungs. He knew there was something he needed to do, but he couldn't focus to think what it was until he managed to open his eyes and saw his lover working his own dick, his pants and underwear shoved down enough to let him have a sure grasp of it.

Hell, no! That's my job! Isaac knew the etiquette of lovemaking between a man and a woman, and he didn't think it was any different between men. He reached down and grabbed Adam's arm.

"No. Let me," he said, his voice still hoarse from screaming.

Without waiting for consent, he dropped down to the floor and gathered Adam's thick, cut cock between his palms. It was flushed with blood and hard as stone, and it twitched when he grasped it. Though he knew he wasn't ready to take it into his mouth — he'd have to get used to the idea first — he had the overwhelming urge to press soft kisses down its length, to kiss the leaking tip, to show the thing affection. Which was such a ridiculous thought that he felt his face heat and was glad Adam couldn't see his blush.

Still, he gave in to the urge and bussed the head lightly, needing to slow Adam's roll to orgasm so he could enjoy having Isaac's hands on him for more than a minute. He wanted to share the passion between them by giving Adam a taste of the sweet elixir of pleasure that he had just given Isaac. He feathered light kisses all along the rigid length, and licked the head as though he were enjoying an ice cream cone.

Adam's moans pleased him greatly. It meant he was doing it right, that Adam was enjoying his attentions. That was what he wanted, so he licked him some more, sending his tongue down the sides and around the base before licking his way back up. Then he began to stroke him, using the moves that he knew set him off. Soft swirling twists and hard pulls on his dick had Adam begging him for release.

"Please, Zac, I need…" Adam was now the one gasping for air.

"What, sweetheart?" The endearment slipped out, unplanned but not regretted. "What do you need?"

"I need to cum!"

Adam opened his eyes, their gray depths stormy with the same hunger that had raged in Isaac only minutes before. Isaac leaned in and kissed him hard, wanting to taste the urgency of that hunger for himself. Their kisses grew more fevered while he held

Adam in his hand and when the younger man began to thrust up into his fist, Isaac pumped him until he came. Adam tore his mouth away to howl out his release as cum shot up his chest, over Isaac's hands. Some even hit Isaac's chin, making him grin. He kept pumping him until Adam's hips stopped jerking and he collapsed against Isaac, resting his forehead against Isaac's left arm.

Isaac smiled, reveling in the power he had to give Adam pleasure, and overjoyed that he had done it right. He figured he might have a bit of a freak out later, but for now, he was basking in his first shared sexual experience since Rowena's death.

"You okay there, Zac?"

Isaac opened his eyes, not sure when he'd closed them again, and smiled at Adam.

"I am, thanks. You?"

Adam's smile echoed the way he was feeling. There was joy and affection in his gaze when he said, "Never been better."

Isaac helped him stand up and said, "We'd better clean up. Come with me."

Pulling his boxers and jeans back up, he collected his t-shirt and led the way up to his bedroom.

"If you'd like, you can have a shower," he told him.

Adam's eyes lit up, the smile returning full force as he answered, "Don't mind if I do. But it'll be even better if you share it with me. Will you?"

For answer, Isaac took his hand and led him into the bathroom. They stripped quickly, though he managed to keep his eyes on his lover's body the entire time. Adam was about an inch taller than David, with pale skin and a trail of strawberry-blond hair across his pecs and down his belly to his cock, where they filled out into a pretty bush around its base. He wasn't especially buff, but he very clearly looked after himself. He was fit and trim and sufficiently muscular that Isaac could see the definition in his long arms and legs.

"Sexy beast," he murmured, holding Adam at arms' length and giving him a heated once over. The color that started in his cheeks and made its way down his body thrilled Isaac. "So pretty, sweetheart," he added, before pulling him in to kiss him.

He had such an increasingly overwhelming need to cherish the younger man, to show him how much he was beginning to feel for him. He realized, as he set the water temperature, that this was exactly how it had happened with Rowena. The slow, easy affection that he was allowing free rein in his heart would grow into something more profound if he let it. Did he have it in him to love so completely again? Could he take that chance with a man? Did he have a choice?

"Hey! Come back here!"

Adam's voice brought his gaze back to him. "What?"

"You left me all alone here for a minute. Where'd you go?" Worry edged Adam's voice, and turned his gray eyes muddy.

"Nowhere, really," Isaac told him. "Just reminiscing."

He stepped into the shower stall, not wanting to pursue this thread of the conversation. "Come on in. The water's fine, now."

Adam moved in behind him and he turned, letting the water sluice down his back as he reached for his new lover. He carded his fingers through the blond waves that fell to his shoulders and then turned them so Adam's back was to the spray of water. Reaching for the shower gel, he looked at Adam and said,

"This is a shampoo and shower gel in one. Do you mind using it?"

"You gonna wash my hair, big guy?"

Adam's tone was teasing, but his eyes mirrored warm fondness. Isaac reined in the sudden burst of need that made him want to kiss the stuffing out of him. He had no frame of reference for the feelings he was suddenly dealing with and no way to know how to feel about them. He loved the way they charged his blood, but what if they were fleeting? Could he live after this without the thrill of wanting another human being, of needing his touch, of letting go in his arms?

Not now, Zac! Get it together, man. Stay present. "If you'll let me. I've been dying to get my hands in your beautiful hair for a long time."

Adam took hold of his hands and raised them to his lips, kissing the knuckles on each one before saying,

"Do your worst, babe. You're in luck since I like having my hair washed."

Something hot and piercing stabbed him in the chest as he turned Adam around so his back was to him. What the hell was that? Jealousy? He had no right to expect the hot man under his palms, who moaned lightly as he began to massage his scalp, to have been celibate. Not only was it unreasonable but it was unrealistic. Adam was younger than he was — he'd need to ask how much younger soon — and he was not likely to have spent his entire youth waiting for Mr. or Ms. Right, even if he had become more discriminating as he got older.

Letting go of the feeling, he washed Adam's hair slowly, relishing the heavy weight of it in his hands, and the way the blond strands looked against the darkness of his skin. The gorgeous study in contrasts that existed between them delighted Isaac's sensual nature. He rinsed the soap out, leaning in to whisper,

"Sorry, I don't have conditioner. Bald here, remember?"

Adam turned and slid his hands down Isaac's side to his waist. "It's okay. I don't condition much, unless it's already in the shampoo."

He raised his head and Isaac gave him the kiss he was asking for. When they separated to breathe, he said,

"If you tell me what brand you use, I'll make sure it's here for you. For next time," he added, in case Adam didn't understand why.

And then it hit him what he'd said. Before he could react or retract the words, Adam said,

"Next time?"

The moment of truth was upon him again. So many such moments had already occurred this evening. He wanted to wait, to be cautious, to withstand the pull of Adam's charismatic personality, to withhold some part of himself, to keep control of his emotions until he was ready to release them fully. But the man who was now cupping his butt cheeks and squeezing gently was relentless, and apparently he was helpless against Adam's machinations.

He wondered if Adam thought he was ready for round two. He wasn't in the first blush of youth anymore, and he usually couldn't get it up so soon after an orgasm. But the way Adam was rubbing his semi-hard dick on Isaac's and squeezing his ass was a sign that even if Isaac weren't ready, Adam could soon be again. The idea made his dick twitch, which shocked the hell out of him. He ignored it in favor of answering Adam's question.

"Only if you want there to be."

Because truthfully, no matter how much he was falling for this man, he wouldn't let go until he was a hundred percent sure that Adam was in it for the long haul. And that kind of certainty took time. They'd need to spend more time together than they had done so far. They'd need to have long talks about all sorts of things, important and unimportant. And he'd need to learn what it meant to be part of a male couple. He'd have to learn how to trust that what he was feeling was more than a fluke or the result of being too long without a partner.

Adam kissed him, shutting down his brain with the voracious hunger of his lips and tongue. Isaac sank into the kiss, letting himself relax and just enjoy the taste and scent and touch of the man who held him so securely, so intimately, so completely in his thrall.

"Can we go to bed now?"

The question knocked Isaac for a loop. He had forgotten the time of day, had forgotten where he was, had forgotten everything except the feel of the man in his arms. It was mind-boggling how deep was the effect that Adam was having on him. He nodded helplessly. What else was he going to do? They dried off quickly, and Isaac led the way back into his bedroom. He handed Adam a pair of his pajamas, ones he hardly ever wore, and pulled on his own boxers and a loose pair of sweats and a t-shirt. He wouldn't survive if he slept in anything less.

"Let me just put your clothes in the wash with mine so you'll have clean clothes to wear when you leave in the morning."

He rushed away to do so as he spoke, knowing he was running away and not yet understanding why. As he dumped the clothes into the washing machine and added detergent and softener, he acknowledged something his heart had known before his head had figured it out. He hadn't slept in his bed with anyone since his wife's death. This was huge and he knew it. Could he do this? Wasn't it replacing Rowena to let someone else sleep on her side of the bed? Should he do that so soon? Was he being disloyal to allow it? And as always, though he knew he really didn't care that Adam was a man, would it be okay to let his male lover sleep in his wife's spot after they'd just had sex?

Come on, Zac. Man up! He shut the door to the laundry room and headed back to his bedroom. He had no idea what he'd say or do when he got there, and he didn't have any time to think on it, so he went with his gut. Adam had pulled up the blinds and was looking out into the night, his arms crossed over his chest. What was he thinking? The greenhouse wasn't visible at night unless an animal passed under the motion sensor that would then switch on a light.

"Penny for your thoughts?" That seemed as good a way as any to start a conversation.

Adam turned his head to look at him for a moment before turning back to look into the darkness beyond the window panes.

"I can sleep in the guest room, if you prefer," he began, "or wait till my clothes are dry and go home. I don't have to sleep in your bed."

Isaac's heart hurt him at the carefully neutral tone of Adam's words. How had he read him so easily? He thought he had hidden his momentary panic well enough. What could have clued Adam in to his worry? He studied the younger man's rigid spine a moment before replying, choosing his words carefully. This was as important as his first orgasm with a man, with this man, had been. He refused to fuck it up.

"I panicked," he confessed. "I'm sorry if I upset you."

He stepped closer to him, close enough that Adam would hear him if he whispered, but he didn't touch him. He wasn't sure he should until they had cleared the air. Adam kept his back to him when he spoke again.

"I'm not upset. I'm…confused, I guess, because I don't know what I did or what you're feeling. And if you don't talk to me, I won't ever know, will I? I don't know what's the right question to ask."

Damn! Isaac sighed, because Adam was right. He had forgotten how difficult relationships could get when partners didn't talk openly with each other. He and Rowena had learned early on to be open about what they were feeling and thinking, even if it caused a fuss. Better to get things out and deal with them than to keep them in and let them fester and grow like an open wound.

"I hadn't gotten as far as thinking about you spending the night here," he began, "so of course where you slept didn't come up. Until now. And the only other person I've ever slept in this bed with was Rowena. I just…"

He paused, trying to find the right words to say. He didn't want Adam to think he was rejecting him, but he needed him to understand why he had panicked.

"I've never had to think about what it would be like to have someone else, and now that I've started something with you, I'm forced to answer questions I hadn't thought of before."

Adam turned to face him then, his eyes troubled. "Questions? Like what?"

Isaac held his gaze. Another moment of truth was upon him. He swallowed before speaking.

"Questions like whether or not it's right to have someone else sleeping on her side of the bed. Or if I'm being disloyal to her memory. Or whether we got intimate too soon and sleeping in the same bed this early is a bad idea."

He braced himself for whatever response Adam would make, praying that he was strong enough to take whatever Adam might dish out.

"And what do you think the answers to those questions are?"

Adam's words were softly spoken, his gaze watchful.

"I don't know, to be honest. All I know is that I don't regret what we did together. Not even a little bit. I just need time to figure out the rest."

Adam uncrossed his arms and took Isaac's hand, leading him to the bed.

"Sit with me. I need to tell you a story."

His voice was gentle, tender, warm. Isaac let hope flutter its wings in his heart as he did as requested and sat next to him on the end of the bed.

"Nova's mom and I were friends who became fuck buddies as well. I was too busy for a relationship, and Cheryl wasn't looking for anything more than someone to enjoy no-strings-attached sex with."

He looked down at his hands then, clasping his fingers together and contemplating them a moment more before he continued.

"We were very careful. I always wore a condom, and we tried hard to avoid sex, even protected, when she was ovulating. Then we decided that the condom was decreasing our enjoyment, so we both got tested and she went on the pill. And still, she got pregnant. Neither of us knew what to do. I talked to my parents, and they advised me to marry her. I agreed with them, so I proposed to her. She turned me down."

Isaac rested a hand over Adam's clenched fingers. Sadness radiated from him and Isaac sensed that the story wouldn't end well. He didn't speak, just squeezed his hands and waited.

"I asked her why she would refuse the best offer I could make her and she told me that she didn't love me. Not the way a woman should love the man she married.

"I love you as my friend, Adam," she told me. "But I won't marry you because it's the right thing to do. The right thing is for us to marry the person we fall in love with. I'm not in love with you and I won't settle for less than my ideal. Marriage is too important to fuck it up with obligation."

He chuckled then, a watery sound that made Isaac lift his chin. Adam's eyes glistened with unshed tears. Dear Lord, what had happened?

"Go on," he urged him. "Tell me everything."

He wasn't sure what this story had to do with their situation, but since Adam needed to tell him, he would keep listening.

"We planned everything…how we would co-parent, how we'd do vacations as a family, how I would integrate her into my family as my non-traditional partner. But then she died in childbirth."

Shit! That was not what Isaac had been expecting to hear.

"Oh, sweetheart, I'm so sorry!" Isaac pulled him close enough to drape an arm over his shoulders. "How did she die?"

"Eclampsia. She went into the hospital a couple of weeks before the baby was due complaining of headaches and vomiting. There were also other signs that something was wrong. And she'd been having them for a couple of days before she figured she ought to go in. They had to take Nova by Caesarian section, to try and save her, but she still died."

Isaac needed to hold him. He pulled him to his feet.

"Come on. Let's lie down."

Suddenly, it didn't matter which side he lay on. All that mattered was that he comfort him. Isaac pulled him into his big body, spooning him from behind, just letting him breathe away the tears he knew were threatening. His heart broke for him. He understood grief only too well himself.

"I was a wreck for a long while after she passed away." Adam's voice was still quiet. "I blamed myself. How could I have missed the signs? I went over her charts but none of her visits and screenings had shown any problems."

Isaac felt his chest rise and fall as he took deep breaths. He stroked his hair, soothing him, giving him some of his strength.

"You know it wasn't your fault, right, Adam? There was nothing that you could have done to save her."

One of the hardest things that Isaac had had to face was the fact that nothing he could have done would have spared Rowena's life. And even as he spoke the words to Adam, he realized why the younger man was telling him this terrible story.

"Thank you," he said, pressing a soft kiss to Adam's temple.

Adam looked over his shoulder at him in confusion. "For what?"

"For being as smart as you are. Maybe I need to go to smart school like you did."

He smiled, hoping to lighten the mood without diminishing the poignancy of the moment. He was rewarded for his effort when Adam said,

"Smart school ain't cheap." His smile was rueful, but it was still a smile. Isaac would take that. "So, what makes me so smart this time?"

"You've learned that what is important is to be true to what you believe in and to trust yourself to know what's true and what's right."

Adam turned in his arms and smiled at him, stroking his goatee. "Seems like you may not need smart school after all."

Isaac chuckled. "I'm a quick study."

"So, we're good?" Adam cupped his cheek tenderly.

"Yes. Let's get some sleep. Busy day tomorrow."

He wasn't sure that Adam would want to stay in his arms, so he let them fall, but he stayed on his side and when Adam turned his back to him and settled against him, he breathed a sigh of relief and wrapped an arm across his belly again.

"Goodnight, Zac."

"Night, Adam."

Chapter Seventeen

"Come in, Dr. Kincaid."

Chantal McKenzie's smile and voice were a bright, cheerful beginning to game night. Adam walked in and shook off his coat, which Channing took and hung up for him.

"You know where to go, Doc," she said to him before turning to greet the person behind him.

"Hi, Detective Kincaid," he heard her say.

He waited for Aidan to follow him inside and they walked together into the family room where everyone else was already assembled, snacking on chips and drinking beer. Adam saw Isaac at once and he resisted the urge to look at him, though it took considerably more effort than he would have imagined.

"Evening, everyone," he said loudly.

He received their various greetings with a smile and went to sit next to David.

"Where's Nova?" the boy asked, looking around.

Adam chuckled. "She's with her grandparents till after Sunday dinner tomorrow. I have work tomorrow morning so I'll pick her up after."

"Oh!" David's disappointment was palpable.

"I'm famished," Aidan said, "so how about we break out the food so I can avoid starvation?"

Chantal laughed. "Sounds like you're gonna need more than the slim pickings we've got in the kitchen, Detective!"

Her oldest brother Chandler laughed as he stood up. "Come on, big guy, let's go get you situated."

Adam watched them walk out and then let his eyes trail around the room, finally settling them on Isaac, who smiled and winked at him as soon as he did. He returned the smile and then looked away, hoping that no one else had noticed it. After their night together a week ago, he still wasn't sure — despite the wink — how Isaac would respond to anyone other than David finding out about their relationship. And because they hadn't been able to do more than talk on the phone since, he'd have to play it by ear.

Chantal and Aidan returned bearing bags with tacos. Channing was right behind them carting pizza boxes, while Chance brought in the cooler with the drinks and they all fell on everything like ravenous beasts. There wasn't much talking until they'd had their fill for the moment. Then Chantal said,

"Come on, David. We're gonna head into the living room for our game night, now. Holler if you need me, guys."

Adam watched Isaac's brows rise in surprise and he bit back a laugh. He'd find a time to reassure him that David would be fine. He seemed like a sensible, level-headed boy. For now, he settled in next to his twin and they played some lively poker. Isaac won more than he lost, again, causing a lot of moaning and whining among the losers, including Adam. He just laughed at them good-naturedly and wished them better luck next time.

After another round of snacks, everyone chatted amiably about everything and nothing. Aidan accosted Adam almost as soon as he sat down from taking a potty break.

"You don't fool me, you know," he began

Adam looked at him. "What are you talking about?"

He suspected that he already knew the answer to the question, but he would play dumb for as long as he could.

Aidan rolled his eyes. "So, that's how you want to do this, bro? I don't mind playing twenty questions."

He really didn't, either, dammit! "Not sure why you think I'm trying to fool anyone."

"You haven't looked at him for more than a second or two all night, but I saw the way he looked back when you finally made eye contact. And I didn't miss the wink. So, you may as well tell me what's up with you and the chocolate hunk."

Adam laughed loud enough that Isaac looked up and their eyes met. He could feel his cheeks heating as he wondered how upset his lover would be if he answered Aidan's question without quibbling.

"Chocolate hunk?" he quibbled anyway.

Aidan grinned. "He's hot, bro, there's no denying that. He's got that sexy silver fox vibe going for him."

Adam knew Aidan was teasing him by being so explicit in his praise of Isaac but he still couldn't stifle the spurt of irritation he felt that he was looking at all. Isaac was his, dammit! He squashed the feeling — because really, how ridiculous was that! — and said as nonchalantly as he could,

"We're going on a date next week."

It wasn't a lie, but it wasn't the truth Aidan wanted to hear.

"And? Because I know there's stuff you're not telling me, bro." He paused a moment, turning to look at Isaac before returning his stare to his twin. "In fact, I'd bet you've seen each other already since last game night."

"What makes you think that?"

Aidan's smile softened. "I know you, remember? Once you like something, you go after it. And we've already established that you like Mr. Hot Chocolate over there."

"You're ridiculous!" Adam retorted, but he was smiling, too.

"But I'm also right, aren't I?"

"And relentless as fuck," Adam grumbled, still not answering his brother's question.

"It's my job. Bite me! Now quit stalling and spill."

Adam looked around. Everyone, including Isaac, was listening to whatever story Benny was regaling them with, so thankfully no one was paying them any attention.

"We had dinner at his place last week." Adam glanced warily over at Isaac again before adding, "There, satisfied?"

Aidan smirked but kept his voice low. "Not really, but I'll spare your blushes till we can speak freely."

Benny looked over at them just then and said, "Watch out, boys! When those two get their heads together, trouble is sure to follow!"

General laughter greeted his teasing comment, but Adam was relieved that Aidan let it go. He would seek advice from his twin at a more appropriate time, grateful that he had someone in his corner.

"I can play another couple of rounds before we have to call it quits." Chandler spoke into the hush beyond the laughter. "Ry has an early meeting, so we'll have to head out soon."

"Yeah...I have the early shift at work tomorrow as well, so I'll need to leave soon," Adam added.

"I'll just go tell the kids so they'll be ready to wrap things up when we are."

Chandler stepped out of the room for a moment while Aidan shuffled the cards. Isaac won the pool, because he'd won most of the games, as they had all predicted. He took his thirty-five-dollar prize with a grin, and promised to use it to buy treats for the next game night that he could attend.

"Good man," Aidan said, slapping him on the back as they stood in the front hall getting their outerwear.

Adam liked the sound of that. He admired that can-do spirit in Isaac, the one that said once he'd made up his mind to follow a course of action, nothing would stop him from achieving the goal. It was so nice to be reminded that they had made a commitment to getting to know each other. His cheeks warmed at the memory of how they had cemented that agreement.

"You look a little warm there, big brother. Are you okay?" Benny asked, looking over at him with a playful twinkle.

Adam groaned silently and managed not to roll his eyes at his youngest brother. Although, in the moment, his brothers' nosiness was irritating as fuck, he knew the day they stopped minding his business would be a sad day, because it would mean they also didn't have his back. He would tolerate teasing for the joy of their undying support. So, he just nodded, choosing not to speak. Someone helped him on with his coat and he turned to find Isaac behind him as he shrugged into it.

"Thanks," he said, hoping he didn't sound too breathy.

"No problem." Isaac smiled at him, then turned to help his son with his coat before taking his own from Aidan, who winked broadly at Adam.

Adam shook his head and chuckled. Twin brothers…can't live with them, can't live without them.

"I had a good time," he heard Isaac say to Chantal. "Thanks for having us over."

Chantal smiled. "You're welcome. We loved having David with us. Make sure you bring him next time, please?

David's shy smile at her words brought a grin to Adam's lips. His father's face, when Adam turned to look at him again, was a study in neutrality. Adam resisted the urge to laugh out loud at Isaac's unease. Even though the younger set had spent the whole evening together in a separate space, Adam could well imagine the conversation between Isaac and David on the way home. He may never have been in the Army, but Isaac would probably do a great imitation of a drill sergeant.

"If he's available, I'll do that," Isaac answered, nothing in his tone giving away anything.

They waited until Chandler helped Ry into their Mercedes before Aidan and Adam headed out together. Aidan stopped by his truck, parked behind Adam's SUV.

"I'll call you later, bro," he said, making a gun motion with his hand.

"You really don't have to," Adam said, hoping for a reprieve.

Aidan's evil chuckle was his only response. He gave his twin the middle finger as he drove past him and watched with amusement as his brother threw back his head and laughed. Troublemaker!

He got into his SUV and started the engine. Isaac approached his window so he rolled it down. Isaac leaned down to speak.

"Everything okay?" Adam asked.

"Yeah. Just wanted to have the only private word with you that I could before you left."

Adam chuckled. He had felt pretty deprived of Isaac-time himself. "Sorry about that. What's up?"

"You said you had some free time this week?"

"Yes. I'm off Wednesday and Thursday."

"Morning or evening shift?"

"Morning this week. Why?"

Isaac seemed to consider his response, then said, "I don't like going out on a school night. Would a date on Friday night be okay? I'll come and pick you up. And if you say it's okay, I can leave David with Nova."

Adam didn't mind going out on a work night, since his shift ended at seven on his three-day weeks. Still, he wasn't sure how Isaac would respond to his hesitation, which had nothing to do with the day and everything to do with his proposal. He didn't know if he was quite ready to leave his toddler with an untried teenager. He knew he had to be honest, though, so he said as gently as he could,

"I don't have a problem with him being with her, as long as you're not offended if I have my babysitter be there anyway, just to make sure he can manage on his own the next time."

His heart thudded uncomfortably in his chest. It would be perfectly understandable if Isaac got mad that he wasn't trusting David, but Adam had to go with his gut, which told him it was what was best for Nova. And, if they were both honest, what was best for David, as well. Instead of dumping him into a totally unfamiliar situation, where there was no one around in case of an emergency, knowing someone was close by, even if she weren't visible, would no doubt ease his mind, as well. At least, Adam hoped so.

"That's reasonable," Isaac said. "I should have thought of it myself. I'll contribute to her pay for Friday night."

"You'll do no such thing," Adam said sharply. He held up a hand when Isaac started to argue. "End of discussion, Mr. Hamilton."

He tried for his sternest voice and couldn't decide if he should be affronted or amused by the clear merriment in Isaac's eyes at his tone. He decided he'd go with amused, because he knew the man wasn't laughing at him...well, not in a mean way, more with affection. He didn't mind affectionate laughter at his expense.

"Yes sir, Dr. Kincaid, sir!" Isaac said, straightening to give him a smart salute.

Now it was his turn to laugh. "You sure you never enlisted?" he teased.

"I had a military man for a father. The Major taught me how to salute when I was a little boy and it has stayed with me."

"Hmm. And you call upon the skill when you want to be sassy, is that it?"

Both of them laughed then, and Isaac leaned in again to say, "I'll see you Friday night. Eight o'clock good for you?"

"Eight is fine," Adam said, suddenly wishing he could plant one on the plump lips so near to his own.

"We can't, so stop looking at me like that."

Isaac's voice was just a little bit hoarse and Adam decided that that was as good as a kiss.

"Fine. Be that way!"

He pretended to be annoyed, but the smirk told a different story. Isaac chuckled as he straightened up, slapped the roof of the car, and said,

"Drive safe, sweetheart." He walked away before Adam could reply.

The endearment rang in his mind all the way home. He woke next morning with the echo of it in his head while he showered and got dressed, and even after he had parked and walked into the ER, the sweetness it left behind was still bubbling in his blood stream. Fortunately, the first call came in moments after he'd donned his doctor's coat and for the rest of the day he was too busy to remember more than his name and the things he had to do to do his job well.

Monday and Tuesday rolled by with nothing more remarkable than usual in the ER. A child who had swallowed a button, a mother who had sliced her fingers instead of the vegetables she'd been chopping, a teenager cutting school who had broken his collar bone after a fall from somewhere he shouldn't have been in the first place...these were the biggest dramas of the day, thankfully, and after that it was the usual flu symptoms, headaches that wouldn't go away, mysterious stomach pains. One of those, though, turned out not to be gas, as the middle-aged woman had thought, but a cyst on her liver that needed to be removed ASAP because it was so large it was pushing all her organs aside and had stretched her gall bladder beyond repair.

He thought about the look on the poor woman's face as he told her which specialist she needed to see at the larger hospital an hour away who would take care of her surgery and aftercare. She looked defeated, relieved, and scared all at the same time. She was sixty, in fairly good health for someone her age, and obviously stronger than she knew because she'd been living with the pain for a couple of weeks before her family persuaded her to try the ER since her home remedies for flatulence weren't working.

By Wednesday, though, he was tired enough that when Nova woke him up at the usual impossible hour — why did a toddler have such early waking hours, for Pete's sake? — he had to drag his tired ass out of bed to go help her with her breakfast. He was sipping his first cup of coffee when his doorbell rang. He glanced at the analog clock on the wall and frowned. If it was Benny, he'd have just used his key.

"Finish your breakfast, babygirl," he told Nova, who nodded and kept spooning cereal into her mouth.

Peering through the peephole, he found Aidan looking the worse for wear. He pulled the door open immediately, and his brother stumbled in, his suit pants dirt-stained and his shirt and tie both bloody. His suit jacket was over his arm, and his tie was askew.

"What the hell, Aid?"

"Hey." Aidan could only seem to manage that one word before snapping his mouth closed again.

"Come in." Adam let his twin pass him into the foyer.

"I need coffee."

"Sure. But not till you've cleaned up. Nova's in the kitchen. Go take a shower and borrow some clean clothes. Then you can tell me what happened and why you're here and not in the ER."

Aidan nodded and moved to do as he was bid while Adam went back into the kitchen. As he was pulling out Aidan's preferred mug, Nova asked,

"Who was that, Daddy?"

"It's your Uncle Aidan, sweetie. He just went to have a shower. You'll get to see him soon."

"Okay."

She nodded, satisfied with his response. If only he could be as easily appeased. What the hell had happened to his twin? Whatever it was, it had been bad enough to bring him here instead of sending him home to his lonely house. And also bad enough that he didn't want to tell their parents. But at least he didn't seem to be injured himself. Even Aidan wasn't foolhardy enough to come to him instead of going to the hospital if he was injured...he hoped. He took a sip of his coffee, accepting the offering of cereal and then yogurt that his toddler offered him. He loved her kind heart, even if she did have weird eating habits.

He made sausages and eggs and toasted bagels for Aidan to give himself something to do other than worry. No doubt his twin had neglected to eat, and he knew he'd need to feed him. A sound made him turn his head, but Nova's squeal of delight would have alerted him to Aidan's presence even if he hadn't heard the whisper of his footfall as he walked into the kitchen.

He watched Aidan wince as he caught Nova and lifted her into his arms, hugging her tightly for a long moment, despite his obvious discomfort, before loosening his hold.

"Morning, Pumpkin," he said, kissing her temples before depositing her in her abandoned chair at the table. "How's my sweet niece this morning?"

"Morning, Uncle Aid. I'm okay. Are you okay?"

Adam smiled. His kid may only be four, but she wasn't slow on the uptake at all. Uncle Aidan wouldn't be at her house this early on a weekday if something wasn't wrong with him. He knew Aidan wouldn't lie to her, even if he didn't tell her most of what was wrong, and he was grateful for that. She needed to have men whose word she knew she could trust as she grew older.

"No, babygirl, I'm not so okay right now. But I will be. Now you go on and finish your breakfast, okay?"

Aidan looked up and saw Adam watching him. He slid his eyes to the pan Adam was removing from the stove and smiled a weary thanks.

"Your daddy made me breakfast, so I'll come sit with you and we can eat together."

"Okay, Uncle Aid."

She still had her fruit to eat. Adam plated Aidan's breakfast and his, slid the toasted bagels into a shallow bowl, passed him his full, giant-sized mug of joe, and sat down. Butter and marmalade were already on the table, as well as cream and sugar for the coffee. He watched as Adam breathed a quick grace before filling his mouth with eggs and a piece of sausage. He was dying to know what had brought his brother to his house, but he'd have to wait until Nova was occupied before he could ask.

Eventually, breakfast was done, and while Aidan tidied the kitchen, Adam took Nova into the living room and switched on the television. There was an hour of her favorite shows on, and he didn't mind them since they reinforced what she was learning in preschool. It would entertain her and keep her occupied while he talked to Aidan

Back in the kitchen, Aidan was sitting at the table nursing a second cup of joe.

"Okay, spill. What happened? Why did you drag your ass over here instead of going home? And what the hell is with the bloody clothes? Are you hurt?"

Aidan sighed. "No, I'm fine. We were on a stakeout. Things got a little bit hairy, and a girl was hurt."

Ah! That explained the extra tight hug he'd given Nova earlier. His voice wobbled when he said that, and Adam wondered what exactly he meant by 'hurt'.

"Hurt how?" he asked gently.

"Asshole came after me but his shot went wide and hit this kid who was…" He stopped speaking for a moment, took a deep breath and then continued. "She was just coming around the corner from the back of the bar where we had the stakeout."

Adam frowned. "You said she was a kid. What was she doing there at whatever time you and the others were there?"

Aidan's eyes were tired as he looked into his twin's face. "A guy rushed out a second after she got hit. He was…zipping up." He swallowed. "She was turning tricks, Adam! Fifteen years old, and she was selling her body for money. She's a runaway, and based on what I managed to find out before Captain Mansfield sent me home, she had every reason to be scared to stay home."

Adam's heart broke. His twin saw much more of the awfulness of humanity than he would, and it was times like these that he wished he had more to offer him than a listening ear and a sympathetic heart. He wished he could make him forget, wipe away the memories. But he couldn't. Even words seemed inadequate at this point.

In the next moment, he was thinking about David. Same age, such a different outlook, because he had a parent who cared about him, who took care of him, who loved and cherished him and did his best to provide for his son and to make him happy. Life was shitty that way…some people were blessed and others seemed cursed to suffer. He shook his head.

"You held her till the bus came, didn't you? Hence the blood all over your clothes." He didn't have to ask. He knew.

Aidan didn't answer, which was confirmation enough. Adam sighed.

"Go get some sleep. What time do you need to be back at work?"

"Cap gave me the rest of the day off."

He sounded supremely disinterested, and Adam knew he'd have to push him just a little so he didn't settle into a funk. He loved his twin but hated it when he let his job get to him. He'd figure out something for them to do together in the afternoon.

"Fine. I'll wake you in a few hours and we're going out."

Aidan didn't argue. When he was like this, he was the exact opposite of his usual ebullient, teasing self. Adam watched him drain his mug, walk to the sink to rinse it and add it to the dishes in the dishwasher, and turn to face him.

"Thanks, bro."

"No problem."

Adam reached over and squeezed his twin's shoulder before Aidan walked out. He started the dishwasher, his mind spinning. Where could he take his brother that would take his mind off his troubles for a while? It had to be somewhere that he could also take Nova, since her preschool was closed for repairs. Suddenly it hit him. He knew the perfect place. He recalled that Wine and Roses Flower and Gift Shop had a small selection of acoustic guitars.

Aidan had started learning to play the guitar when he was a little kid and had gotten really good over the years. Maybe he'd see one he liked. And while he was there he could buy flowers for the wounded teenager. It'd be something nice for her to wake up to…if she woke up. He'd have to call and check on her.

He'd take them to dinner somewhere kid-friendly after they got Aidan a fresh set of clothes from his house. He'd spend the night with Adam and leave from his place for work the next day. Perfect plan!

Now if only he could manage to keep his desire for Isaac under wraps while they checked out his gift shop, all would be well.

Chapter Eighteen

The ringing of the bell over the door in the shop brought Isaac out of his funk. He was still feeling grateful for game night, because the guys had distracted him enough that he hadn't had time to think about the way his last visit with his dad earlier on Saturday had gone. He had said his hellos and waited a suitable amount of time before going back to peek around the door to see what was taking David so long.

"What's this I hear about you dating, Isaac?"

The Major's strident voice carried like a trumpet and Isaac cringed, hoping no one else was paying attention.

"I am."

He hoped the affirmation would be enough. Stupid hope. They weren't.

"And David tells me it's the reverend's doctor son."

Isaac hadn't responded. He didn't owe his father any explanations for anything he chose to do with his life. And he wished that David hadn't mentioned it, but he knew his father asked his son about him all the time, so it would have been good if he had remembered to prep David. His lack of response hadn't fazed his dad, who just kept on speaking.

"Have you lost your mind, boy? What nonsense is this?"

Isaac had bristled. He was not a boy, for starters, but as a grown-assed man, he still needed to show the proper respect to age and allow his son to keep as loving a relationship with the Major as he could. Before he could answer, David piped up.

"Dr. Kincaid is cool, Maje. And he has the cutest little daughter."

Isaac could still feel his father's beady eyes glaring at him. "Didn't I teach you any better? How can you stoop to this…this kind of behavior? And with a white boy saddled with a child, too? What are you thinking?"

"I'm thinking it's my business who I date, Major, not yours."

He had leveled a hard stare at his dad then and told David to hurry up. Then he'd walked out, seething with a rage so deep his hands shook with it. Rage…and hurt, if he were to be honest. They'd never been close, even when he was a small boy, but they had not had words like that in years. It angered him that the Major would choose to speak ill of someone he didn't know, and that he had done so in front of David.

He knew he'd have to talk to his son about that, but he hadn't been in the right frame of mind to do it before game night, and he had just kept pushing it off. He sighed heavily as he stood up from the back of the refrigerator he'd been looking at for the last fifteen minutes. It was on the fritz and he needed an appliance man to come out and see to it. Who knew, he might even need to buy a new one.

He shook off the unpleasant thoughts. "We need to call a repairman, Peaches."

Pulling off the work gloves he was wearing, he walked through the swinging doors into the shop.

"I need him to come out ASAP," he continued, not looking up until he was behind the counter.

His shop assistant's silence finally brought his head up. She was nowhere to be seen, but as he listened, he could hear her talking to someone in the far corner of the gift shop, at the back, where he kept his music inventory. He searched through the Rolodex that she had next to the vintage landline phone which she had insisted was the perfect sales pitch for the gift shop. He grinned at her refusal to modernize her contact-keeping system, though she had been right about the phone. It always drew folks' attention to it, which gave her the chance to start a conversation. They'd sold quite a few based on those conversations.

"If it ain't broke, don't fix it," he mumbled as he searched for his electrician's phone number.

"That's not always true."

Isaac's head snapped up at the sound of Adam's voice. He remembered the last time the doctor had shown up unexpectedly in his shop, and he hoped Adam hadn't forgotten his words then. After their lovemaking, it had been a torturous six days. He'd gone to bed hard every night, and had woken up wet one morning, embarrassed and confused. Weren't wet dreams in grown men a sign of illness? Maybe he'd see a doctor, but not until after he'd…

"What is it about me that makes you go off in your head, Zac?"

Adam's voice brought him back from his meandering thoughts. Good question! He shook his head at the amused expression on the man's face.

"I have no idea," he answered honestly. "Sorry."

"Hey, as long as you come back to me, I don't have a problem with it. Unless…" he moved away from the doorway between the flower shop and the gift shop and stopped right in front of Isaac at the counter, "unless you're thinking about someone other than me. That's a no-no."

He wagged his finger in front of Isaac's face, quirking his brow and pursing his lips. His eyes danced merrily, but Isaac sensed that he was serious. As he should be. It was bad form to be messing with one person while thinking about another. Still, he felt the urge to tease him.

"What if I'm thinking about my son? Is that okay? Or about your dad and what a great preacher he is? Or what about if I'm thinking about your little princess?"

Adam eyed him suspiciously. "Were you thinking about one of those people?"

Isaac laughed. "No, I wasn't."

This was neither the time nor the place to tell Adam what he'd actually been thinking about. And even though the man was a doctor, he wasn't sure he could ever tell him the questions he had about how his body worked. That would just be humiliating. He'd Google it. He changed the subject.

"So, what brings you to Wine and Roses today?"

Adam's eyes shadowed. "Aidan needed a distraction. I noticed you had a small selection of acoustic guitars the last time I was in, so I brought him in to have a look around. Good thing I did, too, since there are fewer than there were before."

Something bad must have happened on the job if the detective needed a distraction. It probably wasn't his place to ask, but he could still be supportive.

"He plays guitar?"

"Like a dream, when he has the time." Brotherly pride sparkled in Adam's eyes and sounded in his voice.

"Well, I'm sure Peaches will help him decide what's best for him." He looked around. "Where's Nova?"

"She's with Aidan. I think she senses that something bad happened and she wants to make him feel better, so she's sticking with him. Holding his hand, specifically. He had to ask for it back so he could try the guitar Peaches was showing him." He chuckled at that.

As if on cue, they both heard the sound of a guitar as Aidan played the melody to an old hymn. Isaac was impressed.

"Wow! He's good!"

"I told you!"

He smiled at Adam, as it suddenly hit him what the other man had done. It was a great compliment that Adam would think his gift shop was interesting enough to be a distraction from whatever painful thing had happened to his twin.

"By the way, thanks for introducing the store to a new customer. I appreciate the support." He didn't want to be too effusive, but he did want to show his gratitude.

"It's no big deal. You've got some pretty sweet items in the shop. I even noticed the wine cooler in the opposite back corner. You've got one or two I like. And it makes such sense, given the name of the store."

"Rowena was all about being practical as well as poetic. Originally, we had wanted to sell wine and roses for the romance. Then we realized adding gifts to the mix allowed lovers to find things other than flowers, in case their loved ones didn't want or couldn't have flowers. But we didn't want to give up the name Rowena had come up with, so we just added the rest, for clarity's sake."

Adam beamed at him. "You've got some interesting stories to tell, don't you?"

"I've lived a good life," Isaac agreed. "I have no complaints."

Well, he had none now, but Isaac remembered how when Rowena was killed, he had been a bitter, angry man in a world of hurt with a lot he felt righteously indignant about. He was glad those awful, hurting days were over, and it seemed he might be on the cusp of something new and bright, with the man standing across the counter from him, looking at his lips with undisguised hunger.

"The last time I came in unannounced, we had a falling out because I did something I'm dying to do again," Adam informed him, eyes never leaving his lips. "It's such a pain being grownup, sometimes."

His complaint made Isaac laugh out loud. "You're a troublemaker, just like your little brother said," he declared when he got himself under control. "Now stop trying to distract me. I have to make a call. One of the fridges that I keep some of my blooms in is acting up. I need to call the electrician."

He looked away from the seductive gleam in Adam's eyes to the number he had to dial and made the call. By the time he had made arrangements for the technician to come in the following afternoon, Adam had retreated to the doorway between the two parts of his store. Isaac was caught between disappointment that he'd done the sensible thing and given them both some space, and elation that he wasn't the only one struggling with desire.

He listened a moment more as Aidan played another familiar tune and hoped he'd find something he wanted to buy. The few guitars he carried in the shop ranged in price from the fairly inexpensive for a musical instrument in good condition to the very expensive because of brand and material. He couldn't be mad if Aidan couldn't afford to buy anything from him, though he also knew his prices were somewhat more reasonable than the detective would find in any exclusive music shop.

"Seems like you've done a good job of distracting him," Isaac complimented Adam. "Glad I could help. But why didn't you just take him to the real music shop in Larkmount? You know they're the premier dealers in this area."

Adam shrugged. "Aidan goes there all the time. I wanted to give him a new experience. If he doesn't buy a guitar from you, maybe something else will catch his eye and he'll buy that instead. Or maybe he won't buy anything, but he won't be in his head."

"Can you tell me what happened?"

Isaac was curious. He only had a general idea of what life as a detective was like, and all that he thought he knew came from the television shows he sometimes watched. So, he understood that his information was unreliable at best.

"There was a shooting and a teenager got hit. He happened to be there."

Isaac sensed that that was the précis version of events, and he didn't push. It really wasn't his business, anyway.

"I can imagine how he must have felt. When I got to the scene of the accident, they wouldn't let me see Rowena at first, but I made such a stink…"

Adam's eyebrows shooting up to his hairline stopped him mid-sentence.

"What?"

"You made a stink? You? Mr. Deliberate? Mr. Cool? Mr. Calm and Collected? You're fibbing!"

Isaac laughed, the first time he could recall ever laughing in the middle of recounting the horror of that morning. How had it come to this? When had he let go of his grief enough to laugh while recalling what he'd seen when he had arrived at the place where Rowena breathed her last?

"You're a bad influence," he said, wagging a finger at Adam. "It's not funny."

"No, the story isn't funny. You are. Fibber!" Throaty chuckles accompanied the accusation.

"I promise you I'm not lying. I was fit to be tied."

"How did you know to go there? I would have thought no one would contact you till her body was in the morgue."

"One of my business neighbors saw it happen. He called me and told me where to go."

Adam's hand over his was a warm comfort that eased the memory even more than the laughter had done. He had someone to share the memory with at last, someone he could break down with, if he ever needed to do that, if the memory ever blindsided him in a weak moment again, as it sometimes did.

"I'm so sorry, Zac!"

"Thanks." He smiled and turned his hand so their palms were connected. "It's okay. It doesn't hurt to talk about it today."

He squeezed Adam's palm before releasing him. This was still his place of business, and even though handholding wasn't French kissing, it was still more than anyone who might enter the store needed to see. Even Peaches wasn't yet aware of his new relationship status, and he didn't want this to be the way she found out. He was relieved when Adam didn't object, but placed his hands in his pockets.

Aidan eventually left the gift shop, bringing with him another music box for his niece. Isaac smiled at the purchase. Nova didn't seem like she was a spoiled child, but she was certainly very much loved and doted on. And that was as it should be. He also ordered a small bouquet to be sent to the girl in the hospital.

"Wanna carry your music box, Pumpkin?" her uncle asked her.

"Yes, please, Uncle Aid." She nodded vigorously and smiled up at Isaac as he handed her the bag with the gift.

"Thanks, Mr…"

She looked up at her father anxiously. Adam supplied the name she didn't remember.

"Mr. Hamilton, babygirl."

"Thanks, Daddy." Her grin was infectious as she turned back to Isaac. "Thanks, Mr. Hamilton. When can I come back to play with David and the kitties?"

Isaac glanced up in time to see a smirk on Aidan's face. Adam meanwhile was doing his best not to blush, and Peaches' eyebrows were raised in surprise.

"I'll have to see when David's available, little one," he said, not really knowing how else to answer her innocent question.

"Thank you." She smiled at him again and turned to her father. "Can we please go eat now, Daddy? I'm hungry."

Everyone chuckled at that and the moment of tension eased. They walked out, Adam with a backward glance and a small wave. Isaac braced himself for an interrogation, because Peaches had not moved, and was now standing with her arms crossed over her chest like the bad cop in a detective show.

"Something you wish to share with me, Boss?"

Isaac smirked at her, feeling suddenly lighthearted. "I'm sure you think there is," he hedged, teasing her.

"Have I ever been wrong?" she demanded with a superior smile.

Isaac had to shake his head, both in agreement with her and in amusement at her.

"Can't remember the last time you were," he admitted.

"Because I've never been wrong. So, all I really need now is confirmation of my suspicions. Is there something going on with that handsome Dr. Kincaid?"

"We're dating."

The smile he couldn't keep off his lips was probably megawatt bright, but there was nothing he felt like doing about it. His heart was light and it was all because of Adam.

"Well, it's about damned time!"

Peaches' exclamation was heartfelt and accompanied by tears, relieved that his concern about her reaction had been unnecessary. He should have known better. She walked around the counter to pull him into a tight embrace. He wrapped his arms around her and held her while she got herself back under control. When she released him, he stepped back and handed her a tissue from the box on the other side of the cash register.

"All right?" he asked her with a gentle smile.

She nodded, blew her nose, and then looked up him sharply. "I have been praying so hard for you to find someone," she told him. "Because it's not right for you to be alone. And after all these years, you finally decided to give it a try again."

She sighed and leaned down to dump the used tissue in the waste basket under the counter. Then she straightened up and said,

"Please give this a real chance, Boss. Dr. Kincaid looks like a very nice young man. And if the two of you can make it work, David will finally have that little sister he's been after."

Isaac chuckled. "He's already smitten with her," he told her.

"And by the sound off it, she is with him, too." Peaches grinned. "She's a cutie pie, isn't she? And so smart for her age!"

Isaac nodded, then moved away so she could take her place at the counter.

"I've called the repairman. The fridge is acting up again and I don't think I should be the one patching it up this time."

"Maybe you'll finally have to get the new one I've been trying to get you to buy." Peaches rolled her eyes as she said that, and Isaac chuckled.

"Maybe I will. But you know I don't like having to spend money if I don't need to."

"Yes, I know. But I also know sometimes it's better to spend less money sooner than more money later."

"Bite your tongue, lady!"

Peaches had a way of jinxing things with her almost supernatural insight and the last thing he needed was for some prophetic event she had only hinted at to come true. Maybe he'd spend a little time checking out the best refrigerator to buy so if the guy confirmed his fears, he'd be ready to hit the order button.

The rest of the day passed quietly enough, and though he wanted to move the flowers he had in the fridge that was spazzing out into another one, there just was no room for them. One more night couldn't hurt. He'd leave things as they were and once the technician came the next day, he'd figure out what to do. There was at least one fridge he could get immediately if push came to shove.

He locked up on time for a change, went to get David, and they stopped at the market to get fresh greens for the salad he wanted to make to go with the pizza he felt like having for dinner. David was overjoyed — to no one's surprise — and eagerly set the table while his dad made the salad. They had just finished eating and clearing up the dinner mess when his cell phone rang.

"Hamilton."

"Mr. Hamilton, this is Chief Granger in town. You'll need to come back in, sir. There's been a fire."

Isaac's gut clenched. He knew at once what had caused it, and he berated himself as he replied.

"I'll be there as soon as I can, Chief. Thank you."

He cut off the call and turned to his son. "I have to go back into town, son. There's been a fire. Will you be okay till I get back?"

He didn't like leaving David alone in the house, but it wasn't as though he had a choice right now. Dammit! This couldn't have come at a worse time, either. Valentine's Day was his busiest day of the year, bar none, and with only three weeks left, and a number of orders already in, he was screwed if the fire had done more damage than he could work around.

"I'll be fine, Dad. I'll lock up after you go and stay down here till you get back."

"It's still a school night, son. Don't wait up for me. If I'm not back in time, just go to bed."

David nodded, though he suspected his son wouldn't fall asleep till he got home. He was grateful to have a child who didn't care what other people thought of him. He was happy being the sensitive kid he was and he seemed comfortable in the skin he was in.

Isaac decided the sweats he had changed into would have to do. He slid his socks and boots back on, added a sweater over the t-shirt he had on, and pulled his long winter coat out of the hall closet. It'd help keep his legs warm.

"See you soon, son."

He hurried out to his truck and drove as fast as he could on the slippery roads back to town. He could see the bright lights on the street, and the smoke curling up from the fire was visible the closer he got to his store. Gripping the steering wheel tightly, he searched for parking beyond the boundary the fire department had put up and walked the extra block to where firemen were still dousing the side of the building where the fire was located with fire retardant foam.

He walked over to one of the firemen who was standing back talking to a tired-looking man in a rumpled suit. He walked up to them and cleared his throat, unable to staunch the emotion that suddenly welled up at the thought of what he would hear, and the fear of what might have happened had he been back there working when it did.

"Excuse me. I'm Isaac Hamilton. I own this shop. Can you direct me to Chief Granger, please? He called me to let me know what was happening. Thank you."

"Ah, Mr. Hamilton. I'm Chief Granger," the firefighter said. "And this is Max Malloy, our fire investigator."

Isaac shook their hands, preparing himself for a barrage of questions.

"What time did you leave here tonight?" the chief asked.

"A little after six."

"Were there any problems? Did you notice anything amiss?"

"No. Everything was fine. There wasn't anything to see, but…"

Having to tell these men that he was responsible for the fire because he'd been negligent was grating on him, making Isaac feel shame and regret and worry about what his responsibility would be if the store on the other side of his had been impacted. But he knew he had to say what he knew. It wasn't in his nature to hide from ugly truths or to bury his head in the sand. Nothing ever got solved that way.

The two men looked at him expectantly, obviously waiting for him to finish his thought. He cleared his throat again and continued.

"I have a fridge, where I keep some of the cut flowers, and it was giving me some trouble earlier. I called a repairman but the earliest he could come was tomorrow."

"What sort of trouble, exactly?" The fire investigator stared at him unblinkingly, no expression on his face.

"Well, mostly, it was getting warmer. I need the flowers to be kept at a certain temperature to preserve them long enough for me to make up the orders I receive on a daily basis."

"Go on." The man seemed to know there was more to the story.

"When I left, I turned it all the way up to keep it at the lowest temperature, thinking that even if it warmed up a bit, I would still be able to salvage my flowers when I came in tomorrow. I was planning on getting a new fridge, if the repairman said that that one was done."

He sighed heavily, shoving hiss hands into his coat pockets. He had forgotten to pull on gloves in his haste to get back to the store.

"So, what caused the fire? Was it the fridge?"

"We know it was an electrical fire, sir," the fire chief said, "but we won't know the source until Mr. Malloy here does an investigation."

"When will I know what my fine is?"

The chief looked at him in surprise. "Why would you think there'd be a fine?"

"Well, I assume if the issue is with the fridge then I'm to blame."

"Let's not jump the gun, Mr. Hamilton." The fire investigator spoke up again, his tone still neutral. "Let me conduct my investigation and then we'll see where we go from there, okay? No use buying trouble."

Isaac couldn't argue with that, nor did he feel inclined to. He was more concerned about how much damage the fire had caused. How had anyone even noticed it, anyway? The part of the store where he kept his flower refrigerators wasn't visible from the street. Maybe one of his business neighbors saw when he was dumping garbage.

"Do you know who called it in?" he asked. He'd need to thank whoever it was.

"Anonymous caller," the fire chief said. "We think maybe it was someone who was where he shouldn't have been."

"You mean like a burglar?"

"Possibly, except I'm not sure what they'd expect to find in your flower shop to steal."

Isaac didn't know, either. No businessman worth his salt left money in his place of business overnight unless it was locked away in a secure place, like a fireproof safe. He didn't usually have a lot of cash to deposit, and he always did the banking before he went home, or else first thing the next day. But he never left money at the store.

"Well, unless you have anything you need to retrieve from the store, Mr. Hamilton, you can probably go on home until tomorrow. We should have more information for you by the end of business tomorrow, once things have cooled down a bit. Thankfully, the fire was mostly easy to contain. There's a lot of localized damage, but it isn't as bad as it could have been."

"Thank you, Chief. Mr. Malloy."

Isaac headed back to his truck, his mind awhirl. He'd have to call the insurance company to make a claim. He'd have to cancel the repairman and find a contractor to come in and have a look around so he could give him a ballpark figure for the cost of refurbishing the store. And he'd have to see if he could work out of the gift shop or if he'd have to do only what he could from home and bring things into the gift shop to sell. Would he even be able to access the gift shop?

He drove slowly back to the farmhouse. All the lights were off except for the one on the front porch. All the exterior lights were motion-sensor ones, so something must have walked by before he drove up. Hoping the critter had already gone, he went indoors, locking the door behind him and leaning against it for a moment. He was worn out. Pouring himself a stiff drink, he took it up to his bedroom where he undressed again slowly and crawled into bed. He would worry about everything in the morning. He really needed to get some shuteye.

Chapter Nineteen

"Sorry, that was Jordan. Did you hear what happened to the flower shop?"

Benny had come over for breakfast after Jordan left for work on Thursday morning, and they were noshing on pancakes and sausages with a side of eggs. Unease prickled its way along Adam's skin as he helped Nova cut up her pancake.

"What happened at the shop?"

"Jordan says apparently there was a fire."

"When did this happen? Was anyone there? Does Isaac know?"

"I imagine he'd know by now," Benny said, finishing the last of his coffee. He rose and took his plate to the sink. "I'd help you clean up but I have a meeting in an hour. I have to go get ready for it."

He walked back to Adam's side, giving him a swift, affectionate squeeze before going round to kiss Nova on the top of her head.

"Thanks for breakfast, Adam. Delicious as always. Call your man. We'll talk later."

After he left, Adam got Nova situated with some television. He needed to call Isaac. He waited impatiently for him to pick up and was relieved when he said, after the third ring,

"Hamilton."

"Hey, Isaac. Morning. It's Adam. What's going on? I heard what happened."

"How did you hear already?"

"Jordan called and told us. I guess he must have seen it on his way into school. Do you know how it happened?"

"I'm not absolutely sure, because the fire department has to finish its investigation, but I think it may be because of a flower refrigerator that I have in the back. It may have caused some kind of short circuit."

Adam hated how upset Isaac sounded, even though he could tell the older man was doing his best to contain it.

"Is there anything I can do to help? I'm off today as well."

"No. No thanks, I'm good." Adam heard his heavy sigh a moment before Isaac added, "Sorry, I have to go. I'll call you later."

Resigning himself to not finding out any more until Isaac called him, and realizing that that call might not come for a long while, he went back to sit with Nova, watching the rest of her show with her, then pulling out the book she wanted him to read and focusing on her. Just before lunch, when Isaac still hadn't called, he dressed her warmly and took her with him "for a drive", he told her, "so you'll have a nice nap this afternoon in preschool."

He drove past and saw the blackened side of Isaac's shop, a part of the roof destroyed, the front windows dark. Where was Isaac? Was he home? In town running errands? Adam figured he'd need to talk to his insurance agent, at least. He'd need money for repairs. It probably wouldn't be good for business if he wasn't able to open his store until everything was back normal. And how long would all that take?

He was pretty sure, given the kind of man Isaac seemed to be, that he had already asked and likely answered all those questions. But Adam wanted to know. He found himself quite worried and struggling to find a way show it without making a pest of himself or putting himself in where he wasn't invited. Fuck it! He'd take the chance to call again even if it was just to say... what would he say? He didn't know, but that didn't stop his fingers from dialing Isaac's number.

"Hamilton."

"It's Adam, Zac. Have you heard anything?"

Isaac's heavy sigh weighed on him. He couldn't imagine him being okay, but he hoped he wasn't as defeated as his sigh sounded.

"Not yet."

"Where are you?"

"In the diner. The fire investigator is there now, but they still wouldn't let me in."

"Want some company?"

"What about Nova?"

Adam's heart warmed at the mention of his daughter. "She's with me."

"Doesn't she have school this afternoon?"

"Yes. So, come home with me after I drop her off. We live closer to the shop than you do. They'll call you when they're ready."

Adam didn't know where this spur of the moment behavior was coming from, where his mouth took over from his brain, but he couldn't feel bad about it, either. He wanted to comfort Isaac, since there was nothing else he could do.

"It's fine. You don't have to…"

"I want to, Zac. You don't need to be alone right now. And what about David? Doesn't he go to the shop after school every day?"

"Yes. I told him I'd be picking him up after school today." He sighed again. "Thanks, Adam."

"Anytime. Meet me at home?"

"Yeah. Sure."

Adam took Nova to his mother's and as soon as Isaac arrived after he got back home, he pulled him into his arms for a hug. The big man was tense for a long moment before he relaxed and wrapped his arms around Adam.

"Thank you," he said when they moved apart. "I'm used to doing everything on my own. It's hard to let someone else help me."

"Did you eat at the diner?"

"Wasn't hungry, really. I just had some coffee."

"No more coffee for you. How about some pie?"

Isaac chuckled, shaking his head. "You're something else," he said slowly, pulling Adam back into his arms and kissing him soundly. "I'm okay, I promise. Let's just go sit on the couch and wait. Maybe play some Ella or Sarah?"

Adam liked the sound of that. Isaac sat on the couch while he went to put an LP on the player. Then he went and sat next to him, smiling when Isaac drew him under his arm and they just chilled. His mind went to ways they could spend the time waiting, but somehow it felt better to cuddle than to fool around.

How very grown up of you, Adam! He chuckled at the thought, and Isaac looked down at him curiously.

"I was just thinking how adult we're being right now," he explained. When it was clear that Isaac still didn't understand, he added, "You know, cuddling instead of kissing and ripping off clothes."

Isaac echoed his amusement. "It happens sometimes."

Eventually, he had to leave to go get David from school, and Adam persuaded him to bring the boy back for dinner.

"You can go home afterwards. It'll give him some time with Nova, and I get to have you a little longer."

He wasn't going to hide his selfish interest in making the suggestion and Isaac's smile said he didn't mind giving in. By the time he returned with David, Mrs. Kincaid had brought Nova home and Adam had reheated the lasagna that she had brought with her. He was finishing up a green salad when the doorbell sounded. Feeling jittery suddenly, he had to smooth his hand down his chest and take a deep breath before opening it.

"Hey! Come in. You're right on time. Dinner's ready."

"Thanks. We'll just go wash up."

When they finally sat down to eat, Nova was all excited at seeing David again and wanted to know everything about his day. While he regaled her with stories about his tests and the classes he liked, Adam watched Isaac. His broad shoulders were so inviting, he almost wished the kids weren't there so he could strip his shirt off them, rub them with oil, and massage the tension out of them.

"What?"

Adam blinked. Isaac had caught him staring. "Nothing."

"The preacher's kid lies through his teeth. Haven't you heard the saying about lying lips? Even if they are beautiful lips."

Isaac's voice was low so the kids wouldn't hear, and the compliment accompanying the chastisement drew his eyes to Isaac's lips. They were curved in a smirk that he wanted to kiss right off them. Dragging his eyes away, because getting a boner at his dining table with two children sitting across from him was not in the cards, he said,

"I was just thinking of how I'd like to relieve the tension you're carrying in your shoulders, that's all."

"That's all, huh?" Isaac's smirk grew wider.

"Hand to God," he said, raising his right hand. "I can't afford to think any other thoughts at the dinner table with children present."

Isaac laughed outright at that, and Adam was pleased to see some of the tension ease from his posture. If flirting was what would make the big guy relax, then he was all for it. Any port in a storm and all that. He decided to go one better, though he remained very aware of the possibility of listening ears at an inopportune moment.

"Not that I'd be averse to trying other methods than a simple massage, mind you. I mean, we both know there are lots of stimulating ways to relieve tension."

Before Isaac could respond, Nova's high-pitched squeal brought his attention back to his daughter and her wannabe big brother. He was holding a forkful of lasagna just out of her reach and Adam listened as he said,

"I'm gonna eat this, since you said you're full."

Adam laughed at them as Nova shook her head vigorously and replied,

"I'm not full. I promise!"

They had already advanced to that, had they? She liked to claim she was full so Adam would feed her, and it seemed that David had now been initiated into the family game. He liked the spin that the boy put on getting her to finish eating. Sweet!

Isaac's phone rang as they were finishing up dinner. He stepped away to take the call while David helped to clear the table and pack the dishwasher. He disappeared with Nova into the living room while Adam waited impatiently for Isaac to return. When he did, Adam asked immediately,

"Any news?"

"Preliminary investigation is done. He'll know for certain in about a week. In the meantime, I can't go in, and I'll need to secure the gift shop, which was thankfully not damaged. I guess I need to go about finding contractors to get things back up and running once I know what's what."

A heavy sigh accompanied the words. Adam reached for him, and Isaac hugged him back. Then he let go and said,

"I'd better be on my way. It's a school night and David has a test tomorrow. I'll call you, okay?"

Adam released him reluctantly. "Okay." He didn't know what else to say.

Nova hugged David goodbye and he promised he'd play with her again soon, said goodbye to Adam, thanking him for dinner, and then they left. Why his home felt suddenly so empty, he didn't know. They'd known each other less than three months, but Isaac was coming to mean more to him with every encounter. He hoped the news would release the insurance funds he'd need to get his store back up and running soon, but he knew in the meantime, Isaac would be without an income unless he could find a way to work in the gift shop and fill people's flower orders for Valentine's Day.

He wouldn't have a chance to see Isaac again until their date on Friday night, assuming he'd still want to do anything. This was a rough time for him and Adam wouldn't push if he called it off. He didn't deny that he'd be disappointed, though. He was jealous of every chance he had to be with him, to learn more about him, to soak in his warmth. He knew he was falling for Isaac and he welcomed the feelings with an open heart. But maybe he'd need to prepare himself for the fallout, in case Isaac didn't end up reciprocating the depth of feeling he was already experiencing. It was one thing to agree to dating, but in his experience dates did not always result in long-term commitments. They didn't always end up in a love fest, either.

He was on his way to work the next morning when his phone rang. It was Isaac. Routing it through the bluetooth speaker, he answered.

"Good morning, Isaac."

"Morning, Adam. I just wanted to know if you were still available tonight?"

"Definitely. I was worried that you mightn't be." And boy am I glad you are!

"Eight still good?" he asked next.

"Perfect."

"See you then. And have a good day at work."

"Thanks."

The day flew by, with only one pretty heavy-duty emergency that required him to stabilize the patient before sending her off to the nearby trauma center where the woman would get the kind of care that they weren't equipped to give in town. The rest of it was patients with high fevers, other flu symptoms, bruised ribs from a bloody fistfight. He had a ton of paperwork to complete for the several patients he saw in his twelve-hour shift, with special attention to the ones for the accident victim and the fight patient.

Eventually, he had done his due diligence and could leave with a clear conscience. He greeted his replacement, made his report, and was out by seven-thirty. Half an hour to get home, get changed, and be ready when Isaac came. He'd have to hurry, but the jangly feeling in his gut was more from anticipation than nerves about how late it was. In his apartment, he found Benny feeding Claus.

"Thanks, bro. I have a date so I can't chew the fat right now."

"With the hunky florist again?"

Benny waggled his brows, making Adam laugh, despite his hurry.

"Yes. Now go bother your man, and let me get ready for mine."

"Woohoo!" his little brother whooped gleefully. "Take ownership, why don't you!"

Adam shooed him out and took the fastest shower known to man. But one look at the clock when he stepped out of the steaming bathroom told him he'd still be dressing when Isaac rang his doorbell. He'd worry about it when it happened, but for now, he took out socks and boxers, pulled a clean t-shirt over his head and stood in front of his closet trying to decide which sweater to wear over it. The doorbell rang. Fuck!

"Coming!" he called out, struggling to get his legs into the first pair of jeans he put his hands on.

Trying not to trip over his feet as he went, he managed to get to the door in one piece and opened it quickly. He hated feeling so out of breath and unprepared, especially when he took in the well-groomed man standing in his doorway.

"Evening! Come in." He stood aside and let Isaac and David pass him, adding as he closed the door, "I'll just be another minute or two. I got home later than I expected."

David walked ahead of them into the living room, but Isaac's hand on his arm stopped him dead in his tracks. And when the big man pulled him closer and planted one on his shocked mouth, he responded at once with the same fierce hunger. He hadn't realized how much he'd needed that kiss till Isaac had given him the gift. And now his limbs were shaky with remembered lust.

"Good evening!"

Isaac released his lips and headed for the living room, where the babysitter and Nova were watching TV. Adam left his bedroom door open so he could listen to their voices while he pulled a thick red sweater over his head. It went nicely with the skinny jeans he wore, and after adding a little product to his long hair, he pulled it back into a ponytail and sat down to put his boots on.

"Take your time, sweetheart."

Isaac's voice brought his head up from where he was lacing up the boots. He was standing in the doorway, shoulder leaning against the frame, hands in his pockets. He looked perfectly at ease, composed, cool as the proverbial cucumber.

"The show doesn't begin till nine. We're going to a supper club. We'll eat while we listen to a live band."

Adam looked down at his attire. "Should I change? I mean, aren't those places high-end?"

Isaac chuckled. "You look fine. They don't stand on ceremony at this establishment. The owner is a former Marine who wanted to make a place for his buddies to unwind. It has grown over time, and he called it The Supper Club because he couldn't think of another name."

Adam finished with his boots, put his wallet and phone into his back pockets, and turned back to his date.

"I'm ready."

He walked into the living room to kiss his daughter goodnight, reminding her that she was to go to bed when David said so. He watched the teenager preen at his words, and he bit back a grin. The babysitter had repaired to his office where she was already on her Kindle. He told her thanks again and wished her a good night.

On the way out the door, he pulled a scarf around his neck as Isaac helped him into his coat. Adam stole a quick kiss before they walked out the door. The drive in Isaac's truck to the club was charged with the potent chemistry that their earlier kisses had unleashed. He was glad when they arrived and Isaac led him into a cozy, intimate space that was packed, it seemed, to the gills.

"Where are we gonna sit?" he asked, pulling Isaac's ear down so he didn't have to shout.

"Special seating for us. This guy's dad and mine are Army buddies and I always get treated like family here."

The date was a smashing success. The food was good pub grub, the drinks were excellent, and the live music was a delight to his senses. Old blues tunes, smooth jazz, soft rock, everything made Adam sink deeper into contentment. He wished he could dance with Isaac, but there didn't seem to be any other male couples on the dance floor, and given how new this thing with him was, Adam didn't want to jinx it by doing anything that would bring them further into the limelight than they already were, even if all he wanted to do was rub himself all over the big man like a cat.

"Ready?" Isaac asked after Adam had downed his third beer, interrupting his wayward thoughts.

"Yeah, sure." He drained the glass and stood up. He hadn't even noticed when Isaac had paid the tab.

Outside it was frigid after the warmth of the bar, but Adam embraced it. He needed to get his body under control and a shot of cold air was as good as a cold shower.

"I had a good time," he said as he strapped himself into the car a few moments later. "I didn't know about this place, but I know Benny and Chandler would love to bring their men here for a night out."

"You know me. I'm old school."

Adam loved that about him, and he said so.

"That's one of the best things about you," he said. "And I love that you're unapologetic about it, too."

"I'm too old to need permission to be me," Isaac said with a laugh, glancing at him. "But it's good that you like that about me. One less hurdle to overcome."

As he turned his eyes back to the road, Adam wondered what other hurdles there were in Isaac's mind.

"Not sure I see any hurdles at all," he said honestly.

He reached over as he spoke and covered the hand that Isaac had draped over the top of the gear shift. Squeezing it gently, he added,

"You're fine just the way you are. I can't imagine you being anything else but this."

When Isaac turned his hand and linked his fingers with Adam's, there was nothing that he wanted to do about the smile that bloomed on his face. He was still smiling when they got back to his place. Isaac shut off the engine and turned to him.

"I'm glad you had a good time. Maybe we can do it again some time?"

"I'd love that."

They were stalling. Adam knew it, and he suspected so did Isaac. The tension in the car had risen once they'd linked hands, and now it was so sharp Adam was sure if he struck a match they'd be engulfed in flames. He wanted more than a kiss goodnight, but there were three people in his apartment and none of them needed to be there when he and Isaac made love again.

"I had a good time, too, sweetheart."

Adam was learning Isaac's tells. When he called him an endearment, it meant Isaac was very aroused and it wouldn't take much to push him over the edge into action. He really wanted to push him right this minute, but he refrained. They had time. Instead, he planted a soft, chaste kiss on his cheeks and said,

"I'll send David out. Have a great night, Zac."

He smiled, realizing that the diminutive was his tell. And who'd have thought that that would ever happen to him, and so quickly?

Chapter Twenty

"Come in, Isaac," Reverend Kincaid said.

Isaac smiled at the rector and walked past him into the office. It had been five days since the fire had halted his work flow, and he was still waiting for the report from the fire investigator. He had filed all the necessary paperwork with the insurance company, but they were also waiting on the investigator's report before they disbursed any funds. And it had been four days since his date with Adam.

They'd talked on the phone in the time between then and this moment where he was sitting in front of Adam's father, still not sure why he'd thought talking to the man would help him decide how to proceed. Their talks had been flirty and supportive on Adam's part, and he had responded in kind and with gratitude. But in his heart of hearts, he knew he wanted more of the chemistry they had found together that one time they had made love. He wasn't sure why he was hesitating, and had thought maybe he just needed an outside perspective.

Settling his spine firmly against the tall chair back, he waited for the priest to retake his seat behind the desk and then he said,

"Thanks for seeing me, sir." He grinned ruefully at Reverend Kincaid's quirked brow. "Sorry, I know you hate 'sir'."

"As I keep telling people, I need no reminders of my advanced years, thank you very much. And especially not from folks like you."

Isaac nodded. "I understand. That's really part of why I'm here. I'm…I'm seeing someone. It's really new, but I feel certain this is my second chance."

The priest kept his gaze on Isaac, not speaking, waiting for him to finish his initial thought. He had always liked how attentive the man was to his parishioners.

"It's happened really fast, so the speed is surprising. But what is even more so is who it is."

This time he waited for the inevitable question that his statement would raise.

"Who it is? I don't understand." The rector's brows rose in puzzlement.

Isaac cleared his throat. He wasn't ashamed of his feelings for Adam, though he didn't understand how he could have them to begin with. He also didn't know how his relationship would be perceived by all the people who had known him for all these years as Rowena Hamilton's widower.

"I don't know what this makes me," he began, still searching for words to express his worry and confusion, "but the person I'm with is a man."

"Ah!"

There was no inflection in the word, but Isaac couldn't help the unease that began to form in his gut. He had no intention of telling him that he was seeing his son. He felt that that was something for Adam to do, but he also knew that the younger man wouldn't make any proclamations until he gave the signal that he was ready. Was he ready? He thought he might be, but he just wanted to be sure he was thinking things through clearly.

"Are you concerned because you've never been interested in men before? And are you concerned about other people's reaction to this new relationship?"

Unsurprisingly, the rector's quietly voiced questions got immediately to the heart of the matter.

"Yes and yes. I don't understand how it's even possible, frankly."

"But you're prepared to ignore that confusion because your feelings are strong."

It wasn't a question. Isaac nodded once.

"Do you think it's wrong to have those feelings?"

Isaac snorted. "Not at all. I just don't understand how I never knew this about myself until now. I'm forty-seven years old, Rev. How could I have lived all these years and not known I liked men as well as women?"

The priest steepled his fingers on the desk in front of him, and Isaac could almost see him gathering and organizing his thoughts before he spoke.

"I have two more questions." He held Isaac's gaze as he continued. "First, do you like men as well as women, or is the feeling just for this one man?"

Isaac paused. He knew he wasn't gay because no other man interested him. Not that he had been actively seeking a lover, but since it was clear his heart had settled itself on Adam, it must mean that he was the one Isaac was meant to notice and to want.

"It's just this one man. I've no interest in men in general."

"You're like me, then," Reverend Kincaid said. "You fall in love after you've formed a more platonic attachment to someone. Friendship comes first, then love. I'm assuming you love this man?"

"I believe I am on the way there, yes."

Admitting it out loud was oddly liberating. Isaac smiled. Maybe this was why he'd needed to talk to his rector...the man got him to admit to stuff he'd been keeping a lid on.

"Which brings me to my second question. Why does your age matter? Is this man significantly younger than you?"

"I don't know exactly how old he is," he admitted, chagrined, "but I know he's younger than I am, in his thirties."

The silence seemed to stretch for a longer time than made Isaac comfortable, but he endured it. Whatever the priest chose to say, whatever counsel he passed on, Isaac was sure it would not only be welcome but wise.

"I have only ever been in love with one person," Reverend Kincaid began, "and I married her as soon as I could. But before Anna, I was infatuated with a few people. One of them was a man."

Isaac's eyebrows shot up in shock. The priest chuckled. "I kid you not. I was in college; he was an older man taking the same philosophy class as I was then." He smiled fondly. "I don't know if I would have fallen in love with him or not, because I discovered, after he passed away, that he was checking off items on his bucket list before he died. He had an inoperable brain tumor that killed him six months after we met, a month after we kissed each other in passion for the first and last time."

Isaac was gobsmacked. He didn't know what to say. That had not been anything he would ever have imagined about his priest, and that he was sharing it with him was humbling. The man had always extended the hand of friendship to him, but Isaac had been resistant, telling himself that he was being respectful of his position. However, perhaps he was just being prideful and refusing to let others in. And maybe he'd need to change that going forward.

"My point is that the human heart is full of the potential to love anyone who accepts us as we are, who makes us feel special, and when that feeling blooms and grows into more, we should embrace it. It wouldn't have made a difference for me back then, because Jake would still have died. But when I met Anna and fell for her, nothing could keep me away from the flame of her love and her light. And it's the best decision I've ever made, bar none."

Isaac nodded. He got it. He had had the same thing with Rowena, and now it seemed he was getting the chance to have it again with Adam. He just had to get over himself and let the love bloom. He smiled at the priest and stood up.

"Thanks for your time and your advice, Rev. I appreciate it."

As they shook hands, Reverend Kincaid said, "I'm happy to help in any way I can. And good luck with your young man."

Isaac laughed aloud at that, and the rector joined him a second later as he realized the words he'd used. Isaac raised a hand in farewell as he walked out and turned to the other task he had planned for the day. He used the time it took to drive to the facility where his father lived to consider what he would say to the man who had raised him on his own after his mother's death.

The Major's reaction to the news that he was seeing a man had been about what he'd expected. He had left without really addressing it, but he knew that he could not allow the angry words he'd spoken to be the last ones he said on the matter. If Adam were coming to feel anything close to what he was feeling, they'd be in each other lives a lot more than they currently were. He was not going to hide him from the Major, and he would not tolerate any disrespect toward him.

He tuned the radio to a jazz station, willing himself to relax as he drove. It would never do for him to show up angry and huffing. He would speak in cool, measured tones. But he would lay down the law in a way he hadn't bothered to do before. He had kept his own counsel, making the biweekly visits more for David's benefit than for his own. But he feared that the bond that existed between the boy and his grandfather might be damaged by his father's opinions and Isaac didn't want to be the cause of any rift between them.

The nurse was surprised to see him again so soon, but she sent him through with his visitor's pass. He found the Major in the common room sitting by himself watching a group of men playing cards. He turned his head when Isaac walked in, and the only acknowledgment he made was to watch his son approach him. When Isaac stood before him, he said,

"Where's David?"

No greeting, no pleasantries, just down to what he cared about. Isaac was grateful that at least he was giving his grandson what he hadn't been able to give him.

"School day, remember?" He took the seat closest to him so they could talk without being overheard.

The old man grunted. "So why are you here, then? Shouldn't you be minding the store?"

Isaac shook his head, hating the brusque tone and blunt questions. But he hadn't expected a hearts and flowers conversation so he brushed it off. Best get to the reason he'd come.

"There was a fire. I have to wait for the investigator's report before I can go back in. I came to talk about Dr. Kincaid."

The old man's eyebrows shot up. "What about him?" he asked belligerently, making Isaac's hackles rise.

"I'm seeing him, and I know that you don't favor that, but I'll thank you to not disrespect me or my choices in front of my son again. We may not agree on much, but I am not disrespectful to you. I'd like you to extend me the same courtesy."

The Major harrumphed. "I don't call it disrespect to speak my mind. And why shouldn't I have an opinion about who my son is spending his time with? That kind of thing doesn't reflect well on the family."

Isaac chuckled mirthlessly. "You mean it doesn't reflect well on you."

"I have my pride." The Major's tone was hard, unyielding.

"I'm aware of how important your pride and appearances are to you." Isaac did his best to clear his voice of any bitterness. "But I don't have to be a party to any of that. You need to keep your homophobia under wraps when you're with David. I don't want him being influenced into wrongheadedness because he wants to please you."

"The boy needs to learn what's right and what's wrong," his father began, but Isaac stopped him.

"That's a hard no from me. Anything the boy needs to learn, he'll learn from me. He's my son. I'll teach him what's right and what's wrong, thank you very much. I don't need your input on childrearing. I managed quite well growing up without you teaching me much. You checked out after Mama died, and all I got from you was Army bullshit. That's not how I'm raising David, and I'll thank you not to try any of that with him."

Something shifted in the old man's eyes then, and Isaac was startled to discover them filling with tears. He had never seen his father cry, not even when his mother had passed, although he had seen him red-eyed and had known what it signaled. But actual tears? Never, until this moment. What had he said to cause this sea-change in his dad's response to him? Was it the mention of his mother? He could barely contain his shock, and he had no idea how to react to this totally unexpected reaction.

He stayed silent, assuming that his father would speak again once he had control of himself, most likely to chastise him for cursing. The next words out of the Major's mouth were therefore all the more shocking.

"David is my last chance. Don't keep him away from me."

Isaac was speechless for a long moment. He had so many questions, but there was only one that he wanted an answer to more than all the rest. And there was no time like the present to ask it, since it seemed he had broken down a wall or something.

"What last chance?"

The word 'Pops' — that he used to call him when he was very small —had almost burst from him, but Isaac refused to let it pass between his lips. He had not come here to have old wounds ripped open by the kind of vulnerability that the Major was displaying. He couldn't allow himself to relax around a man who had stopped showing him any soft feelings when he'd been way too young to understand why.

The Major's eyes were dry when he looked up at his son. "I've only ever failed once in my life and that was with you."

Isaac wasn't sure how to take those words. Should he be glad that his father was finally acknowledging how absent he'd been emotionally, how poor a job he'd done of being a parent to him? Or should he be insulted that his dad thought the way Isaac had turned out meant that he had been a failure as a father? And if he meant the latter, how did Isaac feel about that?

He knew he was proud of all he'd accomplished on his own and with Rowena. And he knew that Adam and his family admired and respected him for who he was, for who he showed himself to be every single day. So maybe the Major's opinion didn't matter. He had managed to live and thrive without concerning himself with it so far. It wouldn't be a problem to keep doing that.

"I'm sorry I'm your only failure. I think I've turned out pretty well, considering."

The old man opened his mouth as if to argue, then closed it again, looking so defeated that something in Isaac shifted. He had no illusions about ever having more with his father than civility, but he also didn't want to be the one to stop whatever breakthrough might currently be happening. Who knew that a long-overdue conversation about boundaries would have caused this? Maybe he should have spoken up long ago. Maybe, if he had, they'd be in a better place now. And maybe he wasn't all that different from his old man.

"Anything else you have to say you should probably say now." He hated how that last unwelcome thought made him sound gruff and unforgiving. But after all these years, it was the best he could manage at the moment.

The Major cleared his throat. His eyes were clear and expressionless. He was back in control. Isaac braced himself for…he wasn't sure anymore what to expect after that revealing bombshell earlier.

"No one in their right mind would consider you a failure. That was not my intention. I simply meant that I haven't managed our relationship in the way I needed to and that that is my failure." He swallowed, then continued. "I treasure the time you let me spend with my grandson. I won't fail with him."

Relieved air whooshed out of Isaac's lungs, leaving him feeling almost like a deflated balloon. This moment felt like a major victory in their until-now-unacknowledged war. He'd stopped biting his tongue, had stopped keeping the peace, had stopped thinking of anyone else's comfort, and had managed to negotiate a truce between himself and his father.

He blew out a hard breath. "Thank you."

He didn't really know what else to say. He stood up, ready to say his goodbyes when his father asked,

"How long do you think before the store is back in business?"

"I don't know. I hope not more than a couple of weeks, but that depends on what the fire investigator says."

Regular conversation about mundane things was not the norm between him and his father. It made Isaac itchy. But today seemed to mark a new milestone between them, and if it meant getting used to the old man taking an interest in him as well, he would handle it.

"I'll let you know as soon as I know." He could offer his own olive branch.

"Thanks, son."

Isaac couldn't avoid the shock that rolled through him at those words. The last time his father had called him 'son' in anything other than a reprimanding tone had been...he couldn't remember. It was like he'd been given an electric charge and his brain was knocked offline. He closed his eyes and took several deep breaths before opening them again to reply.

"You're welcome."

Again, the word 'Pops' wanted to spring free, but he held it back. He needed to process the conversation, to decide whether or not he could trust this new, suddenly more open man. It wasn't anything obvious, and the Major was certainly not demanding hugs and kisses, but something was clearly happening to him. Isaac would wait to try anything new until he was sure where his father's head was.

"See you in a week or so."

He raised a hand in farewell and walked away, wondering as he did so what it would be like to hug his father again. Even before his mother's death, the

Major hadn't been much of a hugger, but Isaac had enjoyed the rare embraces when they happened. Did he want to get back to that time? He didn't really know and now didn't seem like the time to start thinking about it. Still, that he was thinking about being hugged meant he probably needed the comfort that it would bring. Which made him think of Adam and how much he enjoyed being in the doctor's arms.

He wished he could see him again but they hadn't discussed another date and he knew Adam wouldn't suggest anything with all that was happening with him at the store. So, if he wanted to see him, he'd have to make the next move. He drove back to town, parked in the lot behind his burned-out store, and pulled out his phone. He sent a text message because he didn't think it was kosher to interrupt a doctor with a phone call while he was at work.

Isaac: Hey! Just wondered when you'd be free again.

While he waited for an answer, he let his gaze wander over the back of his shop, the walls marred by soot, the roof partially collapsed. He had never had so many days of enforced inactivity. Though he had managed to fill a few orders from the greenhouse at home, he was very much afraid that he'd lose trade if he couldn't find a way to do more between now and the time when the store was back up and running.

He was thinking about how to get supplies out to the farm, and how to organize his workday so he and Peaches could do some of the work together, when his cell phone dinged.

Adam: I'm off tomorrow. What would you like to do?

Isaac thought about that for a moment and knew he had to acknowledge the truth. He wanted Adam back in his arms for more than a hug. Leaving him last Friday night with just a peck on the cheek had been almost painful.

Isaac: I'd like to see you again. Just tell me when to come and get you.

A tongue hanging out emoji appeared a moment before Adam's reply. Children or no?

Isaac: No. Where are you? Can I call you? He would never enjoy texting over speaking.

A moment later his cellphone rang. "You really hate texting, don't you?"

The amusement in Adam's voice warmed him. "I keep telling you, I'm old school. When will you believe me?"

Adam laughed outright at that. "Oh, I believe you. I just think you're funny."

"Shut up!" He spoke without heat, chuckling himself at Adam's teasing.

"You okay?" Now the younger man's voice was laced with concern.

"Yeah. It's just…it's been a day. I…"

He paused. It was one thing to decide to act, it was another to speak about the need that made his action imperative.

"Wanna come over? I'm with my mom and Nova."

"I don't want to intrude," he began but Adam cut him off.

"You won't be intruding. Come by and have lunch with us."

"How about I come by and take you out for lunch instead? Just the two of us."

Way to not sound needy, Zac! He rolled his eyes at himself but he wouldn't regret the words. He needed to have Adam where he could touch him uninhibitedly. And he couldn't do that with an audience.

"Okay. I'll be ready."

By the time he got to the Kincaid home, Isaac was calm enough that he could wave at Mrs. Kincaid and offer a genuine smile. He refused to wonder about what she might be thinking of him coming to take her son out to lunch. He didn't have enough brain capacity for that when he needed to concentrate on how he would make it home so he could kiss the man settling in next to him and buckling his seatbelt in the way he wanted to.

"Hi! Long time no see."

Isaac chuckled, his tension easing. He needed to laugh, to enjoy just being in Adam's company. He needed to remember that the heady sexual pleasure he had enjoyed with Rowena had usually been intensified when he had let himself flow into them without planning, without worry, without fear.

He was ready to go there again.

Epilogue

"This feels good."

Adam snuggled into Isaac's arms, letting his own drape over the big man's chest. His heart was still beating a little fast after the hardest orgasm he'd had since the last time he'd been in Isaac's arms. He was thankful that he'd been smart enough to ask his mother to pick up Nova after preschool.

His heart had done cartwheels when Isaac had called him earlier, and though he didn't as yet know what had triggered it, he could feel the need driving him all the way back to the farm. Isaac hadn't waited longer than it took to close the front door before he was on him, dragging groans of pleasure from his throat as he kissed him ravenously. That first press of lips had reminded him of how powerful their first encounter had been, and he had succumbed to the hunger that drove them to rip off clothes and suck each other down in front of the fireplace, too needy to wait.

Now, dressed again but cuddling on the sofa, he waited quietly for Isaac to speak. Something must have happened that had driven him to such unexpected, if delightful, action. He hoped he could help with whatever was on his lover's mind.

"I spoke to your father today," Isaac began, shocking Adam completely.

"About...?"

He refused to speculate. That way lay anxiety and he was enjoying the mellow feelings he was currently basking in too much to mess them up.

"About us." When he stiffened, Isaac hurriedly added, "Don't worry, he doesn't know it's you. I figure that information should come from you first. I...I just needed to hear someone older and wiser than me remind me of everything I already know about what falling in love is, about what it means."

Adam's heart tripped over itself. He sat up. "Falling in love?"

"Do you have a problem with that?"

There was no inflection in his voice, but Adam felt the tension nonetheless.

"Absolutely not," he hastened to reassure him. "I just didn't know...we haven't known each other long and I didn't want to assume that you wanted more than..."

"I said I'm falling in love." Isaac chuckled. "That means I've got a ways to go before anything else will happen. But I'm not prepared to deny it any more just because it happened so fast and I don't understand how it did."

He leaned down and kissed Adam's lips, feeding him his tongue and putting a hard pause on their conversation so they could taste the passion that was apparently always on call between them. He opened his mouth to give Isaac access and gave as good as he got, pulling sounds of pleasure from him as he chased his tongue and they tangled together in his mouth. He gasped when Isaac released his lips, gulping in air in an effort to calm his racing heart.

"And I want whatever will keep you in my life," he added, making Adam's heart swell.

"I want that, too."

"I'm glad to hear it." Isaac kissed him again, then shifted. "We haven't had lunch yet. Let's go see what's easy."

Adam would have much rather stayed on the sofa and made love again, but he had just said he wanted whatever would keep Isaac in his life, so if having a late lunch was what his man needed, that's what they'd do next. His gut told him they'd have lots of time to make love going forward. He would do his best to be patient.

After lunch, which they managed to turn into another mini sex event with the hand jobs by the kitchen sink, Adam had to go back to get Nova and Isaac had to go get David.

"I'll call you tonight," he told Isaac, "to say goodnight."

Isaac winked. "Sure that's why you'll call?"

Adam smirked. "Well, we'll just have to see, won't we?"

The echo of Isaac's laugh followed him all the way back into his mother's house. She was just coming from the back when he walked in.

"Ah! You're back. How was lunch?"

Her question was innocuous enough, but her eyes were filled with curiosity.

"It was good. Really good. Isaac cooks well."

"Ah, so you went to his home for lunch. Is that a new thing?"

Adam loved how his mother tried to couch her increasing curiosity in politeness. She was being as direct as she could until he spilled the beans, and really, what was there to hide? He was falling in love as much as Isaac was, and his mother would be delighted to know that he'd finally found someone.

"It is." He'd let her carry the conversation for now.

"He's a lovely man," she began, "but I never would have expected…"

She paused. Adam knew what she wanted but was afraid to say. He didn't blame her. He knew that Isaac had the same thoughts.

"He wasn't expecting it, either," he said, letting her off the hook. He knew she wasn't judging the older man. "But he's decided he wants to go where his heart takes him."

"And what do you think about that?"

The question, so delicately worded, was his mother ensuring that he knew what he was getting into. He smiled at her reassuringly.

"I like that his heart led him to me. And I aim to keep him."

His mother hugged him hard. "I am very pleased for you, son. And I know your dad will be too, once he hears."

Adam chuckled. "He's already heard," he told her. "He just doesn't know it's me." At his mother's puzzled look, he continued, "Isaac went to see him earlier today."

Mrs. Kincaid's eyes widened. "He went to ask…?"

"For advice, not permission to court me, Mom." He laughed at the expression on her face. "I don't know if he'll do that, though he likes to remind me that he's old school. So maybe he will, and I can see how that thought makes you happy."

On the way home, he stopped in the supermarket to get graham crackers, because Nova requested s'mores for dessert. He hadn't known he could be as happy as he was feeling in this moment. Cheryl had been so right to refuse his proposal. What the hell would he have done when he'd met Isaac if she'd lived and they'd been married? Would he still have fallen for him? He exhaled heavily, glad that that was a nightmare he would never have to live out. What-ifs were never helpful.

Benny was heading in at the same time as he was when he got home, and they stopped outside Adam's door, which he opened so Nova could go in to use the restroom.

"You look...well." Benny eyed him and then added, "In fact, more than well. Why don't we go inside so you can bring me up to speed?"

Adam had never been able to hide anything from his brothers and there was really no point in trying. Benny pushed his way into his apartment and raised his brows as Adam shook his head and followed him in.

"Daddy, can I have the s'mores now?"

Adam chuckled. "No, you can't. They're for after dinner, which isn't for a little while. Have some grapes."

He watched her toddle off to help herself to the grapes that he had placed on a low shelf in the refrigerator. Benny followed him into the kitchen where he put away his shopping and checked out what he had in the freezer ready to go.

"Not gonna tell me why you look like the cat that got the cream?"

Benny's eyes lit up, no doubt because Adam's cheeks had pinkened, despite his best efforts to avoid reacting.

"Ah! Cream, huh? You got some!"

"Oh, f...fiddlesticks up your...behind!" he exclaimed, managing not to utter the dirtier version of that wish in the presence of his daughter, who was happily chowing down on grapes at the table.

Benny laughed long and loud before he answered. "Well it's about d...dandelion time!" They both laughed at his substitution. "So, are you happy?"

"Yeah." He smiled at his little brother.

Long after Benny left, after he and Nova had eaten and he'd put her to bed, after he'd answered Isaac's call and they'd had their first phone-sex session, Adam lay awake, his mind full of the promise of Isaac's words to him.

"You're new," Isaac had said, his voice hitching as Adam schooled him in how to play sex games on the phone. "And you make me feel new. So new, sweetheart."

They had agreed to more dates, but Adam had steadfastly refused to slow their intimacies.

"I've been without touch for so long, and you even longer. I don't want to stop that. I'm not saying we need to go at it like rabbits or anything..."

"Don't think I could, actually," Isaac had interjected with a chuckle, making Adam laugh.

"...but I don't want to be without you when I need you. Will that be okay?"

"I may be old school, sweetheart, but I'm no saint. I couldn't stop touching you now if I tried. So yeah, it's okay with me, too."

Just thinking about him was making Adam hard again. It would keep, though. They were seeing each other tomorrow afternoon again, when Nova was in school. David would spend the evening at his friend's home and Isaac would pick him up after he dropped Adam off at home. They had time to explore their chemistry. There was a lot of man to cover and Adam was more than up to the task. He fell asleep thinking about what they'd do the first time they went further than blow jobs and hand jobs.

Next morning, as he and Nova were finishing up their morning story time, his cell phone rang.

"Adam Kincaid, good morning."

"Hey, it's me. Where are you?" Aidan's voice sounded strained.

"I'm home. What's up?"

"I just witnessed a hit and run," he said. "I'm on the way to the ER with the vic. He's got no one to call. Does the name 'Riley Taggert' mean anything to you?"

Adam thought hard but couldn't come up with anything. "Not really. Maybe Benny knows him? What's he do for a living?"

"He's a research librarian at the university."

"Benny may know him. Or Ry. How is he?"

"He's pretty banged up, but I didn't see any blood. He passed out before I could do anything for him. But at least he's still alive."

"Well, I hope he at least has a friend who can help him for a couple of days. Do you know if he has concussion?"

"They most likely won't tell me anything because I'm not his next-of-kin. Except I couldn't find anything about his family in his wallet, Adam. It's a fucking mess."

Aidan sounded upset as well as angry and frustrated and Adam had no idea why this was so important to his brother. Maybe it was because he'd witnessed it himself? Whatever the reason, he knew his twin wouldn't rest until the man he was fretting over had the best help he could get. And he knew that that would include getting the man to choose a healthcare proxy.

"I'm sure he'll be okay, Aid. I know you'll help him in any way you can. If he's still there in the morning, I'll see him and see what I can do to help."

"Thanks, bro."

He hung up and turned to Nova. "Let's go and get you ready for a sleepover at grandma's tonight."

An hour later, they were on their way to the manse when his phone rang again. He answered through the bluetooth speakers.

"Good morning, Mr. Hamilton."

"Good morning, Dr. Kincaid." Isaac sounded amused by his greeting. "Where are you?"

"On the way to grandma's house with Nova."

"Mind the Big Bad Wolf," Isaac said with a chuckle.

"Oh, I'll mind, alright!"

Adam lowered his voice suggestively, glad that Nova was listening to her favorite Disney songs on his iPad through the earbuds in her ears.

"Are you calling me a wolf, Doctor?"

"If the cap fits…"

Isaac's laugh warmed him. They expected to hear from the fire investigator soon, but in the meantime, they'd decided to spend as much of the second half of the day together as possible.

"I'll see you in a bit."

Once they got to his parents' home, Nova hopped out of the car seat as soon as he released her, and ran up to her grandmother who was waiting on the front porch. Adam took her backpack and her lunch bag, handed everything over to his mother, and kissed them both before waving goodbye. He was glad he'd told his mother he had a date, so she didn't try to get him to sit with her for coffee.

Isaac was walking out to his truck when Adam pulled up alongside him in front of the garage.

"Pull in," Isaac told him, gesturing into the garage. "We're going for a drive before lunch."

"Where are you taking me?" he asked as he buckled himself into the seat next to Isaac.

"I need to pick up a special order of blooms for a job I had planned to work on this week. We're going to a friend's greenhouse."

"I assumed you got flowers from your suppliers overseas or on the west coast," Adam said as they drove away from the farm.

"I do, but I also get some of my inventory from closer to home. And I didn't want to get these too much before I was ready to deliver them because I don't have a cooler to keep them fresh in. My flower cooler at home only has enough room for the blooms I'm going to collect today."

"How far away is your friend's place?"

"An hour. We'll have lunch there — Jack's wife Mona runs a restaurant there — and then we'll head home."

Home…Adam liked the sound of that. By the time Isaac was pulling into the unexpectedly crowded parking lot of what looked like a large farm, Adam's stomach was growling. Isaac laughed at his embarrassed expression as he unbuckled his seatbelt.

"I have a fifteen-year-old, remember? So there's always some kind of snack in the truck. All you have to do is ask."

"Noted."

Adam smiled ruefully as they exited the cab of the truck and waited until Isaac came around to his side. For all the years he'd been without a love interest or a friend with benefits, he had never felt any pull to change the way he lived. Being with his family, caring for Nova, and working with hurting people had been the sum total of his existence for so long, it was almost heady to be with someone who set him off like sparklers.

They had a leisurely lunch. He ordered the Loaded Grilled Cheese Sandwich and Hopped Up Tomato Soup.

"These item names are interesting," he said as the server moved away to fill their orders.

"Mona doesn't do anything by halves," Isaac replied, sipping his hot chocolate.

"How did you meet them?"

"They were Rowena's friends," Isaac said. "She and Mona had been besties since high school. When Mona married Jack, who owns a winery and the greenhouse, it seemed like serendipity."

Adam was intrigued. "So you and Jack became friends as well?"

"Not like our wives were, and since Rowena's death, I haven't really reached out except for business."

Adam reached for one of the hands that Isaac had cupped around the fat mug he held.

"Hey, I understand." He squeezed the big hand. "But maybe you'll reconsider that now?"

Isaac smiled at him. "Maybe I will."

After lunch, Isaac collected the blooms he had ordered and at Adam's urging promised he'd visit again, before they drove back home. Adam helped him unload the flowers before they washed up and Isaac pulled him into the living room to sit with him by the fire he'd started. They snuggled together like two peas in a pod. How must they look...two grown men cuddling under a throw by the fire! He didn't care; he felt warm and safe and loved.

Loved...that was exactly how he felt. And that was exactly how he wanted to feel.

"Will you come to family dinner with me on Sunday?"

He kept his eyes on the fire, loving the way Isaac combed his fingers through his hair. It was lulling him into a drowsy state and he didn't want to doze off before asking. Isaac's hands paused in their petting of his hair, and then he shifted, pulling Adam up so he could look into his eyes.

"Are you sure you want to do that already?"

Adam smiled. "I told Mom, and she has no doubt told Dad, who will therefore have made the connection between your visit and my revelation. So yes, I'm sure." He paused, suddenly uncertain. "Unless…am I going too fast for you? Did you want to wait before meeting the family? You don't have to come. I can wait until you're ready."

He was babbling like a fool, but it hadn't even occurred to him that by telling his mother, he had set in motion a chain of events that would force Isaac to do things he might not be ready to do. So inviting him to Sunday dinner might only be adding insult to injury. Fuck! When would he learn not to follow his impulses where this man was concerned? Isaac was a man of deliberation, of forethought. He never made a move without thinking it through.

"I'm sorry," he began again when Isaac still didn't speak.

"Hey! It's okay. I'm flattered that you want to show me off to your family again." His tone was amused, which helped to ease some of the constriction that had begun to tighten Adam's chest.

"Again?"

"I spent New Year's Day with you all, remember?"

That felt like a lifetime ago but he was right. So much had happened in the month since that day.

"This time it'll be different," he said. "This time, you'll be family." His cheeks warmed at Isaac's raised brows. "I know that we're still exploring, but you know what I mean."

Isaac's answer was a hard kiss on his surprised lips. "I know what you mean." His voice was gruff with lust.

Adam relaxed and let him devour his mouth, and before long they were stretched out on the sofa rolling against each other, hard bodies pressed tightly together. The feel of Isaac's steely cock against his sent a seismic wave through him, and he arched up into the bigger man, needing friction.

"Hungry again?" Isaac asked, raising his head to look into his eyes.

Adam gasped out a laugh. "In a manner of speaking, yeah."

"How can I help you, sweetheart?" Isaac's breath was warm against his cheek.

"Maybe start by getting naked." He pushed Isaac off him and stood up, reaching for the hem of his sweater. "Strip!" he ordered, pulling his own sweater over his head.

A minute later, they were naked and rolling together again. Adam loved the contrast between their skin tones. For whatever reason, Isaac's chocolate skin against his own made him ravenous for the taste and feel of him. He rolled his hips up, groaning at the touch of Isaac's heavy cock against his own, flesh on flesh arousing him past all endurance.

"Fuck, Zac, I need you!" He was breathless with desire.

Isaac nodded, a look of wonder on his face. "I know. Me too. But…"

"Hey, just do what feels good to you."

Despite the voracious need that was making it hard for him to focus on anything but their two leaking cocks sliding together, he understood the big man's hesitation. He'd never been with a man before, and though Adam wanted to feel that big black dick inside him, he could wait for that until Isaac was ready.

"What do you want to do?" he asked, slowing his breathing as he stroked Isaac's cheeks and sipped at his lips.

"I want to fuck you."

Adam could hear the shock in Isaac's voice, in stark contrast to the need he could see in his eyes. He understood the confusion. His own body reacted to those dirty words with glee, and Isaac's eyes registered surprise.

"You want that, too, sweetheart?"

"Yes." Adam had no more words left.

Isaac slammed his mouth back on his, and Adam was happy to give back the hungry kisses the big man was laying on him. They ate at each other greedily, all the while sliding their heavy erections against each other. He could come just from this frotting, but Isaac's words still rang in his ears. Pulling his mouth away to breathe, he whispered into the hot air between their faces,

"Let me up. I'll get lube and a condom."

Isaac kissed him again before complying, sliding off the sofa onto the rug to wait until Adam retrieved the items from his jeans pocket. More kisses were a sexy distraction. Then he sipped at the leaking head of Isaac's uncut dick, loving the salty taste of it, before he sheathed it with tender strokes. He loved the sound of Isaac's groans as he tasted him and when the condom was finally on, he went willingly back to the now-kiss-swollen lips that sipped at his own before Isaac's tongue slid between them to taste him and own his mouth.

"Show me how you get ready," Isaac asked eventually, pulling away to spear him with a tender gaze.

Adam had no trouble with that. He flicked open the little bottle of lube that he had and showed him how to stroke in, telling him how he was spreading his fingers in to widen the channel, sending first one, then two, then three fingers up to help him accept Isaac's huge cock. Isaac watched him with naked lust, making Adam shake with need.

Before he could pull his fingers out so he could take what they both wanted, he gasped at the pressure of Isaac's finger joining his, stuffing him so full he could barely breathe. He fumbled until he could move their fingers to where he wanted them, and when Isaac curled his digit up into his prostate, Adam panted as he fought to stave off the orgasm that was suddenly barreling down on him.

"Wait, Zac, wait! Please!"

Isaac was panting as heavily as he was, as though he was also ready to blow. Adam removed their fingers and sank down onto Isaac's lap, his legs trembling.

"Damn, sweetheart, you've got me right on the edge already." Isaac's voice was shaky with emotion.

"Ditto, big guy!" Adam nipped his bottom lip.

Taking a few more deep breaths, Adam raised himself again, planting his knees on either side of Isaac's thighs.

"Ready?" He held Isaac's gaze.

"Yeah." Isaac seemed to have lost his words as well.

"Help me."

He slowly eased his body down the steely shaft that Isaac held for him, and they both groaned harshly as he took him in to the root. Every slow inch down sent a fresh flood of lust pouring through his veins. When he looked up to gauge how his lover was feeling, Isaac's eyes were squeezed shut, a grimace of pleasure and restraint tightening his lips over his teeth, breath puffing from his nostrils in harsh exhales.

"More, baby," he begged after his body had grown accustomed to the heavy weight invading his walls. "Give me more."

Isaac moved, keeping his eyes closed but raising his hands to pull Adam closer until his arms were wrapped around his narrower frame. Adam rode him like he was a gold medal bull rider, bucking and crying out as Isaac surged up into him. No matter how little experience he had with men, Isaac fucked like a champion. He pegged Adam's prostate just often enough to make his head spin before he slammed into orgasm, ejaculating between them without ever touching himself, hot semen hitting his abdomen and Isaac's chest. He dropped his head, howling against Isaac's neck in release.

"Oh, fuck!"

Isaac's harsh words and fierce growls of completion pierced his haze as he shot off into the condom. They were both completely out of breath, sweaty and sated by the time Isaac stopped moving. Adam sought Isaac's lips, kissing him sloppily, pausing to catch a breath before diving in again, needing to keep the connection between them even as Isaac softened inside him and slipped out.

"I didn't realize how much I missed making love," Isaac said after they'd cleaned up and put their underwear back on. He kissed Adam's forehead. "Thank you, sweetheart."

"Anytime," Adam said with a smirk.

Isaac quirked a brow. "Anytime, huh? So it'll be okay if I drag you off to have my wicked way with you while we're at your mom's for dinner?"

Adam snorted. "As if. You know you'd never do that, so stop posturing. But if you ever lost your mind enough to do that, then yes, in a heartbeat."

A minister visiting their home had once told Adam and his brothers that love is the itching of the heart that you cannot scratch. At the time they'd all laughed. It had sounded ridiculous…what did little boys understand about metaphor, after all? But now, as he lay in the arms of the man he knew he loved, he understood exactly what the priest had been saying.

He knew that Isaac was feeling that same itch, but he was not one to rush things. So Adam would wait. But he wanted to give him fair warning, so he said what was on his mind.

"Some day, I'm going to ask you to marry me. Will that be okay with you?" He held his breath.

Isaac smiled at him, affection in his gaze. "Yes."

Adam kissed him, satisfied that when he did, Isaac would say yes again. There was no other possible answer. And he was more than okay with that.

Lightning Source UK Ltd.
Milton Keynes UK
UKHW021817140722
405868UK00010B/895